THE
(secret)
BABY

ALSO BY LEDDY HARPER

Home No More

My Biggest Mistake

Falling to Pieces

Take Your Time

Beautiful Boy

Eminent Love

Resuscitate Me

Lust

I Do(n't)

The Roommate 'dis'Agreement

Love Rerouted

Kiss My Ash

The (Half) Truth

THE
(secret)
BABY

LEDDY HARPER

Published by Montlake Romance, Seattle
www.apub.com

Amazon, the Amazon logo, and Montlake Romance are trademarks of Amazon.com, Inc., or its affiliates.

ISBN-13: 9781503905368 (paperback)
ISBN-10: 1503905365 (paperback)

Cover design by Erin Dameron Hill

Printed in the United States of America

Kevin, I love you.

PROLOGUE

Kelsey

It was like a yeti had thrown up on everything.

White walls. A white sofa. Even white rose petals littered the coffee table. Furniture made of maple—every piece hand carved and likely worth a small fortune. Sheer drapes hung from ivory rods set above a wall of windows.

Everything was crisp, bright. *White.* Even at eight in the morning, there was no need for a lamp. Warm light glossed the room, a luminous sheen of magnificence and perfection coating every square inch.

Staging homes came with a list of pros and cons.

This house was the epitome of a pro. Glancing around, I didn't see much for me to do in the way of making it marketable—hell, I could've *made* a mess, and it would probably still sell for more than the asking price. But I wasn't about to argue with the Realtor. If she wanted to pay me to take down a few pictures here and there, hang a couple of pieces of art, and add some throw pillows and blankets, maybe a rug or two, then so be it. I certainly wouldn't turn my nose up at that.

There was nothing like an easy project to start my day off right.

However, that feeling quickly changed when I turned toward the built-in entertainment unit along the far wall. My eyes didn't settle on the ridiculously large TV in the center or the tall crystal vases filled with twisted sticks of bamboo and pristine white silk flowers. Rather than focus on the polished knobs of the glass cabinets along the top, the ceramic seahorse on a shelf to the right, or even the snow globe of a white mountaintop, my sight fell upon a picture frame that appeared to have been made out of small pieces of dried wood. Antique, maybe. Or possibly leftover logs from a fire—pale with charred accents that gave it an overall ash-grey color.

But it wasn't the frame that made me pause.

It was the photo inside.

And as I stood in the middle of this exquisite room, surrounded by its beauty, wrapped in its brilliance, I couldn't help but feel . . . *cold*. The emotions clawing their way up my throat were a stark contrast to everything around me—red to the white, fury to the calm, chaos to the precision. The only word filling my head was *con*.

Con. Con. Con.

This had to be a joke. A horrible, painful, sadistic joke from the universe. Karma cashing in her rain check from a mistake I had never intended to make in the first place. There was no other explanation for how I had found myself in the middle of *his* house, staring at a photo of him and his *wife*. Her in a white wedding dress; him in a matching tux. His arm around her ridiculously tiny waist. Her eyes set on his profile. A smile painted on his lying, smarmy, manipulative lips.

Everything was white—the color of silence.

How fitting . . .

Slowly, calmly, I pivoted, turning my back on him the same way he'd done to me. My hands curled in on themselves at my sides to keep from destroying the facade he cowered behind. All I wanted to do was shatter his fraudulent existence, demolish the carefully crafted image of perfection he surrounded himself in. I'd wanted to do it years ago, when he had done those very same things to me—crushed my dreams, destroyed my innocence, annihilated my heart. I had wanted him to feel the pain he'd left on my doorstep, but I never did. Doing so would've only wrecked my reputation and killed my character.

But now . . . now I found myself filled with the same acrid urges, the same venomous desires as before—to expose him for the snake he was.

Except, once again, doing so would ruin me.

Instead of giving in to the resentment and desire for vengeance that had been resuscitated by his wedding photo, I pulled my cell from my back pocket and dialed the only person who had ever been there for me.

"I'm starting to think you're more excited about my wedding than I am," she teased in lieu of a greeting. "Seriously, Kels . . . we just got off the phone less than five minutes ago. Did you come up with another idea or something?"

"Yeah . . ." I craned my neck, glaring at the smug grin on his handsome face as it stared at me from behind a pane of glass. "I'm getting a stripper for your bachelorette party. But not a cop. I'm thinking of a lawyer or doctor. Someone prestigious and rich."

She snorted. "I hate to break it to you, but I think those are only costumes. An act. I doubt they fight fires during the day and take their clothes off for cash at night. In fact, I'm fairly certain they don't."

I huffed and moved out of the room, prepared to get this job over with so I could leave and, hopefully, never look back. "That's not the point, Tatum."

My best friend grew silent for a moment, her gentle sigh drifting through the line as if letting me down made her sad. "Jay won't go for that. We both agreed that neither of us would have them at our parties."

Somehow, I managed to make my way into *their* room. I immediately took control of my gag reflex and headed back out, finding myself in a hallway. "Again, Tater, you're missing the point. I highly doubt Jason would have a problem with a surgeon grinding on me in nothing but a banana hammock."

"Considering he's your cousin, you're probably right. I'm sure his issue is more about someone else grinding on *me*. You know . . . because we're getting married in six weeks. Plus, he's the only guy I ever want to see in a banana hammock. Not that he wears them. He doesn't . . . as far as I'm aware. And I don't want anyone else grinding on me. Only Jay. Is it weird for you to hear that? I never know if something will bother you or not, since he's your cousin and all." Tatum had always been a horrible liar, and even worse at trying to cover it up—her sense of guilt led her to ramble.

I stilled and focused on her end of the call. "What are you doing over there, Tater? You seem . . . busy."

"Oh, nothing. Just putting away laundry." Tatum doing laundry was the very definition of a red flag. A giant neon warning sign. A siren blaring in the dead of night.

"Jason's there, isn't he?" When I heard her sigh again, I realized it wasn't some form of sadness over letting me down. I shivered. "Bless all the things. Don't ever answer the phone again when he's doing . . . whatever it is you guys are doing. I promise, I won't *ever* be pissed at you for that. Call me back when you're done."

After slipping my cell into my pocket, I got to work—boxing up any personal effects to help potential buyers imagine the house as theirs instead of someone else's.

A picture of him smiling at her while she posed for the camera—fake.

Another of him kissing her with eyes closed—fake.

One of her tucked beneath his arm, a gentle happiness in his eyes—fake. Fake. Fake.

While I stored away their happy memories, I made a mental checklist of everything I planned to do to the stripper, and all the ways he'd help me forget the existence of the cheating cop I'd once been tangled up with.

Chapter 1

Aaron

Thumping music escaped the walls of the nightclub while I stood in the parking lot, wondering why the hell I was here. I stared at my reflection in the door of my truck, unable to ignore the fact that, while others staggered about in relaxed or skimpy clothes, I was in dress slacks and a pressed oxford shirt, a silk tie knotted loosely around my neck.

A sore thumb had a better chance of going unnoticed.

"Oh my God, Aaron. What took you so long?" A flash of pink hair came into view in the shiny-red paint of my truck. "I called you, like, an hour ago."

I shifted to the side and quirked a brow at the spitfire. Cheryl was just one of many who had turned down my romantic advances in favor of a friendship. In fact, standing outside of this club was just another way of reliving the nightmare that was my sex life.

The problem with staying in a hometown was that no matter where you looked, memories—the good and the bad—were everywhere. I'd been shot down numerous times inside those doors, only to leave with my friends thinking I'd landed a score.

I was living a lie. Hiding behind the need to appear like a player.

At least I could sleep well knowing that if I didn't wake up, I'd have a chapel full of women mourning my death.

Sadly, that thought didn't keep me warm at night.

"Did you wear your watch in the shower again? You called me thirty minutes ago, and I told you then that I was still at the hospital. I had literally just finished dictating a report for a patient when you called."

Pursing her glossy pink lips, she tightened my tie, nearly choking me before she was satisfied. "Where's that thing you people use to listen to hearts? And your science jacket—the white one. Where's that?"

"Why?"

"Just get it, Aaron. Hurry."

"First, tell me why. When you called, you told me you needed my help. I came straight here from the hospital because you said it was urgent. Now you're fixing my tie and wanting me to put on my coat. At a *club*, no less. I'm not doing *anything* until you start talking. What the hell is so urgent, Cheryl?"

"Has anyone ever told you how difficult you are when you're man-strating?" She set her hands on her hips, reluctance dancing in her fluttering lashes. "There's a bachelorette party going on in the VIP suite. They've asked about a doctor at least a hundred times. And being the amazing friend that I am, I figured I could kill two birds with one stone—give them what they want, and in turn, you get what you want. Sex. You're welcome."

I held her shoulders, adding an impatient shake. "Does someone need medical attention?"

"No." She waved me off as if my question were ridiculous. "They just keep asking if anyone has seen a sexy surgeon with—and I quote—an above-average tongue depressor."

Well, if *that* didn't pique my curiosity . . .

"So get your coat and heartbeat checker, and let's go."

"Heartbeat checker? You mean a stethoscope?" I had to fight off the smirk that begged to curl the side of my mouth when she nodded.

"How many times do I have to remind you that I'm *not* a physician? I have my PhD, not a license to practice medicine."

"And your point is? You couldn't have borrowed one from a friend while you were at the hospital today? I'm sure they're a dime a dozen around that place."

I dropped my chin to my chest and shook my head slowly. Laughter lifted my shoulders while hushed wisps of humor slipped past my lips. This was one of the reasons I'd been okay with keeping Cheryl as a friend instead of dismissing her after being rejected. Her amusement made it all worth it.

"Can't you just put the coat on? For me?" She batted her lashes. "Please, Aaron. They dropped a *ton* of money on that suite, and the last thing I need is for their night to be ruined over something that's out of my control."

"Fine," I conceded and grabbed the last piece of my work attire, completely aware of what a bad idea this was. Sure, there was a chance I might get lucky tonight, but if my history with the entire female population had taught me anything, I knew better than to get my hopes up. "Lead the way, princess."

It wasn't like I had anything to lose.

Except my dignity and self-respect.

Then again, I didn't have much of either one left.

Case in point: I walked into a club on a Saturday night dressed like a medical professional making rounds in an emergency room. I could only imagine this was what it would feel like to show up to a Halloween party and discover that, somewhere along the way, there'd been a misunderstanding, because no one else was in costume.

Mortifying . . . that's what it was.

Cheryl patted my back and winked, as if her encouragement would somehow eradicate my humiliation. It didn't, but at least it gave me something to think about during my stroll through the swaying crowd.

A few people swung their attention my way, but after a quick, inquisitive stare, they returned to what they were doing—drinking or dancing. One was drinking *and* dancing. And if I weren't on my way somewhere, I would've stopped and watched how long it took before she ended up *wearing* that drink.

My heart rate increased when I approached the rear corner draped in ambient lighting. The music pulsed through my veins as bodies swayed together. Rented booths lined the entire wall behind the dance floor. While the smaller sections I'd passed were a few feet above the main floor and only semiprivate, this one sat high enough to boast a view of the entire place and was enclosed by a wall of glass that offered total privacy.

And *that* was what had me the most freaked out, considering I didn't even know who was up there.

However, by the time I stepped inside and made my way beneath the blue fluorescent bulbs and black lights, I'd managed to get a grip on my nerves. Either I'd discovered my confidence, or adrenaline had flooded my veins, because my voice was full of conviction when I called out, "I heard someone was asking for a doctor?"

Holy shit, I'd walked into the mother lode of sex appeal.

Five sets of eyes found me. Five pairs of breasts practically spilled out of tight dresses and low-cut tops. But the best part was, all five women appeared to be my age or less; one might've been slightly older, though I wouldn't turn her away if she showed any interest.

Before I could assess each of them individually, a beautiful blonde ran toward me, squealing and bouncing on the balls of her feet, hands clapping wildly like she'd never seen a man before. The way she hopped and spun reminded me of a merry-go-round with fried electric cords.

"Guys! The stripper's here!" she shrieked, turning to the others in the room.

Excited commotion broke out around me, yet I couldn't understand any of it. The only thought I had at the moment was that these ladies were under the impression that I was here to take my clothes off. And dance.

At the same time.

Yeah . . . this was a *horrible* idea, one Cheryl would pay dearly for.

I attempted to slowly retreat out of the room, though I should've known it wouldn't be that easy. Luck was *never* on my side. I managed to take two steps before the animated blonde foiled my plan. She grabbed my arm and dragged me to the middle of the group, stopping—I wasn't sure if it was on purpose or if my feet had simply quit moving—in front of a tall goddess I wouldn't mind worshipping with my lips.

I took my time dragging my attention up her body, starting with the pair of blue heels on her feet. They were the kind that induced fantasies of seeing her in nothing *but* them while I had her bent over, ass in the air. Then again, those fantasies might've also been caused by the long legs that were made to wrap around my waist. A white dress hugged her drool-worthy thighs, and as my eyes continued to travel upward, I couldn't help but spend a few extra moments memorizing the way the light material held her perky breasts, which were brilliantly showcased by the dress's low neckline. Her long dark hair hung in loose curls over her chest, a sparkly crown sitting atop her head.

This girl was the hottest thing I'd seen since my Jennifer Love Hewitt–crush days.

Just then, she bent at the knees and picked up something from the table next to her. Ducking her head to one side, she slipped a piece of sheer fabric over one shoulder before situating it across her chest. It read: *Bride to Be.*

That should've been my cue to leave. *Should've been.* However, my dumb ass ignored the alarm bells in favor of her pouty lips and smiling eyes. The way her gaze caught the blue lights above us as she held my stare sparked a fire within me. A fire I wasn't sure I had the strength to put out.

"Damn . . . he's one lucky guy." It was deep, barely a mumble, a thought spoken aloud. I hadn't meant to verbally offer my opinion of her—she belonged to someone else. However, she had heard it anyway.

Her eyes brightened like two twinkling stars, mouth forming a rapturous arc. Her chest heaved with excited breaths, and I didn't doubt I'd find heat along her skin if I dared to touch her. I had to pretend none of that affected me as I stepped away, removing myself from her dangerous gravitational pull.

Suddenly, the music from the club became nothing more than a muted thump through the walls. With a quick glance over my shoulder, I noticed someone had closed the glass partition at the top of the steps, offering us seclusion from the crowd on the other side.

I'd been to Boots enough times to know that while I could see the people and lights through the privacy glass, no one could see in. I was also aware of the security cameras inside these booths and the team who watched the feeds in a back room. Cheryl had given me the ins and outs of this place, and it made me feel like I had an advantage over everyone else.

The attendant for the room came over with his hand out, palm up, expectation in his eyes. At first, I thought he might've been in search of a tip, but I didn't understand why he'd receive one before the night was over. Then he leaned forward and said, "If you have a playlist ready, I'll get it set up for you."

It took only a second to figure out that he meant the playlist of songs I planned to dance to. That's when my skin began to flush, a heat wave washing over me until I felt damp in all the wrong places—not that there were any *right* places to sweat, but I digress.

Even though I wasn't a professional, these ladies believed I was. Which meant I had to play the part *and* leave them convinced. So I slid my cell out of my pocket and began to browse through every available tune I could find until I had what I felt was a solid lineup of beats one might take one's clothes off to.

I didn't have the faintest idea what kind of music was appropriate for this sort of thing. But with the limited amount of time I'd been given to find something, I went with a variety of favorites from the midnineties. If someone had told me twenty years ago that I'd be in my early thirties, single, and so desperate to make it to the second date without getting locked in the friend zone . . . I would've totally believed them. On the other hand, had they told me I'd be here, searching songs from the *Space Jam* soundtrack to strip for a group of horny females . . . I would have laughed.

Just because my friends were under the impression that I was a natural Don Juan didn't mean I was.

That had been my well-kept secret since high school.

I passed my phone to the only other male in the room and waited for everyone to take their seats. The guest of honor took her place on the decorated throne, while her friends piled onto the couch that sat opposite her. I prayed I could pull this off without ending up with five more women in this area who would never date me. Well, four. The fifth was clearly already on that list.

When I turned away from the bride-to-be, ready to start the show for the others, I was surprised to feel a gentle yet possessive grip on my shoulder, directing me back around. Once again, her magnetic grin stole my attention . . . as well as every last brain cell.

Her sexy voice raked over me when she said, "You're mine tonight, Dr. Phil-Me-Up."

I glanced over my shoulder at the ladies on the couch, each of them turned and engaged with the one next to them as if I weren't there. They chatted it up like they were at a Starbucks, not a nightclub. The drinks in their hands might as well have been coffee.

"Here . . ." Her voice drew my attention until I settled my heated gaze on the temptress in front of me again. She had a shot glass in each hand, one held out in my direction. "You look like you might need something to take the edge off."

I would need more than whatever was in this shooter, but this would have to do . . . for now. I took it from her and dropped my head back, filling my mouth with the harsh taste of tequila. It went down as smooth as pouring gasoline on a fire.

After taking the empty glass from my fingers, she twisted around and set them both on a tray that covered a small table next to her chair. I was surprised to find the majority of them flipped upside down, drained of their contents, and a part of me worried she had consumed them all. But I didn't detect the slightest sway or stumble as she lowered herself onto her throne, so I filed that concern away and moved on.

The sound of a train flooded the speakers.

It's now or never, all or nothing.

Fisting the lapels of my coat, I wedged myself between the bride's legs and began to shimmy the fabric off my shoulders, all while hoots and hollers resounded from behind me. My blood thumped wildly, hips swaying side to side with the drunken encouragement of "Take it *all* off, Doc!" from her friends.

However, even with the added commentary, *her* eyes remained on mine. Cool. Aloof.

With the coat now at my feet, I moved to the tie.

"Oh, *baby!*" came from over my shoulder as I worked the knot loose. "You can tie me up!" But I ignored the outbursts and proceeded to focus on the bachelorette, who sat back with a pleased curl to her glossy lips. There was an airiness to her. A certain detachment, like she was waiting for me to draw her in.

In my head, seductively removing my clothes couldn't have been hard. I'd gone through graduate school and defended a dissertation on facial-recognition impairment following traumatic brain injuries. This should've been a walk in the park. However, as soon as I had my tie hooked around her shoulders, inching her toward my thrusting pelvis, I realized how much actually went into the art of stripping. This all became clear when the sex kitten in front of me took it upon herself to help me out of my clothes.

While I moved, she worked the buttons on my shirt. While I rocked my hips close to her face, she unfastened my belt. And while I remained lost in her touch—the touch of the forbidden that I had no right to experience or find joy in—she released the zipper on my pants. I only snapped out of the fantasies she'd provoked when she tugged on my slacks, desperate to get them down my legs.

"Whoa, whoa, whoa." I grabbed her wrists and took one step away. "Take it easy. You can't rush the process."

Her intoxicating lips quirked to one side, a secret hiding in the seductive smirk. "I want to see what you're packing in there, Doc."

"Patience reaps the biggest rewards."

She arched one brow and tilted her head just so. "Are you saying you're big?"

I'd learned that there was no good answer for this kind of question. "Size is relative."

"That means you're small."

I froze, stunned silent. But I shook it off and said, "Not even close."

"Then prove it." She reached out and grabbed both ends of my open belt, using them as a leash to guide me between her parted legs. Rather than look at me, she kept her sights trained on my body as she drew herself closer to my crotch. Then she curled her fingers beneath the elastic band of my boxers and met my stare, the heated desire in her eyes bringing my dick to life. Regardless of the fact that she wasn't mine, that she had promised herself to another man, I was helpless to remove her hands from my body. And when she grazed her lips along my lower abdomen, demanding that I dance, I obeyed—under the lie that it was only to create distance between us.

I tried to keep up with the beat of the song, though it proved to be difficult with the way she continued to touch me. Well, that, and the dollar bills that seemed to float down from the ceiling as they were thrown at me from behind. Even when I turned around and held myself over her lap, I couldn't concentrate enough to move fluidly. However, when she groaned in frustration, I was ready to call it quits.

"You've got to be the world's worst stripper. No wonder you were so cheap." She'd somehow managed to insult me with a genuine smile and infectious giggle, which kept my confidence from splintering.

"If you can do this better, then by all means . . . show me how it's done."

To my surprise, she said, "My pleasure."

She pushed herself to her feet and pressed her warm palm to my chest, adding a slightly forceful shove. With my ass in the plush chair, she stood over me, and I couldn't ignore the smug satisfaction written on her face. It was like she'd won. Which was absurd, considering I was the real winner—a sexy woman was about to grind on me, and I didn't even have to pay her.

She leaned over, offering me a front-row view of the cleavage I wanted to suffocate in, and settled her hands on my shoulders. It didn't matter that another ridiculous nineties song played through the speakers, one that even a professional couldn't keep up with. All I cared about was the way she slid one knee over my leg before settling it between my hip and the armrest, halfway straddling my lap. The hem of her dress crept higher on her milky thighs, though it never rode high enough to expose what hid beneath it.

The older one of the group yelled out, "Give the woman a pelvic exam . . . *with your tongue!*"

Then the brunette, who had been more reserved until now, added, "Yeah, Dr. Phil-Me-Up. She needs a good probing."

It seemed the temptress on my lap didn't appreciate her friends getting my attention, because she cupped my cheek and redirected my eyes to her. Intense desire reflected back at me, heating me up from the inside out.

I had no clue what to do—if I could touch her, if I *should* touch her, where to look, if she *wanted* me to look. It all became too much, and I worried I'd insult or offend her no matter where I put my hands or what I focused on. In the end, I decided to drop my hand to her thigh and go from there.

"You're good at this." My face was close to hers, but between the old-school hip-hop, the cackling women on the couch, and the thumping bass that vibrated through the walls, I wasn't sure if she'd heard me. So I tried again, a little louder this time. "You move like a professional. I bet you'd make a killing doing this as a career."

She met my gaze, her eyes wide in disbelief.

"Wait. That came out wrong."

"How exactly could telling me that I should take my clothes off for a living come out right?" At least she still wore a hint of amusement on her perfect pout.

"I'm not sure, but I thought it sounded better than saying you move like you'd be fucking amazing in bed." *Dammit.* Apparently, it's impossible to speak past a foot in one's mouth. "I just meant that when you roll your hips like that, it's seductive and erotic. Hot. And very tempting."

"If you think this is hot . . . you should see me move while I ride you."

I gripped her waist in an effort to move her off me, realizing the dangerous position we were in. It was wrong, and the alarm bells in my head grew louder, deeper, warning me of what might happen if I didn't put an end to this now. Yet my strength failed, my brain refusing to tell my limbs what to do. I needed to remove her from my lap, but instead, I held her there. I should've pulled myself to my feet, but I remained in the chair.

I was helpless.

And so fucking stupid.

Her lids lowered just enough to give me the universal come-hither eyes while she continued with the provocative dance. I couldn't focus on the fact that her movements didn't match the beat of the song or that four other women cheered their friend on as she air humped me. But when her fingers trailed down my chest to the bulge in my pants, the realization that she had a man at home—a man who wasn't me— slapped me in the face and squeezed my balls at the same time.

Suddenly, we were in a war with each other. A push and pull of right and wrong. Of desire and honor. I shoved against her while she leaned into me. I could've fought harder, made more of an effort to get away, but the second she sat on me, fully straddling my thighs, I found myself in a war of my own making—a battle between *both* heads. And I was convinced that neither would leave here a winner.

Everything changed, though, when she threaded her fingers through my hair. Holding my head in both hands, she closed the distance between our faces. Her lids closed, and a split second later, I felt the soft warmth of her mouth against mine.

It was all over in the blink of an eye, yet the way she'd moved on top of me, rolling her hips into me while her mouth laid claim to mine . . . there was no way in hell I'd forget it anytime soon. In fact, there was a good chance I'd spend a week—at a minimum—stroking myself to the thoughts of another man's fiancée.

As if I needed something else to make me feel like shit.

I gently pushed her off my lap and then pulled myself to my feet. The weirdest part of it all was the way her friends applauded from the couch, as if rooting for her to cheat on her future husband. Honestly, it was sickening. It drove me to secure my pants as fast as my fingers would move, then my shirt. Forgoing my tie—unwilling to spend the time to locate it—I grabbed my coat off the floor and stepped away.

Yet the sight of her kept me from leaving.

Rejection danced across her face. The room wasn't well lit, and the lights used in the space weren't the kind that offered much in the way of visibility . . . but I understood that face. I saw it every morning in the mirror. I recognized those eyes—unable to connect, shining with false excitement and dwindling hope.

"I'm really sorry. I hope you enjoy the rest of your party, and good luck with everything." There was so much more I wanted to say, maybe even ask, but I didn't have the courage to stick around any longer. I was already a fraying thread, and if she gave me the slightest bit of reasoning for coming on to me while celebrating her upcoming union to someone else . . . I wasn't sure how much longer I'd last.

I tried to offer a parting smile to the other ladies, though they seemed to be occupied by the drama of the situation. They exchanged quick glances as if confused why I'd put a stop to the evening; one appeared annoyed. So I reminded myself that these were not the women for me, not the ones capable of a relationship, and while I enjoyed the easiness of temporary satisfaction, I would've so much rather had more.

And these ladies couldn't give me the *more* I sought.

Unexpected emotions furled in my gut with each step I made away from the suite. They grew so intense that by the time I made it into the thick of the dance floor, sweaty bodies surrounding me on all sides, the demanding beats of the music were nothing more than vibrations that kept my feet moving through the crowd.

I'd known this would be a bad idea.

I just hadn't been prepared for how bad . . . or why.

"That was fast." Cheryl stopped me at the edge of the bar, but I couldn't shake out of my thoughts fast enough to hear what she'd said. With a perceptive smile, as if she'd known me longer than five months, she gripped my hand. "Why are you leaving so fast?"

"You knew why they were asking for a doctor, didn't you?" I shook my head, recognizing the unapologetic truth in her eyes. "So you sent me in there, aware that they were expecting a stripper, and you not once stopped to question how I'd feel about it?"

"Loosen up, Aaron. If anyone could pull that off, it was you. And since you *are* a doctor, I figured it was fate or something. Come on . . . you're always complaining about not being able to get a girl. Well, I just led you to five of them. What's that saying about leading a horse to water?"

I shook my head, hating how I couldn't stay mad at her, no matter how ridiculous her antics could be. "Yeah, but someone who's getting ready to walk down an aisle to another man isn't the kind of woman I'm looking for."

"There were others in the group. I didn't limit your options."

To a certain extent, she was right. She hadn't told me to focus on the one with the smoking-hot body. However, she was responsible for putting me in that position to begin with.

"Did you at least get a number? Or a name? Just one?" Her first question reminded me that I'd left my phone with the attendant. And while she tossed out a few follow-up inquiries, I frantically contemplated various ways of getting it back *without* going myself.

I gripped her small shoulders and gave her a little shake. "Cheryl, listen to me. I left my phone up there. I gave it to the attendant, who took it somewhere and hooked it up to the speakers. I forgot to get it back—I had my mind on other things. I need you to get it for me, please."

"You're a mess. And here I thought I was handing you the golden ticket of lady love, and you can't even get that right." She rolled her bright eyes. "Sit. Drink a beer while I go fetch your belongings. Did you leave anything else up there I should be on the lookout for? Maybe your manhood? Testosterone? *Anything?*"

Ignoring her digs at my pathetic life, I took a seat at the bar and waited for her to hand me a cold beer. It wasn't that I wanted it or would even drink much of it—not after the shot of tequila upstairs. I used it more as a way to fit in with everyone else. After all, my attire made me stand out enough as it was . . . I didn't need to be *that guy*. The suspicious one who clearly didn't belong.

A few minutes later, Cheryl came back, my tie dangling off her finger and a taunting smirk dripping from her lips. "By the way, you totally could've gotten that yourself. There was no one up there."

I took a quick glance around to see if I could spot any of the women from the party, but none of them stood out in the crowd. "That was fast."

Her deep-belly giggle broke through the music that consumed the dance floor behind me. "I didn't expect you to be the best stripper in the world, but I didn't imagine you'd clear out a room full of horny drunks. Maybe you're right . . . maybe you are a lost cause."

My intense stare was meant as a middle finger without actually raising one. It was pointless, though, because all she did was laugh that off, too. And the only thing that made her calm down was the cold bottle of beer I pushed toward her.

"This has been fun, Cheryl. Really informative. At least now I know not to come running when you tell me something's urgent. And if you ever say you need my assistance in *anything*, you can bank on the fact that you won't get it. But seriously . . . it's been fun." I nodded and left, leaving her standing next to the stool I'd vacated with obvious disinterest in her rolling eyes.

At least I had an entertaining story to tell.

There was something about being in a loud space for an extended period of time that made the quiet of the outdoors noticeable. When I'd arrived, I could hear the music clear out to my truck. Now, as I left the club, the air held almost no sound at all.

Maybe that was why I heard it; I'd never know.

A heavy sigh sliced through the deafening silence of night. Unlike relief, this one felt weighted with sadness. Defeat. It might have been a sigh, but it sounded more like a gust of wind slamming into a windowpane. Subtle yet devastating.

I lifted my sights and stopped dead in my tracks, finding the bride-to-be leaning against one of the pillars that decorated the front of the building. She had her arms crossed, her shoulder pressed against the brick. Closed off. But I couldn't ignore the way she stood there with her head dropped forward, attention glued to the sidewalk below her as if trying to blend in with her surroundings. There was a good chance she wanted to go unnoticed, remain invisible beneath the lights lining the fascia. However, it was impossible *not* to notice her. And there was no way in hell she'd ever be invisible.

As I moved closer, her details became clearer. Beneath better lighting—unlike the blue hues inside—I could see more than just dark hair and eyes. I was able to notice the deep shade of red that veiled her face in long, loose curls. And when I came to a stop in front of her and she lifted her gaze to my face, I grew lost in the mixture of browns, greens, and golds that stared back at me.

"Where are your friends?" I asked, glancing around, still not finding anyone even remotely familiar.

"They decided to go to a real strip club."

"You didn't want to go with them?"

At first, she shrugged, but then she released another sigh and rested the side of her head against the pillar. "I decided to go home. Call it a night and go to sleep so I can put this all behind me."

My throat tightened as I contemplated the words to use, uncertainty nearly choking the life out of me. "Yeah, that's probably a good idea. I'm sure your fiancé would agree, too."

Wide eyes held mine; then her pink pout tipped into a grin I could only describe as flirtatious. "Oh, I'm not engaged."

I fingered the sash she still wore draped across her body, pinching the thin fabric while taking in the slow swells of her chest, as if each breath were a rolling wave on a creamy beach. "Then who's the bachelorette?"

"My best friend." Her voice was so soft it reminded me of marsh-mallow puff, which didn't seem to fit what I'd seen of her tonight. If anything, I would've imagined her as more of a marshmallow over an open flame, hot and dangerous yet deliciously addictive and satisfying. "She just found out she's pregnant, so she had to cancel at the last min-ute. I guess she's been sick and really tired lately."

I nodded with a hesitant step backward, still unsure of the situation and not wanting to get my hopes up. "Was this just practice for you? Or do you have experience being the guest of honor at a bachelorette party?"

She glanced to the side, avoiding me. "Neither."

I was desperate for her to lift her gaze so I could navigate the uncer-tainties better. Right now, I felt like a blind man feeling my way through a desert in search of a drop of water.

She shrugged again and, finally, raised her chin to meet my stare. "I guess a part of me wanted to know what it'd be like. I'll never get married—never want to—so in a way, this was the closest I'll ever get to experiencing it for myself."

"Then why not go to the strip club with your friends?"

"Because . . ."

Waiting for her to continue, I held my breath so long my breath turned stale in my lungs. Yet she never did. Instead, she dropped her chin again, wine-colored curtains shielding her face while she hid in the shadows. I had pegged her for a confident woman.

It was amazing how destructive a single insecurity could be.

"Listen, I don't know you. And you don't know me. If you think about it, I'm probably the safest person to open up to. I won't judge you, and even if I do, who cares? The chances of us running into each other again are slim to none."

Wonderment shone back at me when she blinked up, and then a careful grin danced at the corners of her mouth. Like the idea of purging her secrets to a stranger had never crossed her mind, and now that it had, the promise of liberation excited her. "I kinda ran into an ex a couple of weeks ago."

Somehow, I'd had a feeling this had to do with an old flame.

"No one has ever made me feel as worthless as he did when we broke up. Not only that, but he completely tainted the idea of marriage for me. So when my best friend couldn't make it tonight, I thought it would be fun to pretend. I used to love playing dress up when I was little—I could be anyone I wanted. I guess the excitement of make-believe never went away, huh?" She covered her mouth with her fingertips, but they did nothing to conceal the innocent smile or silence the soft rush of laughter that drifted past her lips.

"And what was it you were pretending tonight?"

In an instant, she dropped her reservations like a magician dropped his cape. Her cheeks heated, her grin spreading wider, and her eyes bored into mine with the kind of gratification you'd see on the face of an Olympic gold medalist. "That he didn't leave me. That, instead, I chose to leave him for a sexy doctor who adored me, who looked at me like I was the only woman in the room. I wanted to feel like I won instead of the other way around. That I was on the verge of spending the rest of my life with a handsome, rich, successful surgeon or something. I just wanted to pretend that my heart hadn't been broken into such unsalvageable pieces that I'll never be capable of love again."

Her pain furled in my chest until my ribs ached, threatening to shatter. And even though I should've been used to it by now, the idea that she wanted to pretend I was a surgeon splintered inside like shards of glass ripping me apart.

At least it seemed we had one thing in common—the feeling of not being good enough.

I wasn't sure what compelled me to slip my arms through the sleeves of my coat and drape my tie around my neck. It could've been the need to give her what she wanted, to be the *doctor* with eyes only for her. In some twisted way, I believed doing that for her would help me, too. Or maybe I'd just gotten sick of never being seen. Fed up with always being told I wasn't a *real* doctor just because the letters following my name were PhD, not MD. Tired of the knee-jerk assumptions that I was a loser, all because I'd chosen to stay at my parents' house longer than most.

Either way, the reason didn't matter once I stood in front of her, wearing the costume we both needed. The tips of my loafers to the toes of her blue heels. Her hooded gaze drew me closer until I had my hands on her hips. And the instant she wrapped her arms around my neck, my mouth claimed hers.

A brutal dominance I'd never experienced before came over me. I gripped her tighter and pulled her flush to my chest. Her lips parted on a gasp when my fingertips dug into the meaty cheeks of her ass, marking her. Marking this moment for both of us. And when our tongues met, literally everything else in the world disappeared.

I broke the kiss to catch my breath and asked, "How are you getting home?"

"Uber . . . I think. Amanda ordered it for me before they left."

"Well, if it doesn't show up, I can drive you." I pulled a few inches away from her face, needing to read her reaction. "If you want, of course."

"Why?"

"Same reasons as you—to pretend. You don't want to get married, but you want to know what it would be like if you did. I want to settle down someday, but I haven't found anyone who can look past my job or living situation long enough to give me a chance. So it's a win-win for both of us."

"Under one condition." She waited until I nodded before adding, "No names. If we're going to play make-believe, then we can't ever see each other again. Which means no introductions, no chance at being able to look the other person up."

"Okay. Deal."

"And anything we say in the heat of the moment while deep in our roles can't be taken seriously."

"So if I want to recite my vows to you with my tongue over your naked body, I can?"

"Please do."

Chapter 2

Kelsey

Some said tequila made their clothes fall off.

Me? Tequila made me feel like I'd been run over by a train. Eighty-four times.

Then again, I couldn't blame every ache and pain on alcohol. The soreness between my legs and pinch in my thighs had been caused by the stripper—but *after* the tequila had made my clothes fall off. So in a way . . . Jose Cuervo was at fault for *all* the things that had happened last night.

"You okay?" Tatum raised her dark brows, piercing me with those midnight eyes that made it impossible to see the pupils. They always freaked me out. Eyes shouldn't be that dark. "You look . . . rough."

I cocked my head and quirked my top lip in that sarcastic, "you're so funny" way. But even that nearly made me fall over. Damn hangover-induced vertigo. "Yeah. And in case you were wondering, you had a kick-ass bachelorette party. You're welcome."

"*Language*," Mom scolded from the patio through the open slider.

"Seriously?" I narrowed my gaze on my best friend, who hadn't moved away from the counter while she chopped vegetables for the salad. Leaning closer and lowering my voice, I added, "You curse all the time, and she never yells at you. Must be nice to be the golden child."

Tatum threw her head back and laughed . . . two things I physically couldn't do at the moment, thanks to this ridiculous hangover. "No I don't. Not here at least. And I'm not the *golden child*. That's Jay. I just get the perks because I'm marrying him."

I rolled my eyes and waved her off on my way to the bar, where I perched myself on a stool and dropped my forehead to the granite.

Someone came to sit next to me, but since the world had *finally* quit spinning for a few minutes, I didn't want to see who it was. And once she began to talk—loudly, might I add—my question was answered. My sister, Marlena.

"What the hell happened to you?" It might've been the remaining tequila that still swam in my bloodstream, but she sounded like she had her lips right next to my ear, yelling as if we sat twenty feet apart.

I sat up straight—a little too quickly—and stared at the open slider. Then I waited. And I waited. And when nothing happened, I held my hand out, gesturing to the space between us in the kitchen and my mom on the patio. "Are you friggin' kidding me right now?"

"What?" Marlena asked, having *no* clue what I was talking about.

"Mom literally just yelled at me for my language, and then you come in here, say *hell*, and she does nothing."

"Kelsey Peterson." Again, the stern warning came from outside.

Marlena and Tatum must've found that hysterical, because they couldn't stop laughing. I halfway wondered if they'd ever come up for air with how red their faces turned. Finally, my sister cleared her throat and swiveled her stool to face me. "Your voice carries. Mine doesn't."

"Whatever. You're louder than a stampede of monkeys."

"Not sure how that makes sense, but okay."

My nose scrunched while I gave her the nastiest "eat shit" expression I could muster. "It makes loads of sense. At least it does to me.

Right now. Next time you have too much to drink, I'll make sure to tell you how little *you* make sense the following day."

"Oh yeah. Tatum's bachelorette party . . . how was that?" Marlena eyed Tatum over the bar and furrowed her brows. "Why aren't you hungover?"

"She didn't go." I cringed when Tatum glared at me, knowing I'd have to explain without giving away her secret. "She, uh . . . ate something bad for dinner and had to cancel at the last minute. It was too late to get our money back for any of it, so we just carried on without her. You totally should've come."

"From the looks of you, I'd say I'm glad I didn't. Really, though . . . how much *did* you drink?"

"A shit ton."

"Young lady," Mom said from the doorway, her glare pinning me in place. "How many times do I have to warn you about your language? Connor and Lizzie are here. I'm sure your sister and Nick wouldn't appreciate it if their young children went home saying *ass* and *hell* and *shit*."

All the words literally vanished in that moment while I stared in awe at my mother.

This was my life. I couldn't make this shit up.

"Noted." I swung my gaze to Marlena and scowled. "A *crap* ton. Which should tell you just how much fun it was. But if it doesn't, let me tell you. It was a blast. We had drinks and music and a male stripper that we didn't have to share with anyone else."

"A stripper?" Her brow arched perfectly, only adding a slight wrinkle to her forehead—she was a damn fool if she thought *anyone* believed that she didn't get regular Botox treatments. "Gee, Kelsey . . . I don't know what to say. Am I supposed to be sad that I missed seeing a guy dance around in ass floss?"

Again, I turned toward the door, noticing that my mother was no longer there. Not only that, but she conveniently didn't hear Marlena's "language." I found that odd, considering she wasn't the quietest person.

I rolled my wrist, sweeping my hand close to her face. "It wasn't . . . *floss*."

"Testie straps?" She just refused to give this up.

Unfortunately, Tatum couldn't resist chiming in. "Penis ribbon."

Their laughter made my head throb. Which only got worse the more they carried on. Marlena added, "Dick sling."

"Zucchini bikini."

Having enough, I decided to throw in my own. "Ball satchel."

Somehow, some way, I'd pissed the heavens off, because they were hell bent on making me suffer today. Just then, my mom slid into the kitchen and asked, "What's a ball satchel? I might want one of those."

"Sure thing, Mom. I'll get you one for Christmas." Not a hint of a smile shadowed my mouth—I was *that* good at resting my bitch face during a moment of dry humor. "Any particular color, or would you like to be surprised?"

Her bright smile *almost* had me breaking character. "Surprise me."

"You got it." I shifted to face Tatum and waited until she lifted her gaze, catching me staring at her. Rather than aggravate my throbbing head even more by flicking my chin toward the hallway, I simply said, "Come. Let's walk and talk for a moment."

One of the things I loved most about Tatum was the way she followed without asking questions. It made pulling her aside *so* much easier than having to explain everything in front of half my family. She was like a well-trained service animal.

Jason must've been pleased.

"So . . . I slept with the stripper," I admitted once the door closed behind me.

Tatum turned away from me, and with her head cocked, chin slightly angled up, she observed the bedroom that, at one point in time, used to be mine. "How come I've never been in this room before? It's really nice. I love what your mom did with the curtains."

"His dick was the size of my leg."

Still, she seemed far more interested in the lamp on the nightstand than the words coming out of my mouth. The admission I'd offered. The hot, juicy details of my night.

"He split me in half, and I had to go to the emergency room to get my vagina sewn back together." When she continued to mutter inaudible things to herself, I grabbed her arm and shook her, forcing her to look at me. "Did you not listen to *anything* I said?"

"I have to be honest, Kels . . . I stopped after you said you slept with the stripper."

"Why?"

"I have a feeling I won't be able to scrub the images from my brain with a wire brush through the ear. And with as weak as my stomach has been lately, thanks to the"—she leaned closer and lowered her voice—"vomit-inducing fetus inside me, the last thing I want to do is puke all over this really nice room."

There wasn't much I could do but blink dramatically at her. How we'd ever become friends to begin with would remain a mystery. We were nothing alike. Nothing. All right . . . that wasn't true. But still, I refused to admit to anyone how similar we were—no need to make myself look flighty.

"Fine, I'll skip the details. I just need my best friend right now."

Sympathy softened her features as she lowered herself to the edge of the mattress, pulling me down with her. "What happened? Are you okay? I'm sorry, Kelsey . . . I thought you just wanted to brag about getting laid."

"Oh, I did. It was amazing." I ignored her eye roll and continued as if she hadn't nonverbally dismissed me. "But that doesn't negate the fact that he's a stripper. He takes his clothes off for a living, Tater. Who knows how many other women he's boned after a few dances."

"You used protection, right?"

"Of course I did." My head bobbed from side to side slowly while I contemplated her question, not at all caring that I'd already answered. "I think I did. I'm pretty sure he wore a condom."

"Pretty sure?"

"I woke up with an empty wrapper stuck to my cheek. That's about all the proof I have."

"Do you not remember if he put it on or not?" Her incredulous stare was almost too much to look at, so I dropped my gaze to the floor and shrugged. "Kelsey . . ."

"Before you go all high and mighty on me, let me remind you that I was really drunk. The VIP suite had free liquor, and for the money I paid that place, I took *full* advantage of it. And I do remember stuff. Just not that part."

Her face scrunched, feigned disgust dripping from her lips. "I'm afraid to ask what all you remember."

"The good parts. Like the freaky things he did to me. He should become a gigolo. That's a male prostitute, right?" I waved her off before she had a chance to answer. "Regardless of what it's called, he was a god in the bedroom."

"That sounds amazing. Can I go now?"

"He had all the right moves. Knew all the right places to touch and lick . . . and squeeze. And smack. And—"

"Yeah . . . this has been fun."

At this point, I was enjoying this too much to stop. "Oh, and don't get me started on the filth that came out of that man's mouth."

"No worries. I wasn't planning on it."

"My heavens, Tatum . . . he said things that made *me* blush."

"Impressive. You'll have to tell me about it sometime—later. Or never."

It had become slightly harder to keep a straight face, but I wasn't a quitter. I pressed on, avoiding eye contact, knowing one glance at her and I'd lose my composure. "And his stamina . . ." I shaped my lips into an O, cheeks hollow, and fanned myself. "Holy shit. He could give the Energizer Bunny a run for its money. He just kept going and going and—"

"Going. Yeah . . . I vaguely remember those commercials."

"Oh, and his body. Sweet baby Jesus, Tater. Words cannot describe his body."

"Good. Then we're done here." She stood, but I grabbed her wrist, preventing her from leaving. "What? You just said there were no words to describe it, so why try? What's the point in sitting here while you attempt to tell me about something that defies language? It's a waste of time."

A smile broke free on my lips. "Seriously, Tatum. While all those things are true, I was just messing with you. But I do need you. I need you to tell me that I'm not a slut."

"You're not a slut."

"And mean it."

Her head dropped back at the same time a groan filtered past her lips. She sank onto the mattress and threw herself back, arms stretched out above her. "I *do* mean it, Kels. You're allowed to go out and have a good time, even if it ends with you naked and his penis in your vagina . . . as long as you enjoyed yourself."

I patted her thigh. "Thanks, bestie. You're awesome. World's greatest pep talker who ever lived." The sarcasm was thick.

"You know, you're mean when you're hungover."

Giving up, I fell back onto the mattress next to Tatum and turned my head to look at her. "We agreed we wouldn't share names, so I don't even know who he is."

"Would it change anything if you knew his name?"

"Yeah. If I knew who he was, I'd hit him up for a repeat. He was amazing. I wasn't exaggerating about that. Then again, that could totally get out of hand. It might lead to me paying him to have sex instead of going to a gig . . . that's a line I won't cross. A thin line. Slightly blurry. Faint. But a line all the same."

She closed her eyes and took a deep breath before setting her sights on me again. "Then I guess it's a good thing you don't have his name. Anyway . . . how were his dance moves? Anything like Magic Mike?"

"If Magic Mike had two left feet and were deaf, sure." I laughed and held my head to keep the drums inside my skull from getting worse. "Oh my God, Tater . . . he had the guy play the *worst* music. I'm talking about crap that was before our time. You know that one song that goes like . . . *That's the way, uh-uh uh-huh, I like it, uh-huh uh-huh?* That kinda music."

"That's bad." She tried to keep a straight face but lost after two seconds. "I realize I don't have much experience with strippers or the music they dance to, but I can't imagine a professional taking their clothes off to the likes of 'Tootsee Roll' unless their act doubled as a comedy show. Is that what he was? A comedian?"

"I wish I could say yes. But I can't."

Tatum sat up and dropped her head into her hands, her shoulders jumping with the amusement that rolled through her. "Now I wish I had been there to see it."

"You would've been entertained." I dragged myself up until we sat side by side. "I don't know why you like that lamp. It's hideous."

She pointed to the duck with the shade over its head and quirked a brow my way. "It's so cute. How do you *not* like it? I bet it's a collector's item."

"Yeah, if you were a garbage collector."

Tatum reached out and opened the top drawer, finding a leather-bound book inside. "What's this?" She fanned through the blank pages as though it were a new novel from the library. "Looks like a journal no one ever used."

A memory sparked in my mind, one I'd locked away years ago. I grabbed it out of her hands and opened to the very first page, checking the name that had been written in blue ink. Kelsey Peterson. "My grandmother gave this to me when I was in high school. I forgot all about it."

"How did it end up in here?"

I shrugged and closed the book. "Who knows. My mom probably found it when she cleaned out this room after I left."

"You gonna keep it?"

I held it up and said, "Why not? It's mine, after all."

"What are you going to do with it?"

"Hell if I know. But I'm willing to bet it'll be amazing, whatever it is."

Chapter 3

Aaron

Jason stepped into the party bus, took one look at the two gleaming poles, and shook his head. "I swear to you, Aaron . . . if you got a stripper, I'm gone."

I playfully shoved his shoulder, pushing him farther into the bus. "You weren't specific about that."

The bus began to roll away from the curb, setting us off balance on our feet. Jason grabbed one of the poles to keep from falling on his ass and grimaced, as if he'd just contracted a disease from touching it.

"Warming it up for her?" I joked.

He flipped me off just as the bus darkened. In an instant, colorful strobe lights danced from the ceiling and added to the bright lamppost glow that crept in through the heavily tinted windows. Club music thumped through the speakers, filling the space with a steady beat, but not one we couldn't talk over.

"For a neuropsychologist, you're rather dumb." The grin stretching from ear to ear informed me that he wasn't serious. Then again, he was my best friend—I'd known him since high school—so there weren't many insults he could sling my way that would be taken seriously. "I *specifically* told you that Tatum and I had agreed no strippers."

"Yeah, but that's rather ambiguous if you think about it."

With a heavy plop, we sat across from each other. He stared for a moment, mouth agape, narrowed eyes set on me and sending listless questions my way.

I didn't break eye contact once.

It was a match to the death—I'd always been good at this game.

Finally, he blinked and asked, "How so?"

I leaned back, settling in with my hands clasped behind my head. "Well, it's unclear if that also includes women who are already naked. If you think about it, she wouldn't be stripping . . . because she wouldn't have on any clothes."

Jason didn't hesitate to stand, demanding the driver stop and pull over. "I'm getting out."

"I'm just giving you a hard time. Sit back down, dumbass."

"Dumbass? Me?" He grabbed the pole and whipped around, then realized what he had his hand on and yanked it back as though it had scorched his palm. "Next to you, I'm a certified genius. The only thing saving your reputation is the extra years you put in for a fancy title."

His smile gave him away; meanwhile, mine stayed in check, even as I tossed around a few different ways to give him a hard time about his job. "You sure are, Jason. Tell me, how's the landfill treating you?"

With a groan, he reclaimed his seat. "I should've never looked you up when I moved back."

"Imagine how insanely boring your life would've been had you not."

He pinned me with his doubtful stare. "I'm serious, Aaron . . . if you have something stupid up your sleeve, tell me now."

I held up three fingers. "Scout's honor."

"Why do you do that? You were never a Boy Scout."

"Doesn't mean I can't have the same honor they do. You should understand that more than anyone." It took significant self-control to fight off my smirk when he tipped his head in question. "Just because you have a small dick doesn't mean you can't fuck the ladies like the big boys do."

"Are you jealous, Aaron?" A wicked grin spread across his lips. "Listen, just because you can't please a woman in the bedroom doesn't mean every other guy has a small dick. I'm pretty sure part of a Scout's honor is taking responsibility. If you can't perform, you don't have anyone to blame but yourself. Don't hate on others who can satisfy a woman."

"Psh . . . I rocked a chick's world last weekend," I boasted, excited to finally have someone to tell. Noel, my assistant at the office, didn't seem to care much. But Jason? He'd care. Maybe.

"Oh yeah? Have you heard from her since?" Okay, so he didn't care at all.

"No, but that's only because we agreed it would be that one night, and then we'd never see each other again. She didn't even tell me her name."

"I'm not sure that does much to prove your point." He leaned forward with his elbows on his knees. "If you were that amazing, she would want to do it again and again. I should know . . . Tatum can't get enough of me."

"For your information, we set those rules *before* we left the club."

He grinned in satisfaction. "Ah . . . so you met this chick at a club. Was she drinking?"

"Not the point."

"Whose idea was it to keep it anonymous and never see each other again?"

"Hers. But again, that's not the point."

"And then after you *rocked her world*, as you say, did she change her mind about it only being one night?"

I glared at him, burning my feigned annoyance into his face. "No. But she told me over and over how no one has ever fucked her the way

I did. In fact, she said all kinds of things—sexy things. *Dirty things.* And she was a freak. But in a good way."

Before he had his arms stretched out along the back of the bench, I could tell he had something witty to say. His slow-forming smirk told me so. But I let him have his moment. After all, this back-and-forth ribbing was what had kept us friends for so long. In a weird way, it was the most genuine relationship I'd ever had with anyone, despite the fact that we had gone years without speaking while we each pursued a career. When it came to everyone else in my life, I was a fraud, even when I didn't mean to be.

"So you were the best she's ever had, yet she didn't want to see you again?"

I shrugged and played into his game. "You're twisting the whole thing to make it sound bad. You see, *what had happened was*"—I had to look at something other than his face before I lost my composure and laughed too soon—"we had agreed ahead of time that we would be real and honest, not hold anything back. And we were able to do that *because* we didn't know each other. No matter how great the sex was, a repeat would never work out."

"Why not?"

"Think about it. If you knew ahead of time that you'd never see someone again, you'd have no inhibitions, no reason to impress them. And on the flip side, you'd feel no need to lie to them. It's far easier to just tell them like it is without worry."

His head bobbed as he listened to what I had to say, entertaining my deductive reasoning for the time being. That didn't mean he wouldn't come back at the end with some insult we'd both get a good laugh from, though.

"It was rather liberating." That didn't come close to describing my night with her. "I didn't have to worry about never hearing from her again, because I already knew I wouldn't. And she got to play out her fantasy, pretend I was whoever she wanted me to be, say whatever she wanted, all without any fear of judgment."

"That all makes tons of sense. Really, Aaron, I'm impressed with the logic behind this. I'm also wondering why you've never gone about sex with that mentality before. But what I'm *most* curious about is . . . how would you know if anything she said to you—such as saying you were the best she's ever had—was the truth? If she was pretending you were someone else, she might've faked that part, too."

"Doubtful. I knocked her socks off. If she had a way to find me, she'd tell me herself."

"Did this all happen in the parking lot or something?"

I narrowed my stare for a moment before I realized what he'd asked. "What? No. I took her back to her place."

Jason couldn't hold back his laughter. He went from having an amused grin to head back, arm wrapped around his waist, halfway fallen over in a fit of hysterics. After a minute or two, he finally calmed enough to explain what he'd found so funny. "You know where she lives?"

"Yeah, so?"

He shook his head, amusement still rumbling from his chest. "But you were supposed to keep it anonymous? How can you do that if there's nothing stopping you from knocking on her door? Hell, why *haven't* you done that? If the sex was so amazing, you should be beating down her door."

I wouldn't admit just how many times I'd contemplated doing that very thing. Granted, I couldn't remember *exactly* where her apartment was, but it wasn't like I couldn't figure it out if I wanted. In truth, I *did* want to. But there would've been no point. At the end of the day, she was the same as all the others—believing for one reason or another that I was someone else. They heard *doctor* and assumed my days consisted of reaching inside someone's chest and saving their life with my bare hands while earning at least half a million dollars a year. She didn't think that, though. No . . . she just thought I took my clothes off for money.

I wasn't sure which was worse.

"Have you not listened to a word I said? The sex wouldn't be the same. It was so good *because* we didn't have things like rejection or judgment getting in the way. I was able to tie her up and call all the shots, take complete control. Whereas if I try doing that again, there's the worry that it won't be as good as the last time. Or maybe she was only that vocal because she'd had a few drinks, and the next time, she'd be sober and quiet, making me question everything I did. It's always best to go out like Mikey—on top. Leave it as the best night of our lives and move on, always remembering the time that no other can compare to."

The bus came to a stop in front of a house. Through the window, I could see a guy walking down the driveway, and I assumed that meant this conversation had ended, which I was perfectly fine with. Jason didn't need to know the extent of my pathetic sex life. He'd always assumed I had no problems getting laid, and I never felt the need to correct him.

"This thing is huge, Jason." The guy's eyes lit up as he took note of the interior on his way toward us at the back of the bus. "How many people are we picking up? I thought you wanted to keep this low key."

"I did. But this asshat over here"—Jason pointed to me—"doesn't understand the definition of *low key*. We were actually just talking about his need to overcompensate for the *smaller* things in his life."

A barking laugh ripped through my chest. "It's called *mirroring*, not compensating."

"You don't have to lie to Nick, Aaron. It's okay. Just pretend you won't see him after tonight and be yourself." If he wasn't my best friend, I would've told him off. But since he was, I settled for giving him the middle finger.

Shaking my head, I turned to the guy sitting next to Jason. "Ah, so you're Marlena's husband. Man, do I feel bad for you. You have to be related to this dick," I said, pointing at Jason, who smiled proudly, as if being called a dick was a compliment.

I'd gone to school with Marlena, but we'd lost touch after my graduation, and I hadn't seen much of her since Jason had moved back to town eight months ago. She and Jason, being cousins who were only a year apart, used to be close, which meant I'd spent much of my high school career around her. The few times I'd been around Marlena recently, Nick hadn't been with her.

Nick laughed, glancing at Jason for a second before swinging his attention to me. "He's not all that bad. Although, I won't lie . . . after everything my wife's sister had to say about him, I wasn't exactly welcoming when he first moved to town. But then I got to know him and realized he was a pretty good guy."

The fact that tonight we were celebrating Jason's last days of freedom before he married Tatum was a miracle. Her best friend—who also happened to be Marlena's little sister—had brought more problems between them than they had on their own. I wasn't privy to all the details, only the ones he'd shared with me over a beer from time to time, but I knew enough to conclude Tatum's best friend had something against men in general.

"Speaking of Kelsey"—Jason snapped his fingers and leaned forward—"Tatum's old room is still empty. I'm sure Kelsey's the last person you'd want to live with, even for a few months until you get a house, but if worse comes to worse, I can always ask if she'd be okay with you staying there."

"Are you suggesting I live with your man-hating cousin?"

He shrugged and leaned back, the complete opposite reaction I would've expected to come from him. "Why not? It beats you having to sign a lease on something and throw money away on rent—money you've been saving to buy something more permanent. And like you just pointed out, she hates all things attached to a penis, so I wouldn't have to worry about you making a move on her. If you did . . . I might have to report you to someone. I doubt it would be safe to have you treat people with mental conditions if you have one, too."

"Yeah . . . that definitely wouldn't be safe." I took a second to contemplate his idea. It wasn't the best, but it would do in a pinch. "Okay, fine. I have to be out of the house the weekend after your wedding. If I don't find anywhere to go by the end of the week, I'll let you know. That way, if she says no, I'll still have one more week to come up with something."

"I'll have Tatum ask. We'll have a better chance of her saying yes to her."

I jerked my chin in thanks just as the bus stopped in front of another house.

Jason wanted low key, so I decided to give him that. I just refused to tell him what the plan was, because it was far more entertaining to watch him try to figure it out. But at the end of the night, after driving around town for hours, he'd realize I'd given him exactly what he wanted—a night with the guys, hanging out in a party bus with two coolers full of beer.

It didn't take a brain surgeon to know what your best friend needed.

Chapter 4

Kelsey

I'd stared at the screen so long that the letters and numbers had turned into black blobs that didn't translate to anything I understood. Honestly, I had no idea what I was even looking at anymore. Or why I continued to sit in front of the computer. It wasn't like I was doing anything.

"Did you find a sofa for the Huntington model?" Brent caught my attention with his snapping fingers and flapping lips. That man never shut up. "You've been looking online for, like, an hour, and I'm trying to get the inventory spreadsheet finalized."

Turning my back to him, I frantically searched the top of my desk, then the drawer that held my pens. After finding what I was looking for, I spun in my chair and held it out. "Here. I think you might need this."

He took it from me and then promptly narrowed his very confused gaze on me. "Why would I need your business card?"

"Because I think you forgot who owns this company."

Brent being Brent, the disgruntled asshole in the office, he mumbled under his breath and walked away. If he weren't such a hard worker and capable of lifting heavy furniture, he would've been fired years ago.

Unfortunately, he saved me the additional payroll expense—it'd take two people to cover his job.

"Wow." Tatum dropped her purse on my desk, earning my attention. "What was that?"

"Assholes."

She moved the keyboard aside and leaned against the edge, her disappointment thick between us. "Just because you hate men doesn't mean you should treat everyone with a penis like shit."

"Oh, don't let that fool you." I rolled my wrist over my shoulder, as if shooing someone away. "I treat all my employees like that, regardless of which crotch accessory they have. I'm an equal opportunity employer."

"I think your company is by far your biggest accomplishment."

I beamed, sitting up straighter, filled with pride. "You think? Thanks, Tater."

"You're so welcome. The fact that you still have people willing to work for you is truly a remarkable achievement."

This heifer better watch it—the last thing a bride should do is piss off her maid of honor. "What do you want? Why did you come here? I don't have time for this."

"Why not?" Brent asked, literally coming out of nowhere like an annoying genie who stole wishes instead of granting them. "It's not like you're doing anything else around here."

After glaring at him for a few moments, I rolled my seat back to my computer and furiously searched for the biggest, heaviest couch that man had ever seen. That'd show him. And I would've purchased one, too, had Tatum not removed my hand from the mouse.

"Back away from the keyboard . . . nice and slow." She regarded me like an irrational toddler. "A twelve-thousand-dollar couch is a bit much, don't you think? I mean . . . you make good money, but that's a lot to spend on a sofa that'll sit in a warehouse."

"Get to the point of your visit, hash brown."

She rolled her eyes, though that didn't stop the smirk curling the corner of her mouth. She secretly loved it when I called her potato-related names. It made her feel special—she didn't have to admit it. "Okay . . . so you know Jay's best friend, Aaron, right?"

"I know *of* him. Why?"

"You've met him before, haven't you?" She was up to something; I could tell.

Crossing my arms, I leaned back in my chair. "Technically, but it's been years. What's with all the questions?"

"*All* the questions? Kelsey . . ." Her laughter gave her away—it was the dramatic giggle, head slightly tilted back, and hand waving through the air like she was some character in *The Great Gatsby*. Not that I'd seen it, but that wasn't the point. "I asked *two*; you make it sound like I've interrogated you."

"Fine. It was only two. But there's a third coming. Possibly more."

"Whatever. You know him, though. Don't you? He's the best man in our wedding; you're going to have to walk up and down the aisle with him. Jay went to high school with him, and apparently, he used to hang out with Marlena, too."

"Thanks for that refresher course on Aaron. Unfortunately, I wasn't taking notes, so I hope there won't be a quiz." I lifted one brow in a silent challenge for her to get on with it or give up. I wasn't in the mood to play guessing games.

"You're mighty snappy today," she said, squinting as though she were examining me. "Are you on your period?"

"No. I get that in two days."

"Remind me to stay away from you for the next week." Taking a deep breath, she readied herself to *finally* get to her purpose for coming. "Anyway, he needs a place to stay for a couple of months."

"Nope. Sorry. No vacancy." I slapped my hand on the top of my desk and carried on as if I were too busy to finish the conversation. All

I was missing was a see-through green visor, and I could've passed as a hardworking stock market broker.

"You have the spare room just sitting empty."

"It's not empty. It's full of your old furniture."

"Perfect. See? It's all set up for him to stay there until he can find his own place."

"What about *nope* do you not understand? The *no* or the *puh*? And I use that room."

"Oh yeah? For what?"

She should've known not to challenge me. I always won. "It's where I keep my Tatum shrine."

"Fine, but can you at least consider it? Please? For me?"

Damn all the things. I hated it when she asked me to do something *for her*, knowing I couldn't tell her no. "Okay. I'll consider it—but only under one condition."

A full, heavy sigh rushed past her lips. "What's the condition?"

"You let me name your baby."

"No." Well, that was fast. "Not for *considering* letting someone move into your spare room for a couple of months."

"Then if I agree, you'll let me name it."

"Again . . . no."

"It must not be that important to you."

She stared at me for a full minute, the seconds long and dragged out. "Why do you want to name the baby so badly? What's going through your head, Kels? Like . . . what kind of name are you thinking of?"

It couldn't have been that easy. "I don't really care what you call the bambino, to be honest with you. I just know you won't agree to it, which gets me out of allowing Jason's friend to live with me."

"Why are you so opposed to it? He's a really nice guy—smart and funny."

"Whoa." I sat forward and held a hand up to silence her. "Are you trying to find him a place to stay or a wife? I'm not interested in either. And I'm *really* not interested in dating the guy."

"Good. Because I'm not trying to hook you two up. I'm simply pointing out what a great roommate he could be for a few months."

"Few? You said *a couple* last time. What's it gonna be next . . . a year?"

She laughed—though I didn't know what was funny. "He's looking to buy a house, so he doesn't want to sign a lease, and the house he's in right now has sold. He only needs somewhere to sleep until he can get his own place. You have a spare room, *and* you have an in with most of the Realtors in the area. He'd pay you, obviously. He's not looking for free room and board. And from what I know of the guy, he's not a slob."

"Well, that's comforting. After living with you, I don't think I could handle another slob."

The smile vanished, yet I could see through her phony aggravation.

I huffed, and my shoulders fell forward. "Tatum . . . I don't know how I feel about a guy living with me. I get that he's my cousin's best friend, and that I kinda sorta knew of him years and years ago, so he's not entirely a stranger. But he's a man nonetheless."

Regardless of how I felt about the situation, Aaron didn't deserve to hang in limbo just because I hesitated to have a man move in. It wasn't fair to him. And technically, he wasn't the reason I believed all men were liars with shady ulterior motives. Yet for whatever reason, I blamed the entire male population anyway. It was just easier that way.

The list of their useful qualities was short.

And *roommate* wasn't on it.

"Can you just tell me why it's so important that I let him move in?"

She was quiet for a moment, which was unlike her. Normally, she talked—or rambled—and half of what she said never made any sense.

But then she cleared her throat, which was a good indication that she was about to get real with me. "I feel bad for him, Kels."

"You also feel bad for the old dogs at the shelter who never get picked because they aren't puppies. Do you want me to house them, too? What about the kids on that commercial who could eat for only pennies a day . . . I should move them all in?"

"That's not what I mean." Hmm . . . feisty Tatum was on the verge of sneaking in. *This ought to be good.* "He's a psychologist, owns his own practice, and has spent the last however many years taking care of others. And now, he needs a place to stay just long enough to find and buy a house, and no one's willing to help."

I lasered my narrowed gaze on her. "You have a spare room."

"And I'm pregnant—not news we really care for others to learn just yet. Having someone live with us makes that a rather difficult feat, don't you think? Not to mention, we'll be newlyweds. If worse comes to worse and you say no, then I guess we'll offer him the extra room. But we were kinda hoping it wouldn't come to that."

"If you don't want him living with you, then why would I?"

A groan ripped through her throat that sounded far more like a growl than anything I'd ever heard come from her. "I just explained why him living with us wasn't ideal. It has nothing to do with *him* per se and everything to do with the timing and our situation."

"Damn, Tatum . . . I was just giving you a hard time."

"I know." She didn't, but I'd let her pretend she could fool me.

"Okay, fine," I conceded. "I'll consider it. But that doesn't mean I'll say yes."

She beamed and pushed off the desk. "That's all I'm asking for."

"When do you need an answer?"

Pulling her purse strap up her shoulder, she twisted her lips in thought. "He has to move out in a little over two weeks—the weekend after the wedding. So the sooner the better, especially if the answer's no. He'll need time to figure something out."

I nodded. More like my head bobbed while I became lost down the rabbit hole of concerns and what-ifs. "I'll let you know either way by tomorrow. Is that doable?"

"Yes, ma'am." She stepped away with a smile so wide I wondered if her face would split in half. "Thank you, Kels."

"I didn't say yes," I called after her, but she was halfway out the door, so she might not have heard.

Chapter 5

Aaron

"Morning, boss." Noel beamed at me from her desk when I walked into the office.

No matter what day of the week it was or what our schedule looked like, she always wore an infectious smile and spoke with such cheerfulness—as if those two things had been part of her job description.

They weren't, but if she ever left my practice, I sure as hell planned to make them mandatory. Truth be told, I prayed she'd never leave. I doubted I'd ever find another receptionist capable of filling her shoes.

Thinking of that, I glanced down and took note of how small her feet were; then I shook off the irony. "Whatever's in your coffee, I would like some in mine."

"Having a bad day already?" She finished getting her desk set up—computer turned on, schedule open, files set out—and then moved to the waiting area to open the blinds and organize the magazines. "What was it . . . overslept? Stubbed your toe getting out of bed? Hot water not working?"

I collapsed into a seat and watched as she ran through her morning setup procedures, not bothering to help. Granted, that was because she didn't *want* it—a man could be told only so many times that he was in the way before he gave up. If she chose to handle everything on her own, then so be it.

Yet another reason I prayed she'd never leave.

"It's Friday," I grumbled. "Isn't that reason enough to be in a bad mood?"

Noel stopped what she was doing and placed her hand on her cocked hip, regarding me with quirked, pursed lips the color of strawberry Starbursts. "I always thought the end of the week is when everyone's in a good mood. Last day before the weekend and all. Mondays are usually the moody ones."

"Maybe. But looking forward to time passing doesn't help me much. It stresses me out instead of exciting me. Next weekend is Jason's wedding, and then I'll only have one more week before I have to move." It'd been almost two weeks since my wild night with the faux bachelorette; remembering the way her body felt against mine was the only thing keeping me somewhat sane these days.

She offered a small smile while checking the water station along the far wall of the waiting room. "You still haven't found anywhere to stay?"

One thing my parents always nagged me about was my extreme level of procrastination when it came to things I didn't want to accept. And this time, it had really bitten me in the ass.

"I think so, but I haven't heard back yet. Jason said he'd ask his cousin. Hopefully, he'll give me an answer sometime today. If that doesn't work out, I'm officially screwed." I closed my eyes and ran my hands over my face, not caring if I messed up my hair as I pushed my fingers through the overgrown strands.

"And there's no place that offers month to month instead of signing a lease?"

"I found one, but as of right now, they don't have any available units. And once they get notice of a tenant leaving, it'll still be thirty days before I can get in. So that's not even an option."

"Wow, I so don't envy you right now."

I groaned as she strolled back to her computer and sat, continuing our conversation while staying on track with her morning routine. Perching myself on the corner of her desk, I entertained her while she worked on organizing the patient charts for the day.

"In all seriousness, what will happen if his cousin says no?"

"I guess I'll have to stay here. It's not ideal, but if worse comes to worse, sleeping on the floor and bathing in the sink will be my only choice. At least I won't have to live out of my car." I'd joked about it ever since finding out that my parents had sold their house and I needed to find somewhere to go. But the closer I got to the deadline, the less I found it funny. It was more or less my reality, and it was about time I started to accept it.

Her sad eyes met mine, the sympathetic stare only making my day worse. "I don't understand why Jason can't let you stay with him. Obviously he wouldn't be the first option, but I can't imagine he'd let you sleep on your office floor."

"I doubt they'd want anyone living with them a week after they get married, regardless of how temporary it would be. But on the other hand, if I don't have anywhere to go and have to resort to living in my office, I'm sure he'd offer his place. I just don't want it to get to that point. I know I wouldn't want another man moving in with me and my wife as soon as we get back from our honeymoon."

"Well, hopefully, you'll get good news about his cousin's place."

I nodded and slipped off the corner of her desk, leaving her to finish setting up the office. Honestly, I was surprised no one had come in yet. We usually had at least one person sitting in the waiting room as soon as we opened.

I checked my phone after my last patient and noticed a text from Jason. It was exactly what I needed to boost my mood for the day and ease the stress that had been eating at me for weeks. Kelsey had agreed to let me stay at her place. His message said there were conditions, but I didn't care what they were. It kept me from sleeping under my desk and cleaning myself in a sink that many others used on a daily basis.

Noel peeked her head into my office and paused, assessing me with curious eyes and a hint of a smile. There was no way she knew about my text, other than some odd intuition she seemed to have when it came to me. She always joked that we'd been siblings in a past life, possibly twins, and if I actually believed in multiple lives, I would agree.

"Jason heard back from his cousin."

Her grin widened, excitement brightening her entire face. "Based on your expression, I'm going to assume it's good news. I bet you're relieved." She entered my office and took a seat across from me. "So, have you met him before?"

It took me a second to figure out she wasn't referring to Jason, because that would make no sense. "His cousin's a girl. I used to see her around years ago, back when we were in high school and she'd bug the ever-loving fuck out of Jason and Marlena. But other than that, no, I haven't seen her since I graduated high school and Jason left to go to college."

"How old is she?" Skepticism rolled off Noel like a ball on a downward hill.

I had to stop and think about it, do a little mental calculation. "She's Tatum's age, so midtwenties, I think. Twenty-five or twenty-six. I'm not sure exactly, just that she's quite a bit younger than Jason and me. She was only a kid the last time I saw her."

"Well, is she nice at least?"

"Couldn't tell you, to be honest with you." I shrugged and began to tidy up my desk, preparing to leave for the weekend. "I hear she has issues with men, but I'm hoping that it'll be different with me—I'm not looking to date her."

She pinned me with a stare that promised lectures. "Is she pretty?"

"Hell if I know. Like I said, Noel . . . it's been *years* since I last saw her. And back then, she was awkward. She had frizzy red hair, braces, and glasses, and we called her Inspector Gadget because her arms and legs were long and super skinny. I doubt she's changed much, though."

Her eyes rolled with her head, her shoulders slumping forward in a dramatic display of frustration. "Seriously? If you think I'm gonna fall for that, you have another thing coming. Of *course* she's changed. She's not a little kid anymore."

I didn't have to hear her say it to know what she was getting at— she believed I wasn't capable of making smart decisions around pretty women. Even more, she likely figured living with one would be a terrible idea. I couldn't argue, but at this point, I didn't have much of an option, either.

"You don't have anything to worry about. I *highly* doubt I'll find her attractive."

"Does she have Facebook? Instagram? Any kind of social media we can find her on and see what she looks like now?"

I blinked at her, wondering how we could get along as well as we did when there were times it felt like several generations existed between us. "What is this? Twenty questions? You know I don't use any of that shit."

"College really messed you up, didn't it?" She laughed to herself while pulling out her phone. "If anyone spoke to you before making the decision to go for their doctorate, they'd never go beyond their master's degree."

"What's that supposed to mean?"

"Listen, I didn't know you before you started college, so I can't say whether or not you've always been this way. But from the things you've told me, I imagine you entered freshman year as a normal eighteen-year-old and came out of graduate school as a seventy-year-old." She waved off my confusion with a quick flick of her wrist, turning her attention to the device in her hand. "You only have social media because of your practice, and you have me manage it. Name one guy in his thirties—aside from you—who doesn't have at least one social media account."

"I can name a lot. It's just not a wise way to spend my time." Actually, I couldn't name any. However, that had nothing to do with being the only one my age who didn't feel the need to share my every thought and meal with the world. It had to do with my lack of friends—my circle was small, and I liked it that way.

Acquaintances were plentiful. Close friends were a select few.

"Okay, so what's her name?"

I leaned back in my chair, making it recline with my weight, and hesitantly gave her the information she sought. "Kelsey. I'm assuming her last name is Peterson, because that's what her sister's last name was back in high school, but to be honest, I don't have the slightest clue if they even have the same dad. So there's a possibility that—"

"Found her." Damn, she was good. That was the reason I'd given all social media duties to her instead of trying to stumble through it myself. "Wow . . . she's not at *all* what you described."

I was about to ask what she meant by that when she turned the screen around and stopped my world from spinning with one picture. One face. I didn't need to see the other photos on her profile, because I had every inch of her body etched into my mind. Every time I closed my eyes, I could see her clearly—naked, wrists tied to her headboard, cheeks pink with ecstasy.

Fuck. Me.

"Just keep to yourself when you're both home. I'm sure it won't be hard to resist your best friend's cousin, especially if you say she's a man-hater. Don't sleep with her, and you'll be fine."

"Too late." I hadn't meant to say it out loud, but I was in such shock I couldn't help it.

Noel lowered her phone and leaned forward, concern lining her brow. "What do you mean, it's too late? I thought you haven't seen her in years."

I closed my eyes and took a deep breath, hoping it would clear away the disaster that had become my reality. Unfortunately, when I opened them again, I realized I wasn't lucky enough for it to have been a dream.

My luck had to be the worst that had ever existed.

"Do you remember me telling you about that girl from a couple weeks ago? The one I met at the club and took home?"

"The one who thought you were a stripper?" Realization flashed across her face, dropping her mouth into an elongated O. "Seriously, Aaron? That was her? How the hell did you not know that?"

My defensiveness peaked until I sat forward with my palms flat on my desk. "How would I have? I couldn't have possibly guessed she'd go from awkward to fucking hot as hell in thirteen years. It's not like Jason keeps family portraits in his living room for me to see when I go over there. And he sure as hell doesn't keep her photo in his wallet."

She glanced at the screen in her hand and sighed. "Well, what are you gonna do?"

"What *can* I do?" Just then, a thought came to me. "Shit, Noel. I have to see her next weekend at the wedding. She's the maid of honor. I have to walk down the aisle with her."

"I think I'm missing something here. Didn't you say it was a bachelorette party? Which would mean your friend's fiancée would've been there, right?"

"She told me her friend couldn't make it to her own party because . . ." Grey clouds settled over me at the same time the sky parted, truth shining down like the rays of the summer sun. All the scattered pieces finally piled together. I looked up at Noel, eyes wide. "Tatum's pregnant. That means . . ."

"Oh my God." She gasped and covered her lips with her fingers. "Is it not your friend's baby?"

I truly had no idea why she'd jump to that conclusion. "*What?* No."

"Oh. Well, I figured with all the other bombshells you've dropped, that was the most logical. Why else wouldn't you know about your best friend having a baby?"

I stopped to think about it. "Maybe he doesn't know. Or . . . maybe he just hasn't told anyone. Although, if that were the case, I don't see why the girls would've known about it. It doesn't matter, Noel. Whatever the reason, I *highly* doubt it's because it's not his baby."

She rolled her eyes and waved me off, clearly ready to move on with this conversation—while I was ready for it to be over. "Okay . . . so back to what you're going to do. You can't move in with her. Seeing her at the wedding will be bad enough."

The wedding. *Shit.* Her words slammed into my chest. She was right. The thought of seeing her, Kelsey, day in and day out, knowing how she tasted, how good she felt . . . it was the worst idea ever.

Panic gripped the back of my neck. "I think you should let me stay with you for a few months."

She laughed, rolling her eyes. "You want to move into my one-bedroom apartment with me and my husband? And sleep where? The couch?"

"You won't even realize I'm there."

"Right." Her grin stretched so far it made her eyes squint. "No."

"Fine. I guess I'll just have to sleep here. But that means I'll be adding more to your morning routine. You may have to start coming in earlier to get it all done. I can't afford for a patient to find a pube in the sink from where I cleaned myself."

"You're disgusting," she teased. "I'm sure you'll find a solution over the weekend. If not, at least you won't have to worry about this girl wanting anything to do with you. Aside from what you said about her having a chip on her shoulder when it comes to men, I doubt she'll want anything from you after the first time you ask her to clean up your pubic hair."

"You never know. I rocked her world two weeks ago, so there's a good chance she'll be able to look past my flaws."

"If you say so . . ." She stood and headed for the door.

"Why doesn't anyone believe me when I say that?"

She stopped at the door, held on to the frame, and arched one brow. "When you say what? That you rocked her world? Because we hear it every time you get laid."

I couldn't argue with that. Granted, most of the time, I said that because it sounded better than the truth—that I didn't get laid at all. It was like the real-life version of crying wolf.

I wondered how that folktale would work out for me. From what I recalled of the story, the boy had been eaten by the wolf because no one believed him. No one believed me when I said I had satisfied a woman more than anyone ever had before me. So then what would my equivalent be to being eaten by a wild animal?

Considering my luck, something awful.

Chapter 6

Kelsey

"What is so important that you made me run all the way over here?" Tatum waltzed in as if she'd never left, speaking as soon as the door was open and then flinging it closed behind her.

There were times I had to remind myself that we no longer lived together, but then there were other moments when her absence could be felt deep in my marrow. Such as evenings, when I had to cook my own meals—having a chef as a roommate had spoiled me rotten—or when I needed my best friend's advice and had to go farther than her bedroom to get it. Other things reminded me of her absence, too, like not having to empty the dryer of her clothes before putting mine in.

Although, over the last month or so, she'd been here frequently as we planned her wedding. It was nice having her around again. It'd be a lie if I said I hadn't contemplated ways to get between her and my cousin just so she'd come back.

"Don't act like you have such a busy life." I slouched in my seat at the kitchen table in a vain effort to look less unsettled. "You write recipes—ones you make up. Just leave a stack of note cards next to the toilet and jot down ideas while you're crapping. It's called multitasking.

Then you won't be so irritable when your best friend calls you over in the middle of a crisis."

She plopped onto the chair next to me, completely unimpressed with my dramatic performance. "You're right, Kels. I don't have anything else going on other than writing cookbooks. I don't have a wedding in four days, a rehearsal dinner in three, or a pregnancy I'm trying to keep everyone from finding out about. It's a full-time job keeping your aunt from sniffing it out. Oh, and don't forget all the cleaning I have to do at the house on a daily basis."

I slapped my palm on the tabletop and lowered my forehead as laughter rolled through me. "You? Clean? Don't lie, Tater; this is *me* you're talking to."

"I'm not lying. I clean. Every day before Jay comes home from work, I rush around the house and put everything away so he doesn't realize what a slob I am and call off the wedding."

I reached for her hand, leveling with her. "I hate to break it to you, Tater, but he's fully aware you're a slob. Maybe you should learn to pick up after yourself to begin with rather than wait until the last minute and do it all at once. And when will you learn that lying doesn't get you anywhere?" I pointed to her stomach, indicating the baby she hadn't told anyone other than me about.

"It's not lying when one simply omits the information from conversation. If anyone asks, I'll tell the truth. I just don't see the point in volunteering that information."

Tatum had her reasons for holding on to this secret, and I couldn't fault her for them. The last thing she wanted was for anyone to believe they were only marrying because of the baby.

As soon as Jason had a ring on her finger, the planning had begun. And to everyone's surprise, a date had been set for exactly seven weeks later. She knew people would assume the rush to get married was due to her pregnancy, which wasn't the case, so she'd decided to keep a lid on it until after the ceremony. I understood her worry, which was why

I'd gone along with it, going so far as to tell her friends that she'd bailed on her own bachelorette party because she had diarrhea and couldn't get off the toilet.

She wasn't happy about that when she found out.

I sighed with added effort. "Fine . . . it's a half lie, then."

"I prefer to call it a half *truth*. But that's probably because I'm the optimistic one."

"For someone who's *so* busy, you sure do waste a lot of time yapping about how wonderful you are. If you add a little humility to that optimism, you might find yourself with extra time on your hands . . . time that could be better spent learning how to iron." I'd never met another person who chose their outfits based on what was the least wrinkled.

Tatum dropped her head back and let out an exaggerated huff. And just when I thought she'd toss back some off-the-wall retort, she pulled herself to her feet and moved to the kitchen. Without saying anything, she opened the oven and peeked in; then she closed it before scouring the counters with confusion narrowing her gaze.

"What are you doing?" *Please say you're going to make me something to eat.*

Turning her bewildered expression to me, she said, "You wanted me to look at something, so I thought that meant you ruined breakfast."

"I'll have you know that since you've been gone, I have yet to burn or ruin anything before sunset. My breakfast record is perfect."

"I take it this means you don't eat before nightfall?" She wore her smile across her entire face—red lips curled deep, dark eyes bright with humor, and cheeks tinged pink.

"I don't think I like this new, pregnant version of you. You're rude." I didn't have to bother smiling for her to recognize my humor. She knew me—probably better than anyone. I stood from my seat and pointed at the closed door to my left. "I need you to look at something in there."

"Does it have eight legs?"

The mere thought of a spider in my bedroom made me gag, my skin crawling as if those foul insects covered me. "Hell no. I wouldn't waste my time having you come all the way over here for that. It would've gotten away before you showed up."

"There's no need to act like such a badass around me, Kels." Damn her for knowing me so well. "I've lived with you, don't forget. I specifically recall having to rip your phone out of your hands to keep you from calling the fire department over a daddy longlegs in your shower."

"Oh, you must've misunderstood. I didn't say I would've handled one of those demonic creatures myself. I just wouldn't have called you for help. It'd be far quicker to light a match and burn the place down."

"You're ridiculous." Her lashes fluttered with an easy breath of humor escaping her smiling lips. "What is it you want me to look at?"

"Just come see."

She stopped me with a hand against my shoulder. "I'm sure I don't need to state this, but I'm going to anyway. If it's on an area that's typically covered by panties . . . you'll need to call a doctor for that. I love you, but—"

"It's not on me. It's in my bathroom."

I opened my bedroom door and walked in, not giving Tatum a chance to make another comment about seeing my secret garden. She followed me into the bathroom, where I pointed to a wad of toilet paper that sat on the edge of the sink. Long seconds dragged on as she stared at it, then at me, silently questioning me with wary eyes.

"Just look at it and tell me what it is, please."

Again, Tatum glanced between it and me, then said, "If you're asking whether it's Charmin or Quilted Northern, I don't have the slightest clue."

"Did baby brain already kick in? No. It's *inside* the toilet paper."

Tatum reluctantly took a step forward and pinched the edges of the material the way one would pick up a dirty sock. But once she realized there was something inside—well, something *different* than she expected—she grabbed it.

Then dropped it.

Into the toilet.

"What'd you do that for?" I screeched, staring at the white stick floating facedown in the water.

"You could've warned me what it was, Kelsey. Maybe then I wouldn't have been surprised to find myself holding something you've *peed* on."

"Whatever. Did you see what it said before you tried to flush it?"

"No. I didn't get that far." We both leaned forward to take a look at the piece of plastic floating in the bowl. "I'm not reaching in there."

Nudging her, I said, "It's clean. I promise."

"Then you get it."

"If I get it, I might see what it says."

"Isn't that the point?"

"If it was, then why would I ask you to come do it for me? I took it, like, three hours ago, and this is the closest I've come to it. I need you to do this for me. Please? Just reach in there and pull it out."

With her arms crossed over her chest, Tatum stared at me like I was a recipe she was trying to figure out. "What made you take it to begin with? I mean . . . why do you think you might be pregnant?"

"For starters, I'm three days late."

"You've been late before."

"By no more than a day. Which was because I marked the wrong date on the calendar—user error. This is different. I know for a fact I was supposed to start my period on Saturday, because it was exactly one week before your wedding. I remember being excited that I wouldn't have to worry about hiding a tampon in my bouquet . . . and I wouldn't have to worry about Aunt Flo interfering with getting some nuptial nookie."

"It's only Tuesday, Kels. Don't you think it's a little too early to be peeing on a stick?"

I pressed a hand against my chest and winced. "And my boobs hurt. *Bad.*"

"Sore breasts could mean you're about to start your period."

If she didn't put her hand in my toilet and read the results on my pee stick, then I'd have to help her—I was the reigning bobbing-for-apples champion three years in a row when I was younger. "Yeah? Does an impending menses also make you throw up at the smell of coffee? What about make you daydream about strawberry fields and saltshakers?"

"I'm not entirely sure about that last one, but considering we're talking about you here . . . anything's possible. Is there a chance you ate something extremely out of date? I've always told you that those frozen meals aren't healthy."

"Are you not listening to the words that are coming out of my mouth? I have been craving strawberries with salt on them. Not just a hankering . . . but full-on murderous kind of craving."

Being the best friend she was, she held up one finger and then left the room. I figured I'd give her to the count of fifteen before going after her, but I knew in my heart I wouldn't have to. And when she came back, I realized what she'd gone to get—tongs.

I turned my back to her, not wanting to accidentally see the results. For whatever reason, I felt confident that I would take the news better if it came from Tatum. So I stood there and waited for her to either save the day or deliver my death sentence.

At the sound of another splash, I glanced over my shoulder. The test was once again in the bowl, but this time, Tatum decided to close the lid, where she invited herself to take a seat as though the ordeal had exhausted her. The only reason I didn't give her a hard time was the look on her face—part excitement, part sadness, a twinge of confusion, and a hint of intrigue.

Her expression gave me nothing but more uncertainty.

"Will you just put me out of my misery already before I throw you off the damn toilet and dive in there myself?"

Tatum stood, placing her hands on my shoulders. "Don't worry, Kels. You'll get your period." And then she walked out.

An odd emotion ran over me—relief mostly, but there was a slight pang of sadness. I wouldn't get to experience this part of life with my best friend. And it took discovering that I didn't have what I didn't want to realize that maybe, *just maybe*, a small piece of me might have wanted it.

I slowly made my way out of the room and found Tatum washing her hands in the kitchen sink. Feeling lost in a fog of warring thoughts, I fell into a seat at the table, the one I'd vacated before finding out my fate.

"You don't look happy." A spark glistened in her dark eyes as she dried her hands.

"I am. It's the best outcome, really. I never wanted kids, and the idea of getting knocked up by a stripper named Dr. Phil-Me-Up doesn't appeal to me. But I guess it's just one of those things that you don't realize you *might* want until you think you might already have it."

"Wait. Are you saying the stripper you hired for my bachelorette party is the father of your child—if you were pregnant, I mean? I thought you said he wore a condom."

"He did. Well, as far as I know. But it couldn't have been anyone else; he's the only guy I've slept with in months."

"So what you're telling me is . . . you aren't opposed to having a baby, just as long as it's not with someone who dances in a G-string to *Jock Jams*?"

"Let's not get ahead of ourselves. I just meant that—baby daddy aside—I wouldn't have jumped off a bridge had the test been positive. I might've sat on the ledge, leaned a little too far forward, contemplated the distance between the railing and the water below . . . but not jumped."

"For what it's worth, I think you'd be an amazing mom. I mean . . . your kid's first word would more than likely be something vulgar. He or she would think Hamburger Helper is gourmet, and there's a chance you'd be in a parent-teacher meeting at least once a week defending your child's overly dry sense of humor. But you'd be one hell of a mom."

"Thanks, Tater." Oddly enough, her sentiment meant the world to me . . . even if it would never be proven. "Now I just hope my period waits a little longer to come so I don't have to deal with it at the wedding this weekend."

"I'm sure you'll be fine. If I had to guess, you'll get it in about ten or so months—depending on whether you choose to breastfeed or not."

My heart sank, my stomach clenched, and the world started to tilt. I had to have heard her wrong, because she'd specifically told me that the test was negative. I would've assumed she was just messing with me, but Tatum was the world's worst liar. And now I wasn't sure what to believe. "I'm sorry, but . . . *what*? You told me I wasn't pregnant."

"No . . . I said you'll get your period. Which you will, but not until you finish growing that tiny human currently residing in your womb."

"You're a monster. Who does that to someone?"

She sauntered to the chair next to me, a smile on her face. It was times like these I wished she didn't know me so well, because no matter what names I called her, she wouldn't believe for one second that I meant any of it.

"I just gave you what you never knew you wanted. You said so yourself. You're welcome. Think of it as my gift to you." Her arm must've been sore from patting her own back. "And what's even better . . . we get to do this together. Just imagine—our kids will be best friends, too."

"You're missing one giant issue. The baby's father doesn't change in any of this." Breathing became impossible, and the room started to spin like I'd gotten trapped in one of those Gravitron rides at a carnival.

"Oh my God . . . I'm pregnant with a stripper's baby. If it's a girl, I'll have to name her Star or Bambi. She'll be in therapy from the time she takes her first breath."

"Calm down. You're freaking out for no reason. Maybe this Phil-Your-Holes character only strips to pay for college."

"He's older than we are—at least in his thirties. I doubt he's in school, not to mention, he's dumber than a box of rocks. For fuck's sake, what if stupidity is hereditary? My kid is totally going to be a window licker, won't it?"

She patted my hand the way my mom used to when trying to pacify me. "I doubt that. You're one of the smartest people I've ever met. Worst-case scenario, it'll be average. But even then, I don't think that'll happen. I can't see any child raised by you turning out to be anything less than amazing."

"I'm gonna have to tell him, aren't I?"

"That's probably the right thing to do. Plus, giving him the opportunity to be involved keeps you from having to do this by yourself. If he doesn't want anything to do with it, at least you have me. And I'm sure your family would help out, too."

Somehow, I hadn't even thought about my family until she'd mentioned them. "They can't find out yet. Not until I'm ready to tell them. Got it?"

She latched onto my shoulders. "Trust me, I get it. In case you forgot, they're not even aware of my situation, so you don't have to worry about me saying anything."

"That means Jason, too. You can't tell him, either."

"I love you, Kels, but I'm not about to start off my marriage by lying to Jay."

"Oh, whatever. You lie to him all the time. The poor guy thinks the same bag of cheese puffs has been in the pantry for over a month, when we both know that's not the case. You eat an entire bag a day, and before he gets home, you make sure the same amount is left before putting it away."

She gasped and opened her eyes wide, acting offended. It was obvious she wanted to lie and tell me I was wrong, but she wouldn't convince me of it. Finally, she dropped her shoulders and huffed. "What's your point? If he were to ask me about it, I'd tell him the truth."

"Fine. Then do that with this, too. You're only allowed to confirm it *if* he specifically asks if I'm pregnant. And since you're a pro at keeping him from questioning things, you shouldn't have any problem hiding this until I'm ready to share it with people."

"You have nothing to worry about." That was laughable.

"You're either gonna have to wipe that goofy grin off your face and stop staring at my stomach, or I'll have to avoid you until the cat's out of the bag. And considering your wedding's in four days, and I'm the maid of honor . . . I suggest you get a handle on the ridiculous expression you're wearing right now. Otherwise, someone else will have to stand next to you at the altar, because it won't be me." I only meant half of that—I wouldn't miss her wedding for the world. Unfortunately, she knew that, too.

"For the love of fried rice, Kels. Can't you give me a minute to be excited?" Tatum's brows pinched together, yet her eyes turned soft. An emotional moment hovered on the horizon, which left my stomach in knots. "I was terrified when I found out I was pregnant."

That was news to me. "Why?"

"Lots of reasons. Some were valid, such as feeling insecure that Jay would say it's too soon, that it wasn't part of the plan, and that he's not ready for our lives to change this much. But then there were the irrational fears . . . like being the only one of my friends with a kid, or not having anyone to share it with who can relate. It's a lonely feeling. So excuse me for being a little selfish and getting excited to have a partner in crime to go through this new and frightening experience with."

I contemplated her words for a moment, yet I couldn't seem to make sense of them. "But you *do* have a partner in crime. His name's Jason . . . your fiancé. Soon-to-be husband. My cousin. And unless you're keeping something from me—*again*—he's the father of your uncooked tater tot."

Tatum waved me off with a flick of the wrist and a fluttering roll of her eyes. "It's not the same. I wasn't insinuating that I would be alone or anything. But it's nice having someone to share things with—someone who'll understand exactly what I'm going through. Jay can't possibly comprehend tender breasts, or how I can be ready for bed by nine even though I had an hour nap after lunch. And no matter how hard he tries, he'll never get just how terrifying it is to think that a human being will come out of my vagina."

I choked, causing Tatum to gently slap my back until I could breathe again. But even then, I couldn't do more than stare at her, blinking repeatedly as her words echoed in my head. "What have I ever done to you to make you say such awful things to me?"

Her brow dipped with profound confusion. "What did I say?"

"I'm going to have a person crawl out of my hoo-ha and ruin any chances of ever getting laid again."

It took Tatum a second to respond, opening and closing her mouth several times before finally speaking. "While I've never actually seen anyone give birth, I feel quite confident that they don't crawl out. And again, I have no personal knowledge of this, but I've been told it goes back to normal size."

"You're not helping. I haven't even adjusted to the idea of a positive pregnancy test swimming in my toilet, let alone anything that comes after that. Yet you think it's a fantastic idea to point out how my vag will be stretched to accommodate *a head*."

"Are you planning on giving birth to an adult?"

"I wasn't planning on giving birth to anything."

Tatum quietly and slowly pushed to her feet and backed away, her hands in front of her as if telling me to stay put and calm down. "I think you need some time to come to terms with this. And it's probably safest if I leave you alone while you do so. Just know that I'm only a phone call away. If you need me, I'll be here, but for now, maybe a little quiet time might be best. That way, you can cry, freak out, curse the empty condom wrapper, or possibly hunt down Dr. Phils-So-Good and cut off his balls without feeling like you have to hold anything back."

I'd never held anything back around her before, but she made a valid point. There was no need to use her as my verbal-diarrhea catcher when my real issue wasn't even with her. Sure, she'd ended up being the bearer of bad news, although that was only because I'd made her drive all the way over here and then forced her to stick her hand in my toilet, all to give me the bad news in question.

"Whatever you do," she continued, her dark, contemplative eyes boring into mine, "make an appointment with an ob-gyn as soon as possible. Don't make any plans or decisions, and don't freak out or get excited until you see the doctor."

I nodded and offered as big of a smile as I could. "Thanks, Tater. I'd probably be curled into a ball, rocking myself in a corner right now, if you weren't here. And I still wouldn't know what that damn stick said."

"I can stay if you need me."

I shrugged, suddenly feeling like our roles had switched for the first time in our entire friendship. "Nah. Thanks, though. You're right . . . I need to process it, wrap my mind around the enormity of what it all means and how different my life will be from here on out. But I promise, once I get the major things sorted out, and I no longer feel like I wanna jump off a bridge, I'll give you a call. I love you, Tatum."

"Love you, too."

Once the door closed behind her, I headed into my room, where I flopped onto the bed and stared at the wall. My eyes drifted to the clock on my nightstand to check the time, but before I read the bright-blue digits, my sight fell onto the journal I'd found at my parents' house a couple of weeks ago. A strong urge inside me compelled me to pick it up. And within minutes, I had a pen in my hand and was scribbling any and every thought that came to mind.

I didn't think about the words . . . I just purged myself of all emotion.

Chapter 7

Kelsey

For some reason, doctors didn't consider a positive pregnancy test an urgent matter. Thankfully, a clinic in town could get me in soon, though they made me wait two days—which really wasn't anything special, since I was told I wouldn't get more than a confirmation of pregnancy.

Needless to say, it was the longest two days of my life.

"What exactly is considered paying for sex?" I asked Tatum without taking the clipboard from my face. "There seems to be such a grey area around that."

"I'm pretty sure it's having sex in exchange for money. Not much grey there."

"So bartering isn't the same?"

She finally turned to look at me, even though I didn't return the favor. "What are you talking about?"

"You said 'in exchange for money.' If Joe Blow says he'll give it to me real good if I buy him dinner first . . . is that paying for sex? Because technically, I'd be paying—just not him."

"I'm not sure about that . . . though I'm positive you can find a loophole in just about anything." Tatum went back to the magazine in her hands.

And I continued filling out pointless forms. They likely had a purpose; I just didn't see it. "That's good to know. I'd hate to be accused of paying for sex if I buy a plane ticket for Tom Hardy to come here and"—I leaned to the side and lowered my voice—"fuck me real Hardy."

"You have issues," she whispered, laughter filling her soft words.

"It's part of my charm. And one of the reasons you love me."

"Just hurry up and fill those forms out."

I waved her off, though I complied and continued with the papers attached to the clipboard. "This would be a lot faster if they didn't ask every question eighty-four times. I literally just answered how many times I've been pregnant. Then they ask how many babies I've delivered. I just told them I've never been pregnant before. Wouldn't that answer the next seventeen questions about births?"

Tatum's index finger came into view, tapping the questions in front of me. "See this? Where it says *if you answered yes*? And you see this? Where you answered no?" And then her hand was gone; no other explanation followed.

"No need to be a smart-ass. You've already filled these forms out, so it's no surprise you already have the answers. Don't be a cheater and make it look like you know what you're doing just because you've been in my shoes before."

"I haven't been in your shoes," she said with laughter passing her lips. "Never in my life have I been pregnant with a stripper's baby—a stripper I didn't even have a real name for. Speaking of which . . . what do you plan to put on the birth certificate? Dr. Phil-Me-Up? And if so, what's the last name? Oh, even better . . . what last name will your child have?"

Her last question made me stop and think. I hadn't made it that far in my mental freak-out. And now that she'd posed it, I couldn't concentrate on anything else. Not the nurse who called my name or the cup they made me pee in. Not even the needle they stuck me with to draw blood. Everything was an utter blur—the doctor's words nothing more than garble—until Tatum snapped me out of it on the way home.

"How exciting is this? Your due date is only a little over two weeks after mine. Our babies will be less than a month apart!" Her elation was too much for this moment, and if I'd had any strength to summon sarcasm, I would have.

"I don't understand how any of this works."

Tatum stared at the side of my head in silence for a moment. Then she said, "Well, when a man and a woman have sex—"

"Oh my God, Tatum. Not about that. I'm confused how our due dates are so close if I'm not quite three weeks pregnant and you're seven."

"You didn't listen to a word he said, did you?"

I came to a stop at the traffic light and glared at her. "He said a lot of words. It was hard to keep up. That's what I brought you for. So get on with it and explain it to me before I make you get out and walk home." I should really start coming up with more believable threats.

"Since you know the exact date you had sex, and it couldn't have possibly happened at any other time, they can pretty much pinpoint down to the day how far along you are—give or take a couple days. He's going by the fetal age, which will always be two weeks less than gestational age."

"Yeah, you're just confusing me more, Tater. I don't think I'm cut out for this whole mom gig. I can't even understand how old my baby is now . . . what'll happen when it's here? I'll forget its birthday or put the wrong number candle on the cake."

Tatum huffed, but since I had to pay attention to the road, I couldn't do more than give her the middle finger—which she smacked away from her face. "It's quite simple, really. Gestational age starts at the first day of your last period, meaning you're technically two weeks pregnant before you even conceive. Fetal age . . . well, I think you can figure that out."

"For the love of modern technology, can't they just use one form of counting and leave it at that? I already have enough to be confused about as it is. I don't need anyone making it worse."

She laid her hand on my arm and, in a soothing voice, said, "Make an appointment with an OB like I told you to and go from there. No need to freak yourself out over how far along you are. You already know that answer since you know when you conceived. Stop stressing."

Yeah . . . easy for her to say. She was marrying her baby's father in two days. I didn't even know the name of mine.

My cell vibrated in my hand, and when I noticed the number on the screen, I snapped my fingers to get Tatum's attention. "I have to take this. Give me, like, two minutes."

We were in our hotel room, getting ready to head downstairs for the rehearsal. But this was a matter I needed to take care of without any witnesses—especially my family.

"I'm sorry, Ms. Peterson, but there seems to be some sort of mix-up," the woman said on the other end of the line when I answered the call.

After leaving the doctor's office yesterday with confirmation of my pregnancy, I had immediately gotten ahold of the service I'd used to hire the stripper for Tatum's bachelorette party. Unfortunately, the woman I'd spoken to had informed me that they didn't give out personal information about their entertainers. After I'd insisted it was urgent that I speak to him, she'd offered to pass along my name and number and let him be the one to reach out.

I'd been expecting this call for twenty-four hours.

I sat on the edge of the bed to keep my legs from giving out. "I'm confused . . . what kind of mix-up are you talking about?"

"It seems the performer that was scheduled for your party was double-booked that night, and he never made it to yours. There must've been some oversight, since no one had noticed this earlier."

"Had I not called to get ahold of him, it still wouldn't have been *noticed*." My face heated with the rising anger inside. If this woman had been in front of me right now, I'd likely have had my hands around her neck.

"I realize this, and I apologize. We will credit the card you used when booking."

"That doesn't help me. Someone was there—a doctor, much like I had ordered through you. He came. He danced. He took his clothes off. I need to locate him."

"I'm not really sure what I can do about that, ma'am. Whoever came to your event that night was not one of ours. I wish I could help more, but unfortunately, I don't have the answer you're looking for."

I bit the corner of my thumbnail, careful not to ruin the manicure. "What if he lied about where he was? Could that be possible?"

"For safety reasons, we have location tracking on all our associates. This must be frustrating for you, but we've looked into each and every one of them, and none of our men were at Boots Nightclub that night. I'm sorry. Whoever you encountered wasn't anyone from our revue team. Is it possible someone else in your group had also ordered entertainment, and maybe that was the person you saw?"

"No." The word barely squeaked out past the dread choking me.

"Well, I hope you find the person you're looking for."

"Is there a way I could see their locations, just for peace of mind?"

"Unfortunately, no. We take the safety and security of our employees very seriously."

Tatum sat next to me and rubbed my back while I leaned forward, my forehead resting in my palm. "Thank you anyway. I appreciate you returning my call." I tapped the red icon and sighed, fighting off the urge to throw my phone across the room.

I suddenly regretted the decision to leave my journal at home. This would've been a fantastic time to get my feelings out without worrying about the words I used. I trusted that Tatum would never judge me or make me feel bad about anything, but there was just something cathartic about writing on paper without thinking about anything. I could literally move from one thought to the next midsentence and just keep going.

"What was that about?" Tatum's voice interrupted my need to journal.

"It seems the stripper never showed up to the party. So basically, I have no idea who I slept with, or why he was even there. Or how he even knew to come dressed as a doctor. I could be okay finding out I slept with someone who's even more of a stranger than I originally thought. But I'm having this man's kid. I don't have the faintest idea what his name is or how to find him. And the more I think about that, the more I realize I don't have any way to tell him about the baby or get medical information that I might need later on for my child—family history, hereditary diseases, early-onset male-pattern baldness. I could have a son who starts going bald before he learns to drive, and I would have no way to know if it's normal."

Tatum took my hands in hers, silencing my irrational rambling. "There's no point in freaking out about things that haven't happened— or might possibly *never* happen. Okay?"

I could only nod while taking a deep breath to calm down.

"The good thing about pregnancies is that you're given nine months to prepare. A lot can happen in that time. It's March—the baby won't even be born until November."

"What do you think is gonna happen, Tatum . . . I run into him on the street? And then what? Waddle my ass over to him, tap his shoulder, and explain that his offspring is cooking in my oven?" Realization dawned on me, pulling a gasp from my chest before I could smack my hand over my mouth to keep it in. "Oh my God, I'm going to be on *Maury*, aren't I?"

"Kels . . . one thing at a time."

Something about her voice, or maybe the way her hair framed her glowing face, lips painted a deep red, made me stop and think—about where we were. About why we were here in the first place. And immediately, I felt like crap. We were on the cusp of her perfect day, and there I was, casting a grey cloud over my best friend's weekend.

"I'm sorry. I shouldn't be putting this on your plate right now. I'll be okay once I splash some cold water on my face. I just need thirty seconds to pull myself together, and then I'll be ready to head downstairs." I slipped off the bed and headed to the small bathroom.

"Take your time."

After wiping a tissue beneath my eyes and pulling myself together enough to prevent others from suspecting anything, I was ready to get this over with. I followed Tatum into the hallway and headed for the elevators, but before we got there, she stopped at Jason's room.

"I'll meet you down there." She winked as she tapped her knuckles on the door.

"Are you seriously about to have a quickie?"

"Absolutely not."

I rolled my eyes and stepped away. "You're a shit liar, Tater."

The door opened, and she yelped playfully. Luckily, I didn't have to witness that. I just continued toward the end of the hall to head downstairs. I sent a quick text to my sister to see if she was already there and then turned the corner to the elevators.

Glancing up from my phone, I noticed a well-dressed man standing in front of the button. His light hair was cut short, shaped nicely, which gave his angular jaw a sexiness that nearly made me moan out loud. He had his attention on a device in his hand, but likely hearing me, he turned, locking me in the trap of his familiar gaze.

His deep-green stare reminded me of a forest, and it left me with more questions than answers. Intrigue. Curiosity that tugged at my heart and circled my throat, threatening to both give me life and take it away simultaneously.

It was a knife in my chest and a pat on my back, all at once.

"W-what are you doing here?" I stepped closer, then craned my neck to check the hallway behind me.

A hesitant smirk danced to one side of his delicious mouth—a mouth I hadn't gone one night without dreaming of. And then he tugged on his necktie, drawing my attention to the same strip of silk that had opened my world to things I never would've guessed I liked.

"Hey." One word. That was all he offered.

It was all it took to make me want to climb him like a tree.

"Why are you here?" I asked again.

"Uh . . ." He blinked up at the panel above the mirrored doors, likely checking how long he had to answer my question by how many floors stood between the cart and us. Either that or he was desperate to get away from me. "Just waiting on an elevator to take me downstairs."

"Oh, did you have a private party tonight?"

He cleared his throat, once again tugging on his tie. "Something like that."

"What are you supposed to be? Where's your costume?"

"It's not that kind of party." He shifted on his feet before slowly dragging his gaze up my body. "Listen . . . we should probably talk."

That was enough to snap me out of my daze, reminding me that I stood in front of the unnamed stripper, the one I'd been convinced I'd never find. The one who'd accidentally fathered the child I'd never thought I wanted until yesterday.

"Yeah. We *definitely* need to talk."

"All right. You first."

It was my turn to check the numbers, noting that someone must've pulled some strings to give us more time to have this conversation. "So I know we said we wouldn't see each other again. But that was before—"

"Oh, look." Tatum sidled up next to me, weaving her arm through mine at the same time Jason came around the side, moving to stand next to my unborn child's father. "You're still here."

"That was fast." I scrunched my nose, unsure what they could've possibly done in the ten seconds they were in the room.

She rolled her eyes, a smile plastered on her face. "What can I say? He knows my buttons."

"That's gross. I never wanna hear such filth come out of your mouth again." I turned away from my best friend, setting my sights on the man in front of me. It wasn't lost on me that he looked even sexier when my brain wasn't swimming in tequila, which was a dangerous thought to have, what with how close he stood . . . in a hotel. That had *lots* of beds.

Yet my lack of attention didn't stop Tatum from speaking. "I take it you two met?"

His pupils constricted, the green darkening, as he kept his eyes on mine. Only then did I contemplate Tatum's question, wondering why he'd have any type of reaction to it. But before I could ask anything—or even look away from his demanding gaze—he said, "Yeah. We've met."

"Good. That saves us the introductions." The elevator door chose that second to open. But I couldn't move, even as Tatum tried to drag me by the arm. The only thing that got my feet to move was what she said next. "Kels, Aaron, come on. We have a wedding to rehearse."

Aaron.

Jason's friend.

The guy who'd be living with me for a few months.

The *stripper.*

The father of my child.

One and the same.

There was just *no* way this was real life.

Chapter 8

Aaron

Nothing ever turned out the way I planned—*nothing*.

I'd tried to pull Kelsey aside a few times at the rehearsal as well as at the dinner afterward, yet it seemed there was one interruption after another. Her family was the biggest issue—specifically her mother, who did nothing but stick her phone in everyone's face for a picture. And when it was over, Kelsey had taken Tatum back to their room at the hotel, leaving me once again unable to have a conversation with her.

Obviously, I hadn't been able to see her before the ceremony, as she'd spent the entire time with Tatum, and I'd been with Jason. The reception was the first chance I had to speak to her—other than the sixty seconds up and down the aisle, which wasn't the place to discuss where I'd live in a week. But even then, she made it impossible to be near her.

That was . . . until she excused herself from dinner and ran out.

I didn't bother following her into the women's bathroom or even knocking. Instead, I waited just outside the door for her to finish whatever the hell she was doing in there. And several long minutes later, she rewarded me with her presence—glassy eyes, runny nose, and all.

"Everything all right?" I held her wrists to keep her from running off again.

"Yeah." She sniffled, which wasn't typically a sign of being *all right.* "I didn't realize until too late that they gave me veal."

Still, I didn't understand. "Is that not what you ordered?"

"Honestly, I don't remember what I marked on the card. I think I just circled something because I was tired of Tatum complaining that mine was the only one they were waiting on." She shrugged, pulling her hands from my grip.

"I take it you don't like veal?"

"I don't like eating baby *anything.*" She covered her pale lips with her fingers while staring at the center of my chest. It seemed like she might've been on the verge of vomiting . . . possibly again. "Can we not talk about it?"

"Sorry. I got the vegetarian dish if you want to swap."

Disgusted eyes met mine. "You wanna eat the baby cow? What the f—"

"No." I shook my head and fought to keep my laughter under wraps. "I just meant that if you want, you can have my plate. I've barely touched it."

"Why?"

"Um . . ." I wasn't sure how to respond, so I did the best I could with the vague question she posed. "Because you don't like what you have? I'm not going to make you starve. That would be rude of me."

Finally, the tiniest smile danced on her lips. "No, I meant why did you barely touch your plate?"

I glanced to the side and noticed a bench against the wall. Gently taking her hand, I nodded toward it and led her a few feet to take a seat. "Let's talk. Things have been hectic, and we haven't really had a chance to say anything to one another."

"About why you don't want your food? If it's that serious, I don't want it, either."

I couldn't withhold my amusement anymore. "No, not about that. About us. What happened a few weeks ago. What we have ahead of us."

"Listen, I appreciate the fact that you want to take a walk down memory lane, but I don't really think our best friends' wedding is the place to do that. Do you?"

Smirking, I said, "I didn't plan on going over the details, if that's what you're worried about. I just need to make sure you're still good with me moving in next weekend." I held up a hand to keep her from interrupting before I had a chance to get out everything I needed to say. "If you're not, I understand. Trust me. But I'd rather you tell me now than wait until I'm all moved in."

"Tatum said you didn't have anywhere else to go." That sounded like something Tatum would say, especially if her motive was to guilt Kelsey into doing what she wanted. She was a smart girl. "Plus, how are you going to find something else in a week?"

"Don't worry about that. It's not your burden to take on; it's mine."

"I'm not going to be responsible for someone being homeless, Aaron."

My back met with the wall behind me as I expelled a breath I hadn't realized I'd held in. It came out like a huff, though she likely assumed it to be a sigh. And with my sight glued to the ceiling, I grumbled, "I won't be homeless."

"Then where will you go? Tatum said you're being evicted."

That was enough to pull a barking laugh from my chest. "Evicted? Wow, that was mighty nice of her. No. The house I was living in sold, so I had four weeks to find somewhere to go."

"Then why haven't you found a place if you were given so much time? Didn't the owners tell you that they were putting the house up for sale?" It appeared she hadn't been told *anything* about my situation. Tatum could've at least given her *some* of the facts.

"I knew they were putting the house on the market. What I didn't expect was for it to be in escrow three days later. As for the four weeks

I was given to move out . . . I've been looking, but it's hard when I only need something temporarily." And assuming Tatum hadn't told her any of this, either, I carried on. "I want to buy a house, so renting something for the next twelve months would be pointless."

Her eyes lit up, excitement coloring her cheeks until she no longer looked like she'd just finished hugging a toilet in a fancy dress. "I have lots of connections in the real estate business—I stage a lot of their homes for open houses."

"Yeah, Jason told me. That's why he thought you could help me out."

Before she could do or say anything, we were interrupted. By a blonde. The very same one from the bachelorette party—the one who couldn't stop hopping and clapping.

"Have we met before?" She pointed at me and stared with squinted eyes.

"Uh . . . I don't think so." I turned to Kelsey for help.

"He's Jason's best friend. You might've seen him around Tatum."

"Maybe." She took one step and then stopped. Snapping her fingers, she swung her wide eyes back to me, flickering them between the two of us. "I remember where I've seen you. You're the stripper from Boots!"

Heat blanketed my face. "I think you're mistaken. I'm not a stripper."

Never thought those words would ever come out of my mouth.

"You sure? Because I never forget a face."

"Trust me, Rebecca . . ." Kelsey came to my defense. *Thank God.* "That wasn't him. I think I would know more than you."

At least that was enough to appease the bouncing blonde. Yet instead of leaving, she cocked her head to one side and narrowed her gaze. After the short inspection, she gave a half shrug. "You're right, although there's definitely a similarity there. If you hit the gym more, I bet you'd look just like Dr. Phil-Me-Up." She paused with a finger pressed to her lips. "Well, now that I look again, you might be a couple of years younger, too. He had a sense of wisdom to him."

"Uh . . . thanks?" I wasn't sure if that was supposed to be a compliment, but it didn't feel like one. Then again, I'd take any reason for her to believe that I wasn't the stripper from the party and leave.

Rebecca—whoever she was or wherever she came from—smiled and waved me off. "You're welcome." And then she was gone.

"That's Rebecca," Kelsey muttered under her breath with a thumb hitched in her direction. "She's like a stray puppy . . . never leaves you alone, but you just can't find it in yourself to shoo her away because she's disgustingly nice."

"Thanks for the help with that. The last thing I need is for people to know anything about that night." Well, more than they already knew. Jason had heard his fair share, and if he ever discovered that it had been his cousin . . . I'd be a dead man.

Jason wasn't overly protective of Kelsey, but there was some unwritten code about sleeping with a family member of one of your friends. The fact that he'd heard far too much about that night would only add gasoline to the flame.

"Yeah . . . about that night." Kelsey took a deep breath and ran her palms over her silk-covered thighs. She seemed as nervous as I felt.

The last thing I wanted was for her to assume I wanted more. Well, I *did*, but that wasn't the point. We couldn't have more, and I was fully aware of that. Not to mention, I didn't care to hear her tell me what a mistake it was, or how much she regretted our time together. So I did the only thing I could think of—pretended like it didn't matter much to me, either.

I cleared my throat and prepared for the biggest performance of my life. "It's okay. You don't have to explain anything. In fact, it might be easier if we just pretend it never happened; that way, it won't cause a problem while we're living together. If you're still cool with me moving in, that is."

"I wish I could pretend it never happened, but . . ."

"I know what you mean." I leaned toward her and lowered my voice to add, "It was fucking amazing. Unforgettable." The smell of her hair made me pull away—well, that, and I didn't want anyone to see us sharing a secret. I couldn't handle more assumptions that weren't accurate. "But if you do allow me to stay with you, it'd be in our best interest to act like nothing's happened between us. There was a reason we agreed to remain anonymous with each other."

"Agreed. And you're right, nothing can ever happen again." Oddly enough, she appeared defeated. Deflated. Something dragged her down. "I just mean—"

"There you two are." Tatum came out of the ballroom, hands on her hips. She looked like an angel in her white dress, dark hair pinned to her head with curls escaping near her face. Jason truly was a lucky man to spend the rest of his life with her. "You ran off and then never came back."

"I'm not going in there until the baby cow is removed from the table," Kelsey said with her arms crossed, a sudden defiance consuming her.

"Why'd *you* leave?" Tatum pinned me with a questioning stare.

"I came to check on her after she ran off. Now we're discussing the move."

Recognition shone bright in her dark, wide eyes. "Oh yeah. I'm sorry. I forgot you two weren't able to get together last week. Well, is this going to take much longer? We're about to cut the cake, and then it's the bouquet toss. Which you *better* catch, Kels."

"I'm not coming within ten feet of that shit. You might as well hand it to someone else. I'm sure Carrie wouldn't mind taking it from you. Any reason to get Victor to propose, and she's on it like freezer burn on chicken."

Laughter scratched at the back of my throat. I had no idea whom she spoke of, but between the bouquet and the analogy, I almost couldn't contain it.

Tatum rolled her eyes, a smile playing on her crimson lips. "How many times do I have to explain this, Kels . . . only *your* chicken has freezer burn. It's not a normal thing."

"Either way, I don't want the stupid flowers. But I would like some cake." She glanced at me. "We can finish this conversation another time."

I grabbed her hand to prevent her from getting up and following Tatum back into the ballroom. "We're cool, right?"

"Yeah, we're *cool*."

She seemed irritated or upset, so I added, "With living together, I mean." I didn't want her to misunderstand why I'd ask that.

"Yeah." She might've nodded and given me an answer, yet her eyes didn't seem to match. She wasn't aggravated or annoyed. If anything, she was hesitant, as if she had something else to say but couldn't get the words out. After a moment of deliberating with herself, she met my stare and added, "Maybe we can get together this week and discuss the rules and whatnot."

"Sounds good." At least I didn't have to keep stressing that she would pull the rug out from beneath me, forcing me to find somewhere else to live in the next seven days.

The bouquet hung loosely at Kelsey's side as she made her way down the hall, and all I could think about was her terrified expression when it'd landed in her arms, no one bothering to fight her for it. And what had made it even better was the garter I'd managed to snag, only to slide it up her leg to her thigh. I'd figured it'd be the last time I got to touch her, and I'd refused to pass it up.

It still put a smile on my face.

My hotel room was close to hers, so I decided that making sure she got to her room in one piece would be the gentlemanly thing to do. I might or might not have had a few drinks at the reception, making me cling to any ounce of hope I could find that she'd had just as much and would invite me in.

"So I was thinking . . ." I said as I followed one step behind Kelsey. "We could totally finish our conversation now. That way, we won't have to schedule something this week."

She stopped at her room and turned to face me with her back against the door. Hope danced in her eyes, though a small, cunning grin lined her lips. "You're more than welcome to come in—to *talk*. We're *not* having sex."

Well, that was like a bucket of cold water in my lap. "I wasn't looking to have sex with you again. We've already talked about that." Lies. All lies.

"Right . . ." Skepticism brightened the green rims around her irises. "Fine, then. Come on." And with that, she turned, stuck her key card into the slot, and then opened the door, holding it for me to slip in behind her.

I took a seat on the edge of the bed while she moved into the bathroom, likely to change. But that didn't stop me from beginning the conversation, even if she had to respond through a wall. "Provided I find something quickly, I shouldn't be there longer than a couple months. But like I told Jason, I'm not looking for a free place to stay."

"Good. Because I didn't offer a free room." She tossed her dress through the door and pulled it almost shut again. "I guess we should probably discuss the rent aspect of it, huh?"

Just seeing the peach-colored silk sprawled on the floor filled my mind with dirty thoughts I didn't have any right to have. "Yeah—" I cleared my throat, eradicating the desire that had flooded my voice. "That's probably a good idea."

"When Tatum lived with me, she paid half the rent and nothing more, so I figured it'd only be fair if I did the same for you."

"What do you mean, *and nothing more?*"

Kelsey stepped out of the bathroom in a pair of cotton shorts and a tank top, sans bra. Her nipples pebbled beneath the ribbed fabric, calling my attention to the beads I'd paid particular attention to while drawing the sexiest sounds from her lips. It took every ounce of restraint to stay where I was when all I wanted was to go to her and make her scream all over again.

It seemed she recalled the same memory, because she quickly covered her chest with her arms and moved to sit next to me. With her back against the headboard, she hugged a pillow to her chest, shielding me from the finest view I'd ever seen. "It's easier to have you pay half the rent rather than split all the other bills. I'd pay the same amount for cable whether you were there or not, and the utilities don't come until the following month. Unless you take incredibly long showers, leave the sink running all morning while you get ready for work, or turn on every light in the place during the day, it's just easier to call those things a wash."

"Fair enough. What about food?"

"I don't mind if you eat what's there, just as long as you contribute and replace it if you take the last of something. Same with the laundry detergent and cleaning products. And I ask that you pick up after yourself in the common area—what you do in your room is your business, providing it doesn't destroy anything that I'll have to fix or replace myself."

"You won't have to worry about that." A smile broke free and created a slow burn in my cheeks. For whatever reason, I'd expected her list of demands to be something more than this. Although, she did seem a little nervous, and we weren't done listing the rules, so there could've still been more coming.

"Also . . . my apartment is fully furnished, so you'll only need to bring your clothes and personal effects and whatnot. If you have furniture, you might wanna get a storage unit for the meantime until you get your own place."

"What about the room I'm taking? Is there furniture in there, too?"

"Yes. It used to be Tatum's—she didn't need it when she moved in with Jason. All the sheets and blankets are clean, and the mattress is nearly new. There's one dresser in that room, but it should be big enough for you." She scanned my body with her eyes, as if somehow determining how many clothes I had. "If not, the closet is completely empty."

"That's perfect, because I planned to leave my bedroom set behind when I move. It's old—I've had it since I was, like, twelve. And no one wants to buy their first home and then fill it with ancient furniture."

A whispered laugh blew past her smiling lips, but when she glanced up from her lap and met my eyes, she paused. Then she quickly shook off whatever thought had come to her and continued. "One last thing . . . I would appreciate it if you don't have guests over. I'm just not comfortable—"

"No need to elaborate. I get it." That at least saved me from having to explain that I didn't have many friends. "But just so there's no confusion . . . will Jason be exempt from that rule?"

She huffed to herself, slightly rolling her eyes. "Obviously."

"I guess we're all squared away, then." I didn't want to leave, praying something else would come up that would keep me here—even if we only talked. "You said you could help me find a house . . . is that offer still on the table?"

Her gaze softened, the momentary irritation vanishing as though it were nothing more than a breeze. "Yeah, I can do that. I just need to know what you're looking for, and I can ask around. I have connections with quite a few Realtors, as well as builders in case you're interested in starting from scratch."

That wasn't something I'd given much thought to, considering I was on a restricted time frame. I'd had a hard enough time finding a place to stay for a couple of months. Imposing on someone's space for longer than that while I had a house built would've been impossible.

However, thinking about perhaps staying with Kelsey while that happened seemed like an ideal opportunity.

"But you don't need to let me know now," she continued, breaking me out of my thoughts. "Just make me a list before next weekend, and I'll get a few options ready to look at."

"Thanks, Kelsey. You have no idea how much I appreciate this. When I realized who you were, I have to admit, I was worried you'd change your mind."

"Out of curiosity . . . when *did* you realize who I am?"

I scratched my chin, even though I didn't have an itch. It likely made me look guilty, but if I was being honest, I'd stopped caring what things *looked* like long ago. People made up their own minds regardless of how I acted or what I did. "Last Friday, after Jason told me that you said I could move in."

"But how? Like, how'd you figure it out? Because I had no clue until last night at the elevators." The awareness in her eyes when Tatum had said my name was something I'd never forget.

"My assistant looked you up on Facebook."

She nodded, focusing on the pillow in her lap while biting the inside of her cheek. "Any reason why you didn't say anything when you found out?"

"What did you expect me to do, Kelsey? Retrace my steps to your apartment and knock on your door? Say, *Hey, I know you said I can move in, but you might wanna reconsider since I'm the guy who said 'I love you' right before he came*? Yeah . . . *no*." Nothing was more embarrassing than being so wrapped up in the fantasy we'd built that I had confessed my undying love to her—even without knowing her name. I just hoped she hadn't taken that to heart.

She dipped her head even more, tucking her chin to her chest to hide the naughty grin and rosy cheeks. When she finally seemed to have control over her reaction, she glanced up and asked, "Had I recanted my offer, where would you have gone?"

I shrugged, truly unable to give her much of an answer. "I'm not sure. I'd like to believe that Jason and Tatum wouldn't let me live out of my car and would offer one of their spare rooms, but I'm not sure since that's never come up."

"Yeah . . . I don't know how true that is. I'm sure they would've done all they could to help you out, but moving you in? I doubt that would've been much of an option."

"You mean because she's pregnant?"

Kelsey's eyes widened, fear constricting her pupils while she stared daggers at me. "Did Jason tell you? Tatum said no one knew. They haven't even said anything to their families yet. Then again, she told me, so I guess it'd only be fair if he talked to you about it."

"No." I laughed, placed my hand on her bare knee, and was suddenly sidetracked by the heat burning into my palm. But I quickly managed to lock that down and continue with our conversation. "That night, you told me that you dressed as the bride-to-be because your friend just found out she was pregnant and was too sick to come out. Once I realized it was you, I figured Tatum was the friend in question and put two and two together."

"Shit. Have you said anything to them?"

"Honestly, between work and the wedding—as well as freaking out about seeing you—I haven't thought much of it. I assumed he'd tell me when he was ready, and if he hadn't said anything yet, he had a good reason."

"That could've ended very badly." The tiniest smile curled the corners of her lips before dropping. "Seriously, though . . . if I'd changed my mind about letting you stay with me, would you really have no other place to go but your car?"

Shifting on the edge of the mattress to face her, I pulled one knee up and shrugged. "Technically, I could find something else—maybe a motel, my office, moving between friends' couches."

"But I thought you had a lot of friends? At least, that's how my cousin made it sound."

This was the downside of living a double life, of not correcting others when they assumed things about you. "I *know* a lot of people, meet up with most of them when I go out. But that doesn't make them viable options to live with."

"Why not? You don't know me, but you're moving into my place. How would living with an acquaintance be any different than moving in with a stranger?"

"It's just not the same. End of story." I refused to go into the details of why I couldn't move in with Cheryl or any of the other women I'd attempted—and failed—to date. "But to answer your question . . . no. If you changed your mind, I wouldn't have to sleep in my car. I'd be able to find somewhere to stay. Just as long as you don't wait until the last second to tell me I can't move in with you."

"Nah. I wouldn't do that. I already told you that you can stay in Tatum's old room. It'd be a bitch move if I took that back now . . . no matter how I feel about it."

I felt like shit. It was clear she didn't want me there and had only kept her word out of a sense of honor. On the other hand, if I released her of this self-imposed obligation, then I'd be screwing myself over. As much as I wanted to do the right thing, I couldn't risk not having a place to live for the next few months. And oddly enough, my decision not to give her an out had nothing to do with wanting a repeat performance from a few weeks ago.

"I just don't understand why you didn't get more of a notice from the owners of the house you were staying in. Isn't that against the law or something?"

I dropped my attention to the bedspread and began to pick at an errant thread. "It might be, but who knows. I don't think my situation would fall under those rules."

"Why not?"

"Because I lived with my parents."

She was silent for a moment, and it almost made me glance up to survey her expression. But when she started to laugh, I knew I didn't want to see the look on her face. It would be no different than everyone else's when they found out.

"Wait . . ." She slowed the amusement rolling through her long enough to catch her breath. "How old are you?"

Here we go again. I met her stare, giving her exactly what she wanted to hear. I knew this because it was what everyone wanted—what they expected. There was no reason to give them anything else; it would only ruin their entertainment. "Thirty-two."

"And you still live with your parents? Why?"

I shook my head and glanced around the room. "Why not? Free room and board. Home-cooked meals. My mom does my laundry. Why else do you think?"

Something about my response made her still, and when I turned toward her again, I found her eyes on mine, sad and full of guilt. "What am I missing, Aaron? Tatum said you're a psychologist. You have your own practice. It's obvious you do well for yourself, so I can't imagine you as the type to mooch off your parents into your thirties."

For the first time, I found myself *wanting* to explain it. "I moved back in just before graduate school. I had racked up a lot in student loans, and even more would follow. Living with them made it easier to study without having to worry about a full-time job to pay the bills, and after graduation, they let me stay while I paid them off. They wanted to help put me through college, but they couldn't afford it. Letting me stay with them was their way of financially helping me."

"Then why didn't you just say that?"

"Why would I?" I fisted my hands to hold back my irritation—she didn't deserve it. "As soon as anyone finds out that I still lived in my childhood bedroom, they immediately think I'm lazy or entitled.

No one bothers to consider that there might be other reasons why a thirtysomething-year-old guy would still be at home."

"Exactly. I would think you'd want to set the record straight."

"There's no point, Kelsey. I understand what you're saying, but I refuse to defend myself time and time again. People will think what they want anyway. Why waste my time and energy forcing them to see me for who I am instead of all the assumptions they've made along the way?"

Her shoulders fell as she leaned forward and took my hand. "Is that why you don't tell anyone that you strip for extra cash?"

"Wait . . ." I had to have heard her wrong. *"What?"*

"I'm pretty sure Tatum would've told me that you're a male dancer if she knew. So either you don't tell anyone about your weekend gig—which I would completely understand—or you're not really a stripper. Which would make a lot of sense and explain *so* much."

A smile tugged at my lips, burning the muscles in my cheeks as I stared into her eager eyes. "My friend works at Boots—Cheryl. She called me that night and told me she needed a favor. I had no idea what she wanted me to do. In fact, I didn't know it would involve taking off my clothes until I walked in and that one girl—Rebecca, the blonde who kind of recognizes me—said something."

"And what was your reason for playing along?"

"Seemed like a good idea at the time. Gave me a chance to meet a few ladies, possibly get a number or two. Why wouldn't I?"

She slipped her hand off mine and sat up straight again, as if my admission had physically pushed her away. "Listen . . . about that night—"

"You don't have to say anything." I covered her smooth, warm thigh with my palm, calling her eyes to mine. "I won't lie . . . it was amazing. Hands down the best night of my entire life. But we had agreed to never see each other again for a reason. No matter how fantastic we were in bed, trying it a second time would never be the same."

"Oh, I wasn't insinuating we should do it again."

Boy . . . was *my* face red.

"Then good. Looks like we're on the same page." I stood and took a hesitant step toward the door, hoping she'd tell me to stay—just for one night. The issue was more or less falling into bed while living together, but we weren't roomies quite yet. "Anything else you need to tell me?"

She closed her eyes for a moment, took a deep breath, and then slowly lifted her lids. "Nope. See you next weekend."

"See you then."

Chapter 9

Kelsey

This was a bad idea.

A very, *very* bad idea. One I couldn't get out of easily.

Had I known who Aaron was when Tatum asked me to let him stay in her old room, I would've said no. Hell, if I'd known I was pregnant when she asked, I would've said no. Now, I was living with my one-night stand—who doubled as my baby's father—and no matter what I did, I couldn't get away from him.

Such as right now . . . at my parents' house for our weekly Sunday barbecue.

When he'd caught me getting ready this morning, he'd asked where I was headed. I'd been too busy to contemplate the pathetic look on his face while he sat on the couch, reminding me very much of a puppy being left behind while its owner went out to have fun. Had I given that possibility much thought, I wouldn't have told him. Unfortunately for me, I hadn't . . . so I told him. After that, I couldn't *not* invite him along. Although, in my defense, I'd hoped he'd say no.

He didn't.

Then again, I probably should've guessed that'd be his answer. Jason and Tatum would be there, and if he still had anything to do with Marlena, he'd know almost everyone in attendance. Really, having him there made more sense than leaving him at the apartment alone all day.

"He's cute," my mom said while staring at Aaron's profile. She didn't care who was around, who could hear, or even how uncomfortable the things she blurted out made anyone feel. She was who she was, and by this point, there was no changing it.

We were on the patio with Tatum and my aunt, Jason's mom. My sister was inside somewhere with one of her kids doing God knew what—things I'd eventually have to do unless I could find a way to afford a nanny. Shit, even a poop nanny would be okay. I could handle the rest as long as someone else dealt with the shitty diapers. Well, that and throw up. And drool. Okay, fine . . . I'd have to have a full-time nanny to handle everything.

Or . . . I could let Marlena raise the little booger until it could use a toilet and wipe its own nose. She'd had two, and they were both still breathing, so why not? At least my kid would be in safe hands.

Mom nudged me with her elbow, breaking me out of the manic delusions that had taken over my brain. "Are you spending time with him? Getting to know him at all?"

I glanced past the pool to the dock, where Aaron stood next to Jason and my dad around the grill. He laughed at something that was said—tilted his head back and just let the sexy sound roar out like a werewolf howling at the moon. Even if I hadn't been able to hear the sound, the sight alone would have been enough to offer me plenty to think about later when I was all alone in my room.

No one needed to know the level of desperation my sex life had reached.

"He's only been at the apartment for a week, Mom. There hasn't been much time to spend with each other." I pointed at her, mere inches from her face so she knew I meant business. "Don't play matchmaker, and don't get your hopes up. I'm not interested. *Ever.* Got it?"

Mom had this annoying way of pushing me toward a guy, even though I'd repeatedly told her that if I wanted to settle down, I would do so. That had never stopped her from finding *every* guy around my age to be perfect for me.

Technically, she'd gotten to a point recently where age no longer mattered. As long as they were still in their prime and could have kids, she was all about it. God save my soul.

"Where's my camera?" She shifted in her seat as though she was about to stand up, but I put a stop to that by grabbing her arm.

"Please don't make this awkward. I have to live with him for the next couple of months." *And be tied to him for eighteen years.* I inwardly groaned at that thought. "Cool it with the camera today, will ya? I'm sure he doesn't want candid photos of himself all over your Facebook page. In fact, he doesn't even need to know you're on social media, so *please*, don't send him a friend request. That's just uncomfortable on so many levels."

Apparently, she'd lost her sense of hearing. Either that, or she ignored anything I had to say. There was a good chance the latter was more accurate. At least she'd given up on the camera—for now. "I hear he's a doctor. It'd be amazing to have a doctor in the family, wouldn't it?"

I stared off into the distance, watching the way he interacted with my dad, occasionally glancing up at us before returning his attention to the grill or whatever it was they were talking about down there. The weather was warm, although there was a faint breeze that swept through at a consistent pace, keeping most of the humidity from settling on our skin. Yet I couldn't help but imagine how hot he had to be standing beneath the sun in jeans and a collared shirt.

Sweat. Glistening skin. Slick abs . . .

I shook my head, hoping to rid myself of any image that would induce arousal.

"He's a therapist," I answered without taking my eyes off him. Off his smile or the slight jump in his shoulders when he laughed. He appeared so carefree, so uninhibited. Maybe it was the fact that he was around a couple of guys, or that he had his best friend with him for comfort.

It also appeared I wouldn't be able to escape becoming aroused where he was concerned.

"Isn't a therapist still a doctor?"

Clearing my throat, I brought my attention back to my mother, who continued to shamelessly regard the men on the dock. "I have no idea, but I assume only psychiatrists would be considered doctors since they prescribe medicine."

Her lips quirked to one side, her brows closing in on each other. And then, because she couldn't let anything go, she interrupted Tatum's conversation with my aunt. "Didn't you tell me that Aaron's a doctor?"

"For the love of all the things, Mom. Must you constantly try to prove everyone wrong every chance you get?"

Tatum, Aunt Lori, and my mom all swung shocked, wide eyes my way. Sure, I could've kept my mouth shut, kept my frustrations to myself, but thanks to the overabundance of hormones in my system, I was powerless to stop it. It was as though my mouth had opened by itself, annoyance lacing every single syllable that flew off my tongue without one ounce of consciousness.

"I just got done telling you that I have no idea but that I didn't think so. I wasn't arguing with you. I didn't disagree. I specifically said I wasn't sure. So there's no reason to cut in the middle of Tater's conversation just to prove a point."

While they continued to blink at me like their eyelids had all synchronized to the same rhythm of surprise, my pulse began to slow. And once that happened, the heat in my face lessened, the fog in my mind thinned, and reality slowly settled over me.

These body changes would be the death of me.

I couldn't control them, no matter how desperate I was to keep a tight lid on every last one of them. Everything either made me cry or caused me to flip out without so much as a warning. And the more frequently it happened, the crazier I started to feel.

"Sorry. I've been so hormonal lately."

My mom's bright eyes widened. "Does this mean . . . ?"

"No. It doesn't." It did, but I wasn't about to go there now. Especially with Aaron here. "And why can't you be like every other parent? I'm not in a relationship, not even dating someone. So if I were . . ." I eyed her, refusing to say the word. "I'd be a single mother. How could you possibly be excited about that?"

Lord knew I wasn't.

"You're the one who refuses to date. Refuses to have anything long term in your life. All I want is a grandchild. Is that too much to ask?"

I pointed to the slider that led inside. "You have two in there."

"*Another* one. From *you*. Stop pretending like this is the first time you've heard me say this." Maybe my frustrations with my mom weren't completely pregnancy induced. After all, this had been going on for quite some time. Her wanting a grandchild from me and my complete lack of desire to give her one weren't new developments.

"As much as I hate to be the bearer of bad news . . . I'm starting my period soon." I had Tatum to thank for that one—her convenient ways of spinning the truth worked out well at times. "Go convince Nick and Marlena to pop out another one."

"Anyway . . ." Mom waved me off, ignoring me like she often did when I didn't tell her what she wanted to hear, and returned her attention to Tatum. "Didn't you say he was a doctor?"

"Who . . . Aaron?" Tatum glanced over her shoulder at the men on the dock—likely for nothing more than an excuse to see her husband, based on the glowing blush in her cheeks. "Yes, ma'am. Dr. Aaron Baucus."

"So he's a psychiatrist? Not a psychologist? Am I confusing the two?" I asked, disregarding the fact that though I'd just flipped out on my mom for trying to prove a point, it seemed I was guilty of the same thing. Although, I could easily pass my question off as a desire to broaden my intelligence.

"Neither. He's a neuropsychologist." Tatum must've been in her own world if she didn't recognize the three pairs of blinking eyes set on her. Finally, she chose to explain without being prompted. "It has something to do with the brain and head trauma. I think. But don't hold me to it; I could be way off. I just know it's super scientific."

It both baffled and intrigued me as to why he hadn't admitted that, choosing to almost downplay his profession for some unknown reason. He'd discussed his practice, and on Wednesday, he'd come home late because of some consultation he'd had at the hospital. Then again, I hadn't asked, so I couldn't be *that* surprised to be hearing of this for the first time.

"Wow," Mom whispered—technically, it was more of a swoon than of a whisper. "He sounds like he's really smart." That's when the nudging started all over again, reminding me once more that I should never sit next to her. "Looks *and* brains, Kelsey. He sounds like a winner."

"And you sound like a shoo-in for the host of *The Price Is Right* meets *Love Connection*. Either way, I'm not interested." Which I wasn't. Except for when I found myself alone in my bed, recalling all the things he'd done to my body.

These damn hormones . . .

"I'm not saying go out and have his baby or anything . . ." Mom didn't get a chance to finish her sentence because Tatum started to choke. She turned to Tatum and asked, "Are you all right? Did you swallow a fly?"

"Yes, Mother," I droned, utter sarcasm dripping like honey from my tone. "She swallowed a fly. There's no telling why she decided to swallow a fly, but rumor has it she might die. We should keep an eye on her before she swallows a spider to catch the fly. I hear it's a vicious cycle after that. If she makes it to the goat . . . I'm out."

At some point, they all stopped and glared at me. Even Tatum, who had been dying a few seconds earlier. "Your level of concern is noted." Her smile might have been fake, but I could see the sincerity in her eyes—she couldn't hide that from me.

We'd share a good laugh about this later.

"What were you saying, Diane? I'm sorry I so rudely interrupted." Tatum was looking at my mom, but her words were directed at me.

Mom sat back and lifted her eyes to the sky beyond the patio. Then her lips curled, a sign that she remembered what we'd been in the middle of discussing. "Give the guy a chance, Kelsey. It's not like you have to go out of your way. He's living with you, for Pete's sake."

"I'm well aware of his living situation, Mom. But thanks for the reminder."

"All I'm saying is . . . it'd be nice if you spent some time with him, got to know him a little better. After all, you had no idea he's a doctor. Imagine all the other things you could find out about him if you just gave it a chance."

If she only knew the things I'd *found out* about him during one night of tequila-induced sex, then she wouldn't want me to have anything to do with him. I was her little girl. There was no way she'd be okay with some of the things he'd done to me in the dark.

"I think I hear Marlena calling for me." I got up and excused myself, thankful that no one bothered to stop me, even though I hadn't fooled anyone. Marlena didn't call for me—and if she needed anyone, I'd be the last person she hollered for.

There was only so much bonding time I could take with my mom. She meant well, had the biggest heart of anyone alive . . . but damn, that woman hadn't gotten the memo that just because I was her child, it didn't make her the puppeteer of my life.

"Why didn't you tell me you're a doctor?" I asked as soon as we were in the car, buckling our seat belts.

Aaron had pitched a fit because I wouldn't let him drive to my parents' house—something about how a man in the passenger seat was equivalent to castration. I'd ignored most of it, so I wasn't exactly sure what his issue was, but at least he didn't seem to have it on our way home.

"Considering I was in a white coat the first time you saw me, I guess I didn't think it was necessary to bring it up. How was I supposed to know you didn't think I was a doctor?" The way he fidgeted with the strap across his chest and kept his attention out the window, he appeared nervous.

I didn't understand why, though. "Well, I was under the impression you were a stripper at that point, and when I found out it was all a ruse to get laid, I—"

"It wasn't a ruse to get laid. I already told you this."

"Fine . . . to get *a few numbers*. Better?" I glanced to the side and noted his awkward nod, as if agreeing to that somehow made him feel like crap. Which, again, made no sense, considering *he* was the one who'd admitted that part to me. "Regardless, once I found out you aren't a stripper, the white coat was the last thing on my mind."

"It hasn't come up. And there hasn't been a need to give you my credentials or educational background. I guess I could've given you my business card, but I didn't exactly see a reason to." He had a point, even if I didn't like the way it was delivered.

So far, the worst part of pregnancy was how unbalanced my moods were. For example, my mom could piss me off in a nanosecond by doing nothing other than saying my name in the wrong chord. Tatum didn't have to do much more than breathe to be on the other end of my sarcasm—although, to be fair, I'd always reserved that special level of dry, feigned acrimony just for her. It was kind of our thing.

However, with Aaron, I didn't fly off the deep end or cut him with my sharp tongue. It was rather difficult to be irritated with him when all I could think about was his hands on my body and his tongue on my— *Dammit. I did it again.*

"Can we just go back to why you didn't tell me you were a doctor?" We literally had a five-minute drive to the apartment. If he didn't answer soon, I'd likely never get the answer to my question.

"Go back? When did we ever leave? Did we have another conversation I'm not aware of?"

Bless all the things. Thank God he couldn't read my thoughts and discover that *he'd* been my distraction . . . unknowingly.

"I'm being serious, Aaron. I look like a fool in front of my family when Tatum or Jason say something and I'm in the dark. What do you think that looks like to my parents?" Not giving him a second to respond, I answered for him. "I'll tell you what it looks like . . . that I have a strange guy living with me, and I don't know a single thing about him. If I go missing—"

He placed his hand over my thigh, effectively ending my moment of panic.

Aaron had a way of pulling out *other* reactions that I wasn't proud of. I guess in the grand scheme of things, irrational panic-laced outbursts were better than rage-filled lashings. Plus, it gave him a chance to calm me down. And I liked the way he calmed me down. If freaking out meant he'd put his hand on me . . . then I'd invent anxiety-ridden opportunities every chance I had.

"I don't tell anyone I'm a doctor because it tends to give off the wrong impression. I'm sick and tired of not being what everyone wants or expects. I'm damned if I do, damned if I don't."

"That doesn't make any sense."

He sighed as I pulled the car into the parking lot of my complex. I worried this conversation would be over, but when he didn't budge from his seat, I began to think I just might get the answers I sought without having to resort to throwing a tantrum.

"People hear *doctor*, and the first thing that comes to mind is *Grey's Anatomy*." He cut his eyes at me, making a point.

"So? TV has ruined us—not all doctors are super sexy surgeons."

An infectious grin brightened his face. He closed his eyes, tucked his chin as if embarrassed, and shook his head slowly. Oddly enough, it was hot as hell—the way he timidly gathered his thoughts before saying, "That's just it, Kelsey. Just like we're not all surgeons, we're not all medical physicians, either."

"Okay. Now you're really confusing me."

Instead of responding, he opened the car door and slid out. It took me a second or two, but I eventually followed after shutting off the engine. And while I fell in line behind him on the stairs and then down the hallway to our apartment, I wondered if I'd ever get a response to my question.

I pressed my back against the door and locked my eyes with his so he couldn't mistake the seriousness of my next words. "I'll only let you inside if you answer me. And I want a *real* answer. Not some stupid bullshit about stereotypes."

With an even bigger smile than the one he'd worn in the car, he slipped his keys from his pocket and stepped into me. His closeness was almost more than I could handle, and as soon as he had his arms wound around my waist, it took everything in me not to jump him right then and there, where anyone could see.

But all that vanished when the door behind me opened. I would've fallen on my ass had he not held me against him, and I couldn't push away fast enough. I didn't care to let him know just how badly I wanted a repeat of the night our little bean had been conceived—well, without the conception part.

I was ready to go to my room, lock myself inside like I'd done for most of the week since he'd moved in, yet Aaron stopped me. He grabbed my hand and led me to the couch, leaving no room for arguing—which was impressive, considering I could argue with a brick wall. But rather than take the seat next to me, he stalked into the kitchen, opened the freezer, then a few drawers, *and then* he joined me on the sofa. Much to my surprise, he'd brought with him a carton of ice cream and two spoons. Whether it was his intention or not, shoving the frozen treat into my mouth kept me from speaking and allowed him the floor without interruptions.

He leaned his head back on the love seat and stared at the ceiling for a moment before speaking. "Maybe I'm just sick and tired of assumptions."

"So you've said before. But seriously, what kinds of things can people assume about you being a doctor? And how can anything they come up with be a bad thing?"

"They hear *doctor* and immediately see dollar signs. I make a decent living, but nowhere near what they expect my salary to be. When they realize that, they want nothing to do with me. Then there are the actual MDs who look down on me, as if having a PhD somehow means I'm not a *real* doctor. So on one hand, I'm a fraud, and on the other, I'm a poseur."

"I still don't understand, Aaron."

He shifted on the couch to face me, one knee pulled up on the cushion between us—much like he'd done on the bed in my hotel room two weeks ago. It made me feel like he was giving me his undivided attention. That one gesture gave me a sense of importance that I'd never received anywhere else. Like talking to me was a priority.

That realization was enough to fill my mouth with a spoonful of mint chocolate chip.

Pain lingered in his eyes, though his voice remained emotionless. It was an amazing mask. "Pretend for one minute that you know absolutely nothing about me. We have no mutual friends, no connections, and we've never met. You hear my name—Dr. Baucus. What's your first impression? What picture comes to mind when you hear my name?"

Swallowing the cold lump of ice cream, I shrugged. But when he implored me with his desperate gaze, I gave in and played along. "I guess I'd picture you in a white coat, a stethoscope around your neck. Probably driving around in a Corvette or something."

"Exactly. Now, say you meet me. You see me pull up in my truck that has at least a hundred thousand miles on it. I'm wearing regular clothes. Nothing fancy." Taking his spoon, he mindlessly played with the frozen dessert between us. "What goes through your mind?"

"What does it matter, Aaron?"

"It matters because these are the things I go through time and time again. Every woman I meet expects me to be one thing. When they find out I'm only a Doctor of Philosophy, they're no longer interested. It's like having a PhD is something to be ashamed of."

"Maybe you're just meeting the wrong women." Fearing whatever remark he might come up with after a comment like that, I took a spoonful of ice cream and held it out for him to take. To my surprise, he didn't bother grabbing the spoon from me but rather opened his mouth and allowed me to feed him.

His eyes fluttered to the side in thought as he swallowed, and then he lifted one shoulder, silently conceding. "Either way, I don't offer that information for a reason. Just like I'd rather say I'm a therapist than a neuropsychologist. It's no different than anyone finding out that I was living with my parents until they sold the house. Those things draw a quick image in someone's mind, and it's never the right one."

"Yeah, but everything you just said can be explained."

"Only to those who care for an explanation." Exhaustion laced his eyes, and I could tell it went bone deep—tired of the same song and dance. It was something I recognized. Something I could relate to.

"When someone expects a surgeon and gets a guy with a PhD, they don't stick around. When they expect a genius and find themselves having dinner with me, someone who enjoys beer and lives at home, they run. *Fast.* By that point, the truth doesn't matter, because it doesn't fit with the image they created of me."

"Even when you tell them *why* you were still at your parents' house? That you were paying off your student loans?"

"That'd be fine if I weren't in my thirties, and if my loans hadn't been paid off for the last two or so years." It was his turn to feed me—which I accepted without question. Because . . . well, because it was ice cream.

Either I'd missed something or he hadn't been completely truthful with me when he'd admitted his reason for needing a place to stay. "If your loans were paid off, why did you continue to live there? Wasn't the point of you staying with your parents after graduation to pay off your debt?"

Surprise flashed in his eyes, as if he hadn't expected me to question him. In a way, it made me wonder if this was a test, his way of seeing how long I'd stick around. And as much as I hated tests, I was bound and determined to see this through.

He abandoned his spoon and shifted on the cushion, turning the slightest bit away from me to stare at the front door. "My mom was diagnosed with fibromyalgia just before I graduated from college. Dad was working a lot, so he couldn't always be there for her. Technically, I moved back home to help with her. But with the higher demand in graduate school, I wasn't around as often as I wanted to be. It worked out, though. Between me and Dad, she always had someone there when she needed it."

I continued to gorge myself on ice cream—if for no other reason than to keep myself from interrupting his heartbreaking story. That, and it was cold enough to numb parts of my face, which worked wonders in thwarting those annoying tears that liked to sprout up at the most inopportune times.

This baby had made it its mission to give me an insane amount of compassion.

"After I received my doctorate, my parents suggested I stay and pay down my loans. I saw it as a way to help them as much as they were helping me. Once my loans were taken care of, I didn't feel right leaving my mom. They never pressured me to leave—I'm pretty sure having me around made my dad feel a lot better. In fact, they encouraged me to save my money so that when the time was right, I'd be set."

My heart grew so large that it took up all the space in my chest, making my ribs ache as if they were about to snap like twigs under the pressure of each beat. "I don't see why you can't just tell people that. Anyone who dismisses your reasons doesn't deserve a second of your time."

His eyes met mine, shining like two beacons in the dark, finally locating what they were in search of, as if it'd been lost and now found. "I don't typically tell people about my mom. I want respect . . . not pity."

"That's understandable." I stabbed my spoon into the soft dessert and toed off my shoes. Crossing my legs beneath me, I settled in for what I assumed would be a long conversation—if I had anything to do with it, that was. "Well, they sold the house and kicked you out. That's a good sign for your mom, right?"

"Yeah. She's doing so much better. That, and Dad finally retired, so now he can be there for her when she needs it. In all honesty, it worked out for the best. It's about time I start living my own life. You know? Don't get me wrong—I love my mom, and I'll never be able to repay either of them for all they've done for me. But I have a private practice to run, patients to see, consultations to uphold. On top of that, it'd be nice to have a life outside of work."

"Speaking of . . . explain your job to me. What does a neuro . . . *person* do?"

With a laugh, it seemed all his inhibitions had melted away. He appeared more relaxed, open. Not worried about rejection or assumptions. It had to be the greatest compliment I'd ever received, intentional or not. "Neuropsychologist."

"Yeah. That person," I said around a cold spoon in my mouth.

His smile was infectious, causing my lips to curl and stretch, my face burning from the strain. Scooping another bite for himself, he sank farther into the cushions, as though he intended to hide. "In a nutshell, I treat cognitively impaired patients who have suffered from either an injury or illness."

"Sounds fancy. Wanna dumb it down for me?"

The amusement coloring his cheeks was even more contagious, the heat practically tangible. "Our brains are made up of pathways and receptors—kind of like navigating through various highways in a really big city using Google Maps. Well, when someone sustains any type of severe head trauma or suffers from an illness affecting the brain, it can cause all sorts of issues that interfere with those pathways. In a sense, it throws the GPS off—have you ever seen the map move you off the road you're on and try to reroute you a thousand times? It's like that."

"Oh, damn." I was convinced this man could make the encyclopedia sound interesting.

"Yeah, and none of it shows up on a scan. That's where I come in." Confidence straightened his posture, and I doubted he even realized it. He loved what he did, which was evident in his bright eyes. "I evaluate the patient, perform routine tests, and then I help come up with a treatment plan to get the person back to normal—or as close to it as we can."

"So . . . you're, like, really super smart, huh?" *And I sound really super dumb.*

"That's all in the way you look at it."

"And humble." I slowly bobbed my head, spoon turned upside down and hanging out of my mouth. "Good to know."

Easy laughter seeped past his smiling lips as he reached for more of the mint-chocolate-chip goodness. "I enjoy what I do. It gives me a sense of purpose, and it pays the bills. Which is always nice. I've managed to save enough money over the last several years to either buy a house outright or put enough down to have it paid off quickly."

"Oh! I almost forgot . . ." I passed the carton of ice cream to Aaron and jumped up to grab my laptop from my room. By the time I made it back to the couch, I already had the screen pulled up and ready for him to read. "I have a list of places for you based on what you're looking for—which, by the way, was rather broad."

After swapping the ice cream for the computer, he began to scroll through the listings. "Maybe after I look at a few, I might be a little pickier. It's kinda hard to pinpoint exactly what I want when I haven't really seen what I have to choose from."

"Well, now you can. Just let me know if you want to set something up, take a closer look at any of them."

"Thanks." He swung his gaze to me, holding me captive in the brilliant jade swirls. "Any chance I can convince you to check them out with me? You have far more experience in this field than I do, and honestly, I don't have the first clue what I'm looking for."

My stomach dipped, though I couldn't begin to guess why. He'd only been here for a week, and in that time, we hadn't spoken much. In fact, I'd learned more about him in the short time since leaving my parents' house than I had the entire week we'd slept under the same roof. Not to mention, I'd known from the beginning that he was in the market for a house and would be leaving, so this fiery ball of dread in the pit of my stomach didn't make sense.

Unless this was my child telling me that its father deserved to know the truth.

Still in the womb and already talking back.

I nodded. "Yeah. I can do that." And then I got up, using the melted ice cream as an excuse to leave the room. I had thoughts racing through my head that needed to escape, and since I only let those out in my leather-bound journal, in the privacy of my own room, where Aaron wouldn't find it, I said good night and then closed myself off behind my door.

Chapter 10

Aaron

Over the last week and a half, Kelsey had taken me to see half a dozen houses. None of them were doable—and not because I didn't like them. She had something to say about every last one. I began to wonder why she had picked them out in the first place, but I kept that to myself.

Me: We're still going to check out that listing after work, right?

There was one she'd found and wanted to show me, so we'd made plans to see it this evening. But now that we were less than an hour away and I hadn't heard from her at all, I became worried she'd forgotten. Or I'd gotten the days mixed up.

There was a small chance I'd texted her just because I wanted to talk to her.

But I planned to ignore that possibility.

Kelsey: Yes . . . except I might be late. We should just meet at the apartment.

Me: Late?? What have you been doing all day?

Kelsey: Standing on a street corner hoping to make a few extra bucks. You know . . . same thing, different day.

I laughed so loudly I expected Noel to come into my office and see what was going on. Thankfully, she didn't. And I hoped that meant she was finishing up with the last patient so we could leave and I could see this *amazing* house Kelsey had picked out.

Kelsey: It's called work, asshole. These houses don't stage themselves.

Me: Clearly, because you'd be out of a job

Ever since our chat after lunch at her parents' house, things had been easy between us. Good. *Fun*, even. There were times I had to stop and remind myself that we hadn't known each other for years, or that we weren't in a long-term relationship. That's how comfortable I felt around her. And while there were moments that it frightened me—because I knew it wasn't real and would end at some point, regardless if I wanted it to or not—there were others that left me in a constant state of bliss.

I was fully aware of how delusional I was.

Her response left me puzzled. There was a sock emoji, followed by *it*, but I couldn't figure out what *sock it* meant. I'd only ever heard that used in the phrase *sock it to me*. And the longer I stared at her message, the more confused I became.

Me: What does sock it mean??

Dots appeared and then went away. Several times. As if she'd start typing and then change her mind, only to start all over again. It about drove me insane, and if it went on for much longer, I'd be late meeting her due to wasting time watching her dancing dots on the screen.

Finally, a full message came through.

Kelsey: I wrote SUCK it.

Kelsey: Apparently, my phone changed suck to sock.

Me: I guess it socks to be you! LOL!!

Her only response was a rolling-eyed emoji. Regardless of what she had come back with, I couldn't stop laughing. And in the end, it eventually caught Noel's attention. She knocked on the door, but in Noel fashion, she didn't bother to wait for an invite and just waltzed in.

"Um . . ." She tapped her lips with her finger and hummed, glancing around the room. "Hey, boss. You do know there's no one in here, right?"

I raised one brow and fought to contain my laughter. "Yes, I realize that. I was just texting with Kelsey, and I said something funny."

"Did she laugh?"

"Probably. It was really funny." I proceeded to read it to her, but her face remained blank. "You wouldn't know humor if it slapped you in the face."

"Keep telling yourself that." She could lie all she wanted, but I didn't miss the faint grin that was seen more in her eyes than on her mouth. "Anyway, everything's taken care of up front, and you're all set up for the morning. Don't forget I'll be late. I have *yet* another doctor's appointment, but I'll be here as soon as it's over."

I'd known Noel for a while, and one of the things I hated most for her was her battle to get pregnant. It'd taken a while before she'd opened up to me about her and Pete's struggles to have a baby and how long they'd been trying. And ever since she'd told me about it, I ached for them. If *anyone* on this planet deserved a baby, it was them.

"No worries. If I fuck something up, I know you'll fix it when you get in."

She smiled and rolled her eyes, a soft giggle escaping her as she shook her head. "And knowing you, there'll be a lot for me to fix. Just please, stay away from the fax machine. And the copier. Last time you tried to help out, we had to go without both for days before I could get someone in to repair them. And no . . . before you say anything, photocopies of your hand *weren't* important."

She'd never let me live that down, nor would she ever believe that it wasn't my hand. Granted, it was, but that wasn't the point. In all fairness, she'd just gotten news that their first attempt at insemination hadn't worked, and it was all I could do to cheer her up. It had worked. Even though she liked to complain about how long we'd gone without a copy machine, she'd laughed so hard that day that tears lined her face—and not the kind she had worn earlier, either.

"If you ever go missing, don't get pissed when we can't find you because we don't have your fingerprints." I grabbed my keys from the top drawer on my desk, slipped my phone into my pocket, and walked toward the door. "I, on the other hand, am prepared."

"You have nothing to worry about, Aaron. Nobody is going to take you. And if they do, they'll give you back before anyone can pull the first print off anything." She headed toward the reception desk to grab her purse before meeting me at the door.

"If I ever do get abducted, you'll regret saying that."

To my surprise, Noel fell against my chest and wrapped her arms around my waist. It took all of two seconds before I heard the first sniffle, and another second and a half before her shoulders hiccupped. I didn't hesitate to hold her against me, knowing where this had come from. Every time she had another appointment, her anxiety went through the roof, starting at the end of her shift the day before.

She had to have seen through my act of trying to make her laugh. It usually worked, though not this time.

"It'll be okay, Noel."

She nodded, sniffled again, and then let go. "Thanks, Aaron." And without glancing at me, she opened the door and walked out, leaving me behind to lock up. Which was fine by me, but I hated seeing her so broken.

I'd never had a little sister.

Until I'd met Noel.

I opened the bathroom door to let the steam out from my shower and found Kelsey sitting on the couch. Oddly enough, the TV wasn't on, and she didn't seem to be on the phone. I hesitated at first, but then I thought, *Screw it.*

"What's up, buttercup?" I asked, taking the cushion next to her.

She glared at me, though I could tell it wasn't sincere. "Nothing." She huffed and glanced to the ceiling, eventually giving up on being vague since she'd learned by now that it didn't work on me. "I'm just not ready for bed, but I don't have anything to do, and there's nothing good on TV."

I grabbed her ankles and pulled on her legs until her feet rested in my lap. At first, it surprised her—hell, it surprised me, too. I wasn't a fan of touching anyone's feet, yet I did so with hers without an ounce of thought. And before I could talk myself out of it, I began rubbing the arch on one, stretching out the muscle, which made her groan.

And then I never wanted to stop touching them, hoping to pull every erotic sound from her that I could with nothing more than my hands and her feet. If I couldn't have her any other way, I'd take what I could get. And if this was all I could get, I'd take it without a single complaint.

"Okay, so let's talk." I pushed away any thoughts I had about the noises she made and tried to concentrate on a topic that could keep her talking. "When are you going to find me a house that we both agree on?"

The one we'd gone to look at today was supposed to be a good one—one she had picked out. Yet still, once we were inside, it wasn't good enough. This time, the moldings were the issue, which, in all honesty, was a ridiculous reason to turn it away. Cosmetic things could always be changed. But she'd convinced me that I didn't want a house that I'd end up having to dump time and money into to update.

I'd begun to believe I'd never find anything good enough for Kelsey Peterson.

"I'm starting to question if you're trying to make me stay." It was a joke, but it was clear it freaked her out. Rather than give in, though, I gripped her foot tighter and said, "But we both know that's crazy. I wouldn't be surprised if you kept a calendar tracking just how much longer I'll be here."

At least that earned me a smile. "No, nothing like that. You're not bad to live with. You clean up after yourself, and you cook me dinner. Granted, it's nothing like what Tatum used to make, but I can't fault you for that. She's a trained chef, and I personally like your fish sticks."

There was a chance that hadn't been meant as a compliment, and even if it was, it wasn't a very big one. But that didn't stop me from taking an incredible amount of pride from it. "Maybe you should tell some of your friends how good I am to have around."

I really wished she'd see that and want me to stay, but I wasn't about to go there. No need to scare her off and ruin whatever this was we had going on.

"My friends will break your heart, Aaron. Trust me . . . you don't want them."

"At this point, I'll take anything." That likely made me look desperate.

Oh, what the hell did I care. I was desperate. I knew it. She knew it.

The fucking postman probably knew it, too.

No point in hiding or pretending I was anyone but me.

"Nah, you don't want a bitch. You're too good for that." She chewed on the inside of her cheek for a moment before returning her gaze to my face. "What are you looking for, Aaron? Like, if you could write down exactly what you're looking for, your perfect girl, and have her walk through that door right now, what would she be like?"

You. I didn't dare say that out loud, no matter how badly I wanted to.

"Someone smart and funny—I'd like to talk about anything and everything with her while still being able to laugh. I want a woman who doesn't mind being at home with me, plopped in front of the TV for a movie, but who also doesn't mind going out and having a good time."

"Okay . . . all good points. But what about long term? You want to settle down? Have a family? How big of a family, and how important are these things to you? Is there a time frame in mind?" Good Lord, she certainly got to it, asking all the important questions. It made me wonder what she had up her sleeve.

And I prayed she had a more selfish reason for asking.

There was only one thing to do—give her the truth and see what happened. "You already know I want to get married. I think we established that on the night we've forgotten about." I added a wink for good measure, appreciating the smile she offered in return. "As for kids . . . yes. I want a family, as big a one as I'm allowed. I'm not picky. I just want a good woman I can love every day of my life and kids who'll wipe my ass when I'm too old to do it myself."

She laughed, and it had to be the best sound I'd ever heard. The way she dropped her head back, smile stretching her face and the song of angels filling the room, was the closest thing to heaven I'd ever get here on Earth.

"This is something you want right now?"

I'd skipped this part of the question on purpose, but it seemed she'd picked up on that and refused to let me get away without answering.

"Well, yeah. I'm not getting any younger, and the last thing I want to do is be in the position my assistant's in right now."

"What position is that exactly?"

My heart ached just thinking about it. "Spending years trying to have a baby and still not have one. It pisses me off, you know? That there are people in this world who would give anything to be parents, yet they can't for one reason or another. And then there are idiots who get knocked up on one-night stands or druggies who fall pregnant from a random person they fucked to get high. Why is it that the ones who don't want kids—or were never supposed to have any—are the ones who get pregnant easily, while the ones who deserve it more than anyone else are the ones who struggle?"

Kelsey was quiet for so long I worried she'd fallen asleep with her eyes open.

I switched to the other foot and began to stretch that arch, hoping it'd open her up or break her free from whatever spell she'd become victim of. "I'm sorry. I didn't mean to get so deep with that. I'm just saying . . . the last thing I want to happen is to wait too long to get married, only to find out biological children aren't in our cards. You know?"

"Yeah." She cleared her throat and then pulled her feet from my lap. "Actually, I think I'm more tired than I thought I was. But thanks for the company."

"No problem." I searched my brain for what I'd said to scare her off, yet I couldn't come up with anything. "Is everything okay? You're not upset about anything, are you?"

"Oh, no. I'm fine. Just really tired all of a sudden. But hey"—she placed her hand on my thigh—"you'll find her. I know it. And I have a feeling you won't have to worry about the whole kid thing. You're stressing for no reason."

The only thing I could do was smile and say, "Night, Kelsey."

"Good night, Aaron."

Something I'd done or said had made her run. If only I knew what.

Chapter 11

Kelsey

I'd filled more pages in my journal since Aaron had expressed his concern over women who didn't want kids getting pregnant from one-night stands than I had in all the time before that combined.

My head was all over the place. And it seemed Aaron only made it worse.

Over the last two days, he'd done nothing but give me attention, likely realizing that something had gotten me down. He was a smart guy, so he must've assumed it was something he had done or said, which made him do nothing but overcompensate.

Like now . . . with his frequent text messages. Though I had to admit, most of the time, he made me laugh. His humor was probably the one thing capable of pulling me out of my fear-induced coma.

Dr. Phil-Me-Up: I hope you didn't eat too much at lunch today

The paper sheet crinkled as I lifted my phone and read his message. The doctor would be in any minute; the nurse had told me so about half an hour ago. After a few moments of deliberating—unsure if I should engage in a conversation with him *now* versus waiting until after the appointment—I tapped on the screen and typed up a message.

Me: Why?

Yes, that had taken me a while to come up with.

Dr. Phil-Me-Up: Because I have a fancy dinner planned for you tonight. Gormet

Me: Is that the same as GOURMET?

Dr. Phil-Me-Up: Nope. One step below

I covered my mouth with one hand to hold in the laughter. Which proved to be utterly pointless since I was the only one in the exam room.

After pulling up the emoji list, I found the laughing-face one. But just as I tapped on it, a quick knock resounded, and the door swung open. I jumped in my seat and turned wide eyes to the woman in the doorway, who was smiling like this was some joyous occasion.

Mindlessly, I tapped the blue arrow to send the text. Then I set my phone on the small table next to me and readied myself for the one thing I'd both feared and anticipated ever since finding out I was pregnant.

She went through my chart, discussing dates and terms I'd previously heard at the clinic I'd gone to four weeks ago, all while I just sat there and listened as if it were the first time I'd heard any of it. Then she brought in the ultrasound cart and began going through more things that became white noise in my head. I went through the motions— nodding and the occasional *yeah*—lost under the weight of my reality . . . until a foreign sound filled the room.

At first, it sounded like the garbled sounds of a helicopter. Then the woman who sat at the machine next to me said, "The heartbeat looks good." And suddenly, nothing else mattered. Not the due date, not the situation with Aaron, and not the fact that this lady had a giant wand with a condom over it shoved up my hoo-ha.

Only the sound of my baby's heartbeat.

It was amazing how one sound could completely consume you.

On the way out of the office, my phone vibrated in my back pocket, and even though I was lost in the bliss of my first official appointment, I grabbed my cell. As soon as I saw Aaron's name on the screen, the sun came out, brightening my face and leaving me with the most unexpected smile.

Dr. Phil-Me-Up: I'm starting to wonder if this is a subliminal message about laundry

I glanced higher on the screen, noticing that was his second message, and read the first.

Dr. Phil-Me-Up: Trust me, what I have planned to cook for you does NOT sock.

And then I moved my eyes up one more line to see what he'd meant by that. There, just above that text, was a blue sock emoji. It took me a moment to figure out why it was there, and when I remembered sending him the one of a laughing face, my smile grew wider. Somehow, I'd accidentally tapped the sock . . . again.

Me: I'd love to know why this sock keeps showing up.

Dr. Phil-Me-Up: Me too . . . but now I kinda don't wanna see it go away

Me: Why?

Dr. Phil-Me-Up: Because it makes me laugh

And just for that, I sent it to him again.

I dropped my purse onto the couch, stepped out of my shoes—which killed my feet—and made my way into the kitchen, where Aaron stood in front of the stove, a mouthwatering aroma filling the room.

Sidling up next to him, I couldn't help but laugh. At him. And at the contents of the pot on the burner. "Macaroni and cheese? I thought you said it was gourmet."

"It is." When he turned to look at me over his shoulder, it brought our faces closer together, which stole the breath from my lungs and the beats from my heart. He had me frozen under his stare—willingly. "It's shells and cheese. Not the powder shit. This is as gourmet as you'll get."

It took every ounce of willpower not to touch him, though I didn't bother holding back the smile he painted on my face by just being him. "You're in luck . . . I happen to *love* shells and cheese."

Aaron stilled for a moment. He set the spoon down, turned his body toward mine, and traced the swell of my cheek with his fingertip. "Were you crying?"

I shoved his hand away and wiped my face. I'd dabbed a cool cloth on my eyes before leaving the office and blasted cold air on my cheeks all the way home. There was no way he could've possibly been able to tell I'd been crying. "No."

"Well, if you start to, you can always talk to me about it over a carton of ice cream."

I smiled—it was weak, but a smile nonetheless. "Thanks, Aaron."

"Go get changed and meet me on the couch for some of the best gourmet shells and cheese you've ever had." He winked, and I had to literally force myself to leave his side.

I had no idea what this man was doing to me.

I reclined on one side of the couch, my empty bowl on the floor next to me and my feet in Aaron's lap. I had no idea how we'd started this—his rubbing my feet while we talked or watched TV—but I had no complaints. It seemed my body ached worse as each day passed.

"I heard back about that house today," he said without making eye contact.

Every time we spoke about his moving out, my stomach twisted and my heart raged against my ribs, desperately trying to escape my tightened chest. And the longer this went on, the worse it became. My biggest fear was that he'd buy a house and move out of my apartment, and my world would just quit spinning.

And that thought made me freak the hell out.

"The one you saw yesterday?" I held my breath and waited for the punch in the gut I knew was coming with his response.

"Yeah. I put in an offer once we got back. I guess someone else did the same thing but offered more than I did, so they went with the other guy." The hopelessness in his tone gutted me, as if all his hopes and dreams lived in that one house and someone had stolen them out from under him.

Meanwhile, I couldn't have been happier, though I chose not to dissect my elation. "It'll be okay, Aaron. There are other houses; we just have to keep looking. You'll find something you love even more, and it'll make this one look like a piece of crap."

"Thanks, Kelsey," he said with a smile. Then he stilled, his hands stopping midrub. "Wait a minute . . . I know why you've been sending me sock emojis."

"Because I don't pay attention to what I hit before I send a text?"

"No. I was convinced you were trying to drop hints that I've left my socks lying around. Now I realize it's your subtle way of hinting at a foot massage."

"Yup. That's it. You caught me, Aaron."

With a sinful smile, he dug his thumbs into the soft spot right above my heel, pulling a long groan from my chest. Had it not felt so good, I might've been embarrassed. "Next time . . . just ask. It's amazing the things you can get by simply asking for what you want."

"So you don't want me to send you any more sock emojis?"

"I didn't say that. It'll be a sad day when I stop getting those from you."

And it would be a sad day when I stopped getting foot massages from him.

I didn't want to think about that happening. I wanted to continue to live in the moment.

And in this moment . . . it was easy to pretend that he was mine, we were happy, and we *both* wanted this baby.

Chapter 12

Aaron

"Just remember . . . act surprised," Kelsey told me for the hundredth time tonight.

Tatum and Jason were finally going to tell everyone that they were having a baby. Considering I wasn't supposed to know, and Jason had yet to say anything to me about it, Kelsey felt the need to remind me that I had to react appropriately.

As if she needed to tell me that.

"I got it, Kelsey. Stop freaking out." I grabbed my keys at the same time she reached for hers. And before she could say anything, I picked hers up from the bowl next to the front door and tossed them over my shoulder. I had no idea where they landed, nor did I care. "You're not driving. End of story."

"Who died and made you the supreme ruler of what I do and don't do?"

"My balls." I stopped for a moment, realizing what I'd just said. Yet instead of trying to make it work, I chose to shrug it off and move along. "Let's go."

Unfortunately, she didn't get the memo. Nearly falling over, she held herself up with her hands on her knees, laughing so hard I could barely understand her when she said, "Did you just insinuate that your balls are dead?"

"With all the times you've made me ride in the passenger seat while you drove . . . yup. They shriveled up and died. This is my way of reviving them."

"I hate to be the one to tell you, Aaron . . . but I don't think you can ever come back from that. You may want to consult with a physician to be sure."

Every time we'd gone anywhere together, Kelsey just *had* to drive. Whether it was to look at real estate or go to her parents' house for Sunday meals, she refused to let me behind the wheel. Well, it was time to take charge . . . no matter what opinion I'd given her regarding my testicles.

"Can't you let me have this one thing? I give in to you all the time."

"Oh yeah?" She cocked her head, that ridiculous, satisfied smirk on her lips. "When?"

"Two nights ago, I wanted Chinese. You told me the smell of egg rolls made you sick, so we ate pizza instead. Last weekend, when we went over to Jason and Tatum's place, I wanted to stop on the way and grab a twelve-pack. You told me we didn't have time to do that *and* hit the bakery before it closed. Guess who drank water all night?" I pointed to myself. "And guess who munched on cookies?" I pointed to her.

"I wouldn't consider that you giving in to me. I'd call it me being better at negotiating than you." Oh, she was about to see who was better at what.

I grabbed her wrist, and she reluctantly followed me out of the apartment. "We're taking my truck. And I'm driving. If you don't like it, then you can drive yourself and follow me there."

"Fine." She tried to get away, but I refused to release her. "I'll drive myself."

"Please, Kelsey?" It was almost a whine. And I was almost embarrassed by it. *Almost.*

"Why is it such a big deal who drives?"

"I grew up with my dad always behind the wheel anytime he and my mom were in the same vehicle. He opened her doors, let her into a room first. It's how I was raised. To me, it's a masculinity thing. Maybe it's stupid to you, but it's not to me." My heart pounded against my sternum as I waited for some sort of reaction from her. Anything. I would've taken her laughing in my face right about now—just as long as the suspense was over.

Instead of speaking right away, she pressed her hand against my chest and stepped forward, closing the space between us. "I'm sorry, Aaron. I didn't know it meant this much to you. I'm just used to driving everywhere."

I believed her reasons went beyond habit or what she was used to. Even though I'd only lived with her for three weeks, I knew enough to recognize her need for control. She was a stager—it's what she did. And as I had come to realize, her desire to control everything extended into her personal life as well.

But I didn't need to point that out to her.

"Ready to go?" she asked, peering at me from over her shoulder, and the sight nearly took my breath away.

I made sure to let her walk ahead of me while I took my time locking the front door, just so I could have a moment or two to admire her without getting caught or being questioned.

Her plain, light-pink dress hit her midthigh, and all I could think about was how those legs had felt wrapped around me. How soft her inner thighs were against my lips, and how perfectly I had fit between them. And as she took the stairs one at a time, I couldn't ignore the way her ass moved or the memories it called to mind when I gripped it as I moved inside her.

Dammit. I'd end up with a hard-on by the time I reached the truck if I didn't put an end to this. As much as I didn't want to look away, I had to. For my own sanity.

"You look really nice tonight," I admitted while opening the passenger-side door for her.

She offered a genuine smile as she climbed into the seat. It was warm and inviting, and it made me question what the hell I was doing with her. She was dangerous—something I'd already come to realize—and if I wasn't careful, things could blow up in my face.

After all, I was fully aware of how shitty my luck was.

"Thank you," she said once I settled behind the steering wheel. "You don't look too shabby yourself, Mr. Baucus."

I had one hand on her headrest, prepared to look behind me as I backed out of the parking space, and I glared at her. "That's *Doctor* Baucus to you."

"My apologies. Should I add *PhD* to the end of that? Or is the full title not needed here?"

God, I wished she'd flirt with me like this all the time. Then again, that would only make me fall for her harder, and nothing good could ever come from that. "Nah. That just sounds ridiculous."

Her laughter made it hard to concentrate on getting out of the parking lot.

"You're positive they're going to tell everyone tonight?" I asked after pulling out onto the road in the direction of the restaurant Jason had told me to meet him at. "What happens if they don't announce it?"

"They're definitely telling us all at dinner. Trust me; Tatum's been freaking out about it since last weekend. And if they guess—for *any* reason at all—that you already knew prior to them saying anything, you better not tell them I told you." She could be scary when she wanted to be.

"But you *did* tell me."

"Yeah . . . accidentally. When I thought you were some sleazy stripper. Oh, and I might add I was rather intoxicated when I said it, too. So don't go making it sound like I spilled the beans knowing who you were or anything."

I held up three fingers and said, "Wouldn't dream of it. Scout's honor and all."

"Were you a Scout?"

"Why does everyone focus on that part? Isn't the freaking honor enough for you people?"

Kelsey rested her head against the back of the seat and laughed, filling the cab of the truck with the most glorious sound in the world. "I take it that means no."

While sitting at a red light, I took the opportunity that had presented itself by turning to her and pinching her chin between my fingers, forcing her to look at me. In that one instant all the air around us vanished. Even with the sun long since faded and the traffic light casting a red glow across her face, I could see the way she stared into my eyes, surprise filling her. Though I couldn't be sure what had surprised her to that extent.

Unable to handle the intensity much longer, I smiled and added, "A Scout never tells."

"Are you confusing Boy Scouts with Freemasonry?" Thank God her teasing nature returned without all the awkwardness that I'd invited into our bubble by touching her. "Because I don't think it's much of a secret who's in the Scouts. I could be wrong, though. Maybe those green shorts and stiff-looking tan shirts are simply a ruse to keep us normal folk from discovering who the *real* members of the troop are."

"Damn." I shook my head and pulled into the right lane, getting ready to turn in to the restaurant up ahead. "You know what that means, right?"

"Now you're gonna have to kill me?"

"Yup. Which is a darn shame, because you were really starting to grow on me."

"Aww." She patted me on the arm as I made the turn into the parking lot. "That's sweet. You were growing on me, too. Like mold on a strawberry. All fuzzy and infectious-like."

After parking, I reached to the side to unbuckle my seat belt but stilled while facing her, catching her attention. "For your information, mold is used in antibiotics. It heals. So if you think about it, maybe this was fate."

Her forehead creased as she narrowed her gaze, questioning me without speaking.

"Your stripper not showing up; me inadvertently filling in for him. Tatum not going to her own party, making you take her place as the bachelorette. Then finding out that we actually know each other—*after* you agreed to let me move in. See? Fate."

"So what you're saying is . . . it was our destiny to have sex that night."

"If you want to get all philosophical, then yeah. It's quite possible." I cocked my head to the side and held her stare for a moment, dramatically contemplating a thought. "Although, we were supposed to pretend that night never happened. Kinda hard to do when you keep bringing it up."

"You said it was fate. I'm just trying to figure out how that makes sense."

"I'm your penicillin. I'm here to heal you." How I kept a straight face was beyond me, but once she cracked a smile, I lost the will to hold back and let the laughter out.

She shoved against my arm and opened her door. "You're so lame."

As if walking into a restaurant with everyone already seated at the table wasn't awkward enough, try walking in with smiles on your faces, an inside joke clear to all the outsiders. It was amazing how quickly everyone quieted down and interrogated us with silent stares.

"For someone who's annoyingly on time to everything, you're the last one to arrive," Tatum teased, laughing at Kelsey, who suddenly resembled a deer caught in headlights. "Hurry up and sit down. I told them to give us a few minutes for the drink order, so they should be back soon."

There were two empty seats at the table, side by side. And as I helped Kelsey into one of them, Jason started the introductions. "Not sure if you remember Rebecca or not, but she's one of Tatum's friends. She's the one who made our wedding cake." The blonde glared at me, obviously still not convinced that I wasn't Dr. Phil-Me-Up. "Next to her is Carrie and then Amanda, also friends of Tatum. It's about time you showed up so I can finally have a friend at the table."

I pushed Kelsey's chair in with a laugh and slight headshake rather than a rebuttal that might well get me kicked out. At the very least, it'd make Kelsey's family think twice about allowing me to come over on Sundays.

"What would you like?" With a cocktail menu in my hand, I leaned closer to Kelsey, as if asking her what beverage she wanted was some kind of secret. Regardless, I liked the way it felt to be this close to her, to be able to get a hit of her intoxicating scent without making it obvious. And at this juncture, I didn't give a rat's ass who had what to say about it.

Let them assume—hell, I was used to it.

"I'll just take a water."

I swung my eyes from the list of specialty cocktails to her, not caring that I had to stare at her profile while she studied the entrée section in front of her. "I'm driving, so you can have whatever you want."

She tilted her head just enough to meet my gaze and smile, and then she returned her attention to the paper in her hands. "That's okay. Thanks, though."

"You sure? You only want water?"

Finally, she set the menu down and turned in her seat to face me. "Yes, Aaron. I have work tomorrow. Not to mention, I'm not much of a drinker. But if you'd like something, don't let me stop you."

"I'm driving."

"I bet you're wishing you had let me drive, huh? That's okay, though . . . I'm sure I can handle your truck. I've handled bigger things before."

"Never gonna happen." I raised my brows, eyes opening wider to make my point known.

She shrugged, acting as if it didn't bother her. However, her eyes told a different story. They gave away all her secrets, and I would bet my last dollar that she had no idea. Like right now, her lids lowered just enough to shield her without taking away her ability to see. I'd seen it that first night while standing outside Boots, just before I took her home. Back then, I didn't have the faintest idea what it meant, but now, I recognized it for what it was—her protecting herself from pain or rejection.

It was impossible to guess why she'd reacted that way, though that didn't stop me from making it right. When the waiter came to the table for our drink order, I asked for a glass of water with extra ice for Kelsey—I'd only needed to hear the ice maker at home so many times before I'd picked up on her desire for *really* cold water—and a rum and Coke for me.

"Do I need to ask someone for a ride home now? Or just wait to see how many you have tonight?" Kelsey whispered, keeping up with this secret we'd been caught up in since taking our seats.

Without turning to her, I pulled my keys out of my pocket and slid them into her hand in her lap. And even though there were people talking around us—both at our table and the ones surrounding us—as well as subtle clatter from dishes in the room, I still heard the soft, faint sound of her breath hitching in her throat when my fingers grazed hers.

Nothing else was said about it. She took the keys, slipped them into her purse, and then carried on as if it'd never happened. But one thing did change—when she looked at me, her eyes were fully open, bright, no shield in place. Which was all I truly wanted anyway.

"Everyone got your drinks?" Jason asked, holding up his and searching everyone at the table. "Well, there's something Tatum and I would like to share with you all." He leaned into Tatum's ear just as the murmurs started around the table.

Kelsey nudged me, whispering, "Act surprised," to which I simply rolled my eyes and smiled. But when I took a second to notice her, I couldn't miss the hesitancy on her face, and it made me wonder if I had missed something. And to get the answer to that, I kept my attention set on her as Jason and Tatum continued from across the table.

"It's much sooner than we'd planned, but Tatum and I are thrilled to announce that we're having a baby." Instantly, gasps rang out, mixed with a few squeals, and, of course, the abundance of congratulations from nearly everyone at the table.

I was supposed to act surprised.

And I was.

Because as I regarded Kelsey, nothing surprised me more than the soft, heartbreaking expression on her face. The simple smile meant to brighten a room didn't even offer a spark. And the excitement I'd expected to roll off her like waves on a beach didn't exist.

I followed her line of sight and watched the scene unfold, learning more about her in that moment than I'd ever thought possible. Her aunt regarded Jason and Tatum with bright, glistening eyes, fingertips covering a heartfelt smile. Complete and utter happiness filled her entire face. Next to her, Kelsey's mom had a very different reaction. Excited, yes. Surprised, absolutely. However, there was an overwhelming sense of pride I hadn't anticipated, almost a personal interest. It was something I would've expected had it been her own daughter sharing that kind of news, not her nephew and his wife. The concept of a tight-knit, loving family was not lost on me, but this seemed to go beyond that.

When I turned my attention to Kelsey's dad, I found him sharing in the celebration with Jason. I understood that. Jason's dad wasn't around, and his stepdad—the one who had basically raised him—had passed away last year. So his uncle was the next best thing. And from what I knew, Kelsey didn't have any brothers, which meant Jason would've been the closest thing Fred had to a son. Still, it seemed odd to show that much excitement. Then again, I'd only been around the family a few times, so this may very well have been normal for them.

Marlena, Nick, and Tatum's friends all celebrated, sharing smiles and patting the parents-to-be on the back if they could reach, clapping if they couldn't. Yet when I'd made it around the entire table, returning my attention to Kelsey, all the pieces fell into place.

Maybe this was how their family reacted to happy news no matter who it came from. But the small smile on Kelsey's lips, coupled with her glistening eyes, told me it wasn't. It was a conclusion that deepened along with the lines on her brow when her mother exclaimed, "It's about time we get another baby in the family!"

I moved my hand from my lap to Kelsey's, keeping my eye on her as I laced our fingers together. She stilled for a moment, yet she didn't reject my advances. And when her sister announced, "See, Kelsey? Now you don't need to get knocked up. Mom's happy," she squeezed my hand as though Marlena's words were a physical dagger lodged deep in her chest.

There had to be a way out. Some reason that would excuse us from the table, if not from dinner completely. It was a shitty thing to do, with Jason being my best friend and Tatum being Kelsey's. But at the end of the day, it wasn't any shittier than what her family had unknowingly done to her since the news broke. As I ran through a list of possible excuses, none felt right. In fact, almost all were rather absurd.

There was only one idea that hadn't been immediately rejected—though it should've been—and I had to go for it before it was too late. I reached over Kelsey to grab her glass of water. My right hand still rested in her lap, which meant I had to use my left, causing me to reach farther for it. Somehow, through all this, Kelsey didn't once notice that I had leaned into her, or that I had my arm stretched out in front of her. Nope. She kept her fake smile and pained eyes on the people around her. And once I had her water halfway to me, the condensation on the glass caused it to slip from my grasp.

All over Kelsey.

Technically, that hadn't been the plan. But it seemed to work anyway.

She yelped and jumped back, shoving her chair away as she stood. In some twisted, sick example of the universe's humor, a waiter just so happened to be behind her at the exact moment her chair slid back. Had he not been holding a tray of food, it wouldn't have been so bad. But unfortunately, that wasn't the case. And no matter how hard he tried, he couldn't keep the plates from crashing to the ground.

At some point, I'd gotten to my feet. I didn't recall this happening, though. And when I took a peek around the table, I noticed everyone else had stood, too. All eyes were on Kelsey—and the fumbling waiter behind her. It also didn't help that nearly the entire restaurant staff had come out to see what was going on.

It was a real circus.

Or shit show. Whichever you preferred.

"Oh my God, Kelsey . . . I'm so sorry." I dabbed her chest with my napkin, trying to dry the wet fabric that clung to her skin.

She pushed my hand away and scanned the circle around us, stopping on every one of her family members and friends, who stood gawking at her. Then she lifted her chin to meet my eyes. "What the hell?"

"I'm sorry. I didn't mean . . ." I shook my head and tossed the napkin to the table. "I think I have a T-shirt or something in the truck. At the very least, I know my coat's in there."

"Really, Aaron? I'm in a dress. Your shirt won't do jack for me, and wearing your lab coat over this will make me look more stupid than I already do." It was amazing how she could lecture me with such sternness without once raising her voice. Anyone watching us right now would think we were in the middle of a very calm and rational conversation.

"Then let's go."

She glanced around the table again, but this time, when her eyes met mine, gratitude outshone the terror from earlier. "Tatum and Jason just shared really big news," she said, louder than last time. "I don't wanna miss the celebration."

"Don't worry about us, Kels." Tatum met her friend with sincerity. "We know you're happy for us, and we know you wouldn't leave if you hadn't taken a bath at the table. Honestly, you won't hurt our feelings."

Diane, Kelsey's mom, came around the table and paused behind her, whispering something over her shoulder that no one else could hear. Defeat swarmed her until her posture weakened. It was such a visible reaction to whatever her mother had said, and I couldn't believe that no one else could see that.

Regardless, Kelsey nodded at her mother and then turned to me. "I'll be right back."

With Kelsey and Diane gone, the commotion behind us nearly taken care of, we all resumed our seats. Most of the conversations had picked up where they'd left off—except for one. Rather than converse with her friends or husband, Tatum stared at me from across the table. Questions creased her brow and extended the laughter lines next to her eyes, even though she didn't appear to be anywhere close to laughing. The only thing I could do was shrug and hope she'd understand later when I had a private moment to explain.

I knew more *about* Tatum than I could say I knew *her*. I'd listened to Jason talk about her for months, but I had only met her a couple of times. Even then, it was obvious they had something special—just the look in his eyes when he'd say her name. It was something I'd yearned for. And once they had officially started dating, and I got to be around her more, I could see exactly why Jason loved her. It was hard not to. So even though I hadn't spent years with her or been through anything major with her, I believed, deep down in my soul, that she would under-stand the situation once I explained.

Not to mention, Kelsey had already known about the pregnancy before tonight, and I'd bet they'd had their own private celebration away from everyone else. Really, there was no need for Kelsey to have even come tonight other than to complete the circle.

Fred was to my left, leaning over Diane's empty chair to engage in conversation with Lori and Jason. Tatum had gone back to her friends, nodding and speaking with a genuine smile stretched across her lips, cheeks glowing with the excitement of her news. And I was the lone ranger. It was hard not to sit here and create a list of all the things these people had that I wanted—longed for. I craved a big family. My parents were amazing people, but aside from my mom and dad, I didn't have anyone. No siblings, no cousins, no aunts or uncles. I'd only had one set of grandparents my entire life, and they had long since passed.

Kelsey was incredibly lucky, and she probably didn't even know it.

Just then, in the middle of my mental comparison—and jealousy—Kelsey and her mother returned to the table. She didn't take her seat, though. Instead, she stood behind me while Diane resumed her place between Fred and Lori.

"What's going on?" Marlena took the question right out of my mouth. Granted, had I been the one to ask, no one else at the table would've heard. Yet Marlena hadn't bothered to lower her voice. The heat in Kelsey's cheeks was so tangible, the entire room grew warm.

Not letting Kelsey respond to her sister, I pushed myself to my feet and carefully slid my chair back—after making sure no one stood behind me with a plate of food or tray of drinks. Didn't need that happening twice in one night. I took her hand, met her stare, and whispered, "You okay?"

"Yeah. I just really need to get out of this dress. It's freezing." She softly slapped my bicep when she caught my eyes dropping to her chest. In my defense, I only wanted to see just *how* cold it was. But once my gaze returned to her face, I was surprised to find a hint of a grin curling her lips and a shimmer of peace dancing in her hazel eyes. "Just take me home, will you?"

"Gladly." I nodded at everyone at the table who hadn't lost interest in our Cirque du Shame performance. Stopping at Jason, who pinned me with his questioning, narrowed gaze, I mouthed, "Call me tomorrow."

After tossing a twenty onto the empty plate to cover my drink, a tip, and a little extra for the scene we'd caused, I grabbed Kelsey's hand and led her outside. She kept her mouth shut, her thoughts to herself, which could only mean I was in for it once we got to the truck. No witnesses. That was never a good thing. Even though I was still getting to know her, I'd heard enough *about* her through Jason—and, subsequently, through Tatum—to anticipate a raised voice and two or three curse words. At the *bare* minimum. And that was if I was lucky.

I led Kelsey to the passenger-side door and held out my hand. Her arched brow and quirked lip told me she didn't know what I was after, so I said, "Keys?"

"Oh yeah . . . I forgot you ordered an alcoholic beverage tonight and gave me permission to drive." That damn smirk drove me crazy for several very different reasons. She reached into her purse and grabbed my key ring, clicking the button on the fob until the doors unlocked. "Go ahead, climb in, cowboy."

I opened the door and gestured for her to hop in. "I didn't even have a sip of my drink, so I don't need you to drive anymore."

"No, but you did pour a glass of freezing-cold water all over me. That should count for something." At least she wasn't yelling; that was a plus.

I wrapped my hand around her fist, lowered my mouth to her ear, and growled, "Give me my keys and get in the truck, Kelsey. I'll let you drive another night. Not tonight."

She huffed, though not any normal huff. It was more like an erotic exhale, full of heightened arousal and desperation. Need. Excitement littering the outskirts of the heavy sigh. It was enough to redirect the blood in my body from my brain to my . . . well, head. But before I could question it, act on it, *do* anything about it, she released my keys and climbed into the passenger seat.

After that, it took a few minutes of static filling the cab as we drove down the road before either of us spoke. And of course, any ounce of sexual frustration or desire was gone. Defeat had resumed its place in her voice when she asked, "Why were you reaching for my drink in the first place? You had your own. So why mine?"

Navigating through her question was no different than wandering through a minefield. Granted, I didn't know that for certain, considering I'd never *seen* a minefield, let alone wandered through one, but if I had to guess, this was *exactly* like it.

I gripped the steering wheel and prepared myself for the backlash. "Honestly, I had meant to pour it on myself. I reached for yours because I figured it would make more sense that I had dropped yours rather than mine, which was right in front of me. I had to stretch to get your glass, and in my mind, that made sense."

"Let's back up to the part where you said you had intended to spill the water on yourself. Why the hell would you do that?"

I shrugged. "To get us out of there?" It seemed like an obvious answer to me.

"But why would you want to leave? They had *literally* just announced they are having a baby. That's big news. *Exciting* news. Why wouldn't you want to stay and celebrate with your best—*oh*." Sitting sideways in her seat, she stared at me with wide eyes, hand clapped over her mouth. "Are you in love with Tatum? Was hearing their news too much for you? Are you like . . . jealous or something?"

The traffic light turned yellow, and I slammed on the brakes—unnecessary and maybe a little premature, but totally worth the yelp it caused. Once I came to a complete stop, I leaned into the center console with my elbow to bring our faces a little bit closer. "It had nothing to do with Tatum and everything to do with you."

"Huh? You were going to spill a glass of ice-cold water on your lap because of me? Why? What'd I do?" She seriously didn't get it.

"I needed an excuse to get you out of there."

Wrong choice of words, because it caused her to pull away, a scowl lining her nude-colored lips. "I'm sorry, but . . . say that again?"

"I saw how uncomfortable you were about your parents' response and what your sister said. Lie to me about it, say it didn't bother you, tell me I misread the entire situation. But I know what I saw. And whether you admit it or not, you were bothered by it. Be it upset, hurt, betrayed, mad . . . you had a strong reaction to it all, and no matter how happy you are for your friend and cousin, it didn't do a damn thing to mask your emotions."

Her confusion waned, her expression softening. Understanding flashed in her wide eyes as if someone had lit a match behind the hazel orbs that stared back at me. Unfortunately, it didn't last long. As soon as the light changed to green, she glanced away, shifted in her seat to face the window, and visibly shut down. It was like a switch.

"If you're so opposed to getting married and having a family, why did that bother you so much?" I doubted she would answer me, but it was worth a shot anyway.

"It doesn't matter how I feel about marriage or having a family. Whether I want one or not, whether I'll have one or not . . . it doesn't mean I want to feel replaced. I can't help but think that if I *did* have a baby, it wouldn't be special—it'd just be another kid in the family. Mom doesn't care who gives birth, just as long as she has someone to spoil, and in my mind, that lessens the value my own child will have. *If* I ever have one, I mean."

I could've been wrong, but to me, it seemed like deep down she truly did want the fairy tale. She wasn't as opposed to it as she tried to make it seem, and because of that, I wondered what had happened to her that made her this way. Recalling what she'd said outside Boots that night about her ex, I had a strong feeling her aversion to love stemmed from that relationship.

"What happened with your ex?" In my peripheral vision, I caught her turning her head to look at me, her body still angled toward the door. "You mentioned it before, when you were explaining the need to pretend. You said he made you feel worthless and ruined the idea of a happily ever after for you."

Her posture softened, and she leaned into the seat with her attention set on the road ahead of us, as if pretending to be somewhere else while she opened up to me. "We met at a concert. He was a cop, and he was supposed to be working the event—crowd control or something. We hit it off right away, and for the next two years, we were inseparable. He practically lived with me, and he came to most of the functions at my parents' house. Everyone loved him." She leaned her head back, closed her eyes, and whispered, "He was supposed to be my forever."

"What changed?"

"I can't really say that anything *changed* per se. I just found some things out that had always been there; I just wasn't aware of them. Such as the fact that he was married the whole time we were together."

Luckily, I had just pulled into a space in front of the apartment complex and put the truck in park. Had I still been on the road, there was a good chance I would've slammed on the brakes in both shock and anger that assholes like him got women like Kelsey. Without worrying about shutting off the engine, removing my seat belt, or even getting out of the truck, I shifted in my seat to completely face her and then held her attention with a gentle grip on her chin. "He's a fucking dick, and he never deserved you. No man worthy of breaking your heart ever would, and those who do were undeserving of your time from the start."

"I appreciate that, Aaron. I really do. But it doesn't matter anymore. That was a while ago, and I'm totally over it." She pushed my arm away and reached for the door handle. "Well, I'm over it for the most part. Just as long as it isn't thrown in my face."

"Then what was the issue with tonight? Unless I missed something, no one mentioned him. He wasn't brought up, yet you still felt something. I wouldn't call that being over it to *any* degree." Arguing hadn't been my intention, but I couldn't stop it now.

"Tonight wasn't about him. You're the one who brought him up."

"Explain this to me, Kelsey. Please, because I'm trying to understand."

She shoved open the door and hopped down. "You don't need to understand anything." And with that, she slammed it closed and headed for the stairs.

It took me a moment to absorb what had just happened; my mind was all over the place. But once I realized she had made it up the stairs and had disappeared down the hall, I yanked the key from the ignition, tore off my seat belt, and jumped out of the truck. Taking two steps at a time helped me catch up quicker, and by the time I'd made it to the front door, she hadn't gotten past the couch. Which meant she hadn't reached her room yet.

I still had a chance to salvage this.

"Wait. Don't just run off like that. I'm trying to talk to you."

Kelsey swung around like I'd cracked a whip behind her. "Yeah, well, maybe I don't wanna talk to you. Maybe I don't care to dredge up my past or go into details of why I was upset tonight. I appreciate your efforts to get me out of there, even if I was the one who ended up soaking wet and embarrassed. But that doesn't mean I owe you any explanations."

Slowly, I crossed the space between us until I stood within breathing distance of her, surprised she hadn't backed away as I grew closer. I reached out and captured her hands between us while I held her panicked stare. Every part of me prayed she could see the truth in my eyes and use it to calm down.

"You don't have to tell me anything if you don't want to. I get that it's personal and likely painful to think about it or talk about it. But the discomfort in your eyes tonight was real. It was raw. And if you don't find a way to deal with it, it will only get worse until it's unmanageable. It'll only get bigger until it swallows you whole."

"What could you possibly know about how I feel or what will happen if I don't share my darkest secrets with you?"

"I know what it's like to exist in two different worlds depending on where I am or who I'm around. I understand the weight of a mask and how heavy it can be at times. How difficult it can be to keep it in place so no one sees the *real* you."

She balked and tried to take a step back, but my hold on her prevented it. However, she didn't fight it; she didn't let go of my hands. She just stood there and stared at me, hopelessness swimming in her eyes. "You don't know anything about the *real* me."

There was so much I could say, so many things I could bring up to prove her wrong. We'd shared an entire night together under the guise that we were strangers, that we knew nothing about the other. Not even names. And when I'd had her in my arms, beneath me, surrounding me in all aspects of the word, she was bare. Every inch of her was naked— including her face. Her mask was nowhere to be found.

I'd spent the night with the *real* her, whether she wanted to admit it or not.

"Come with me," I whispered, leading her by the hand to her room.

"What are you—" Her question vanished the second I had her pressed against her closed bedroom door . . . from the inside.

It was dark—no lights were on—and aside from our heavy breathing, no sound filled the space, either. I waited a few seconds until the strain in her posture receded enough to relax her body in my arms. "It's just us. No one else. No masks, no pretenses, no exes or assumptions. Be *real* with me, Kelsey. What upset you so badly tonight?"

She sniffled, and when I reached for her face, there was no mistaking the tracks of wetness on her cheeks. Her tears filled her words when she finally spoke, blowing me away with what she had to say. "My mom won't love my baby as much as she loves theirs."

Chapter 13

Kelsey

Aaron had me caged against the door, his arms on either side of me. His chest to my front. His face so close to mine that I could feel his every exhale. This man was an enigma, and I found myself desperately wanting to figure him out.

One minute, he'd be my best friend while we lounged on the couch with a tub of ice cream between us. The next, he'd come swooping in to save the day like my very own personal superhero. Two seconds later he could piss me off like a brother would—or like Jason always had. And in the blink of an eye, his entire demeanor would soften, as if he were a teddy bear I could use for comfort. But the most surprising of all was how a minute later he could have such confidence, such dominance, such control with no more than a look or a touch or a single sentence. When he flipped that switch, every part of me wanted him.

"My mom won't love my baby as much as she loves theirs." Normally, I'd feel foolish for even uttering such shit. Hell, under any other circumstance, I would've realized what I had said and immediately attempted to retract it before he could pick up on any ounce of truth to my words. But not this time. Not while he kept me safe in the cage he'd offered with his body in the dark room. And certainly not while he ran his fingers along my face, drying my tears.

He didn't speak, just dropped his forehead to mine and trailed his touch from my cheeks to my stomach, making sure to pay special attention to all the important parts along the way. And then, with his palm flat against my abdomen, he held me by the back of my neck, pulled me closer, and covered my lips with his. It was dark, not an ounce of the faint moonlight from the window reaching us. But even still, he knew exactly where my mouth was. He didn't miss the mark. And after the most intense kiss I'd ever experienced—which didn't last nearly as long as I would've liked—he pulled away just enough to speak.

"Everyone will fall in love with your baby," he whispered while rubbing his thumb back and forth along my lower stomach.

I froze, silently freaking out. Every muscle in my body became rigid, and no matter how hard I tried, I couldn't find the strength to speak. There was no way he knew. *No* way. But I couldn't come up with any other explanation as to why he would've said that. Why he would've continued to touch me the way he was.

"Pretend with me," he begged, his voice even softer than a moment ago. While his body held on to the dominance from before, he sounded more like the teddy bear side of him. And what was worse, there seemed to be aspects of all his personalities with me tonight—the best friend wanting me to play along, the hero wanting to save me.

Thankfully, the only one missing was the one that resembled an older brother.

I didn't need to ask, but I did anyway. "Pretend what?"

"*This* . . ." he whispered, holding my stomach as if I were round with child. "Pretend it's real, that everyone was excited for you tonight at dinner. Excited for *your* news."

There was a good chance this might prove to be the worst idea ever—worse than the first time around—but I couldn't stop myself from giving in. "*Our* news, Aaron. Everyone was excited to find out that *we* are having a baby."

In an instant, my feet were off the floor, and I was in his arms, traveling through the dark room. And when my back met the mattress, he wasted no time fitting between my legs while owning my mouth.

Never in a million years would I have thought a man would get aroused over this.

But oh boy, was he turned on. And that passion hit me in the right spot with every roll of his hips. Each thrust. It brought me higher and higher, never wanting this moment to end. And as though I was testing him, I muttered, "I was worried you wouldn't want the baby."

Aaron stilled—*not* the reaction I wanted. But then he changed the game. Flipped the script. Revised the plan. "Why wouldn't I want a little girl with red hair like yours? Or a little boy with your sass and determination? Shit, Kelsey . . . I'd take as many as you'd give me."

Fuck all the things. *All the damn things.*

"A little girl with my red hair and your green eyes." The faintest glow of night that drifted through my bedroom window called my attention to the smile on his face. "Or a little boy with my sass and your smarts."

"Yes, please," he whispered across my lips before sealing his words with a kiss.

My dress came off easily, and at first, I was terrified he'd see my stomach and realize this wasn't an act. I prayed it was too dark to see anything, and if he touched me, he wouldn't notice the softness that had settled along my waistline over the last two weeks. I didn't have the typical bump yet, which was the only reason I hadn't stopped this—the idea of him noticing anything was nothing but paranoia.

Which was proven when he made his way down my chest to settle between my legs, lips hovering over my belly button. "God, you'll look fucking amazing with a round stomach." He circled my navel with his tongue, uttering sexy yet scary things against my skin. "If I had my way, you'd never wear clothes at home. You'd watch TV, make coffee, fold laundry, and brush your teeth completely fucking naked so I could see every inch of your body—knowing you were giving me the greatest gift."

I pushed up on my elbows to see him better, and when he glanced up, his eyes twinkling in the haze of night creeping past the blinds behind me, I couldn't stop myself from tracing the lines on his face with my fingertip. "Either you're an amazing actor, or you're a special breed."

There was also the possibility that he was certifiably insane. Pretending to be married to someone and going along with the act that you're expecting a child together is odd enough. But as a sexual kink? Something wasn't right about that. Then again, I couldn't say much since I was in the role right there with him.

Soft laughter filled his words when he asked, "A special breed?"

"Yeah. What guy gets excited about finding out he's having a baby with someone he's not even with?" I no longer knew what was make-believe and what was real, and a very large part of me didn't care.

Aaron was quiet for a moment, and then he climbed on top of me again, pushing me onto my back once more. As he hovered over me, he gently grazed my face the way an artist painted the lines and angles of a model. "Don't think about it, Kelsey. Don't ask questions; don't pick this apart looking for explanations. Just go with it like you did last time."

"Last time I was drunk."

He stilled, as though he was unsure how to proceed. "Do you want to stop? We don't have to do this if you don't want to. I was just trying to give—"

I grabbed his face and brought his mouth to mine, silencing him. It didn't matter how fucked up this was, or how either of us would feel in the morning. I needed it. I needed him. And I wasn't about to let him put a stop to it now.

It didn't take long for his pants to land on the floor, or for his shirt to fly across the room.

It took even less time for me to forget this wasn't real—well, except for the baby.

♥ ♥ ♥

I awoke the next morning with Aaron on my mind. Well, not *just* Aaron, but *all* the things he had done to me last night. I just lay there with my eyes closed, recalling every touch, every word, every *thing* he'd made me feel.

Of course, the pessimistic side of my brain told me he hadn't meant any of it. It had been a fantasy played out—pretend. Make-believe. It'd been nothing more than a role he'd acted out, a way to calm me down and get in my pants.

But the other side, the one filled with ridiculous dreams and outlandish hopes—thanks to the bun in my oven throwing my hormones all out of whack—refused to believe that last night wasn't real. It refused to believe that the way he'd looked at me had all been an act. Or that the words he'd whispered had lacked all sincerity.

That was . . . until I rolled over and found the other side of the bed empty.

There was a chance he'd gone back to his room after I had fallen asleep last night. Maybe he'd worried about whether I wanted to wake up next to him, so he decided to take the safe route and sleep in his own bed. There were a hundred possible reasons why he wasn't next to me. He very well might've stayed all night and gotten up early for work. The only way to know for sure was to talk to him.

And *this* was the biggest reason I had wanted to stay anonymous with him the last time. It would be stupid to carry on as if last night hadn't happened. No matter how hard a person tried, no one would be capable of forgetting the things we'd said to each other. In a way, I had confessed everything to him. I'd told him I was pregnant and he was the father. Now . . . if only I could figure out how much of his reaction had been an act, and how much had been genuine.

After getting my feelings and worries out on paper—which had become my therapy these days—I got ready for work. Today was an office day, so I didn't have to be there until ten. Granted, I was the boss, so I could've shown up whenever I wanted, or not at all. But since I expected everyone else to arrive by ten, I felt obligated to do so as well.

Only two rings filtered through the speakers in my car before Tatum's voice filled the empty space around me. Except rather than starting off our morning conversation with idle chitchat, I blurted, "I'm going to tell him today about the baby." I'd spoken so fast all my words ran together. It was as though I'd held on to a secret for too long and couldn't hold it in any longer.

"Wait. What? Tell who?"

"The . . . uh, stripper. My baby's daddy. Sperm donor. Whatever you want to call him."

"You found him? How?" It wasn't until right then that I realized just how little I'd filled her in on regarding this baby. Normally, I would've felt like a shitty person keeping such important details from my best friend, but that wasn't the case this time. I would've felt worse having to lie to her longer than I already had to.

"As ironic as it is . . . I ran into him."

After a few moments of silence, two beeps resounded through the car's speakers, signaling the line had disconnected. I had just turned onto the bridge that took me from Samson to Langston, where my office was, so I assumed I had dropped the call. But before I could try her again, my phone rang.

But this time, it was a FaceTime call.

"I'm driving, Tatum. I don't really think this is very safe." I held the device against the steering wheel so I could focus on the road without her having to look up my nostrils from my lap. It was the best I could do.

"Sorry, but you're going to have to start over, and I need to see your face when you do. It's the only way I can tell if you're messing with me or not. Your voice doesn't give much away. So tell me again . . . how'd you find him?"

"Are you alone? Or is Jason home?"

"It's Tuesday. He's at work."

"Good. Just checking. I wouldn't put it past you to trick me into spilling the beans."

Tatum sighed, which diverted my attention to the screen. Her sad eyes were distracting. "How much longer are you gonna wait before you tell your family? You don't have to keep it a secret, nor do you have to do this alone. Your family—especially your *mother*—will be happy no matter how it happened."

"I'm just not there yet. Not to mention, you *literally* just told them last night."

"So? I had a reason to keep it under wraps. I didn't need any negativity surrounding my wedding, and whether anyone means to or not, questioning our decision to get married so quickly is hurtful. And it's even worse when it's behind our backs."

"And you don't think it's any less hurtful for them to talk about *me* behind my back?" Thank God for traffic lights. I came to a stop, able to give my full attention to Tatum.

"Waiting until you're too big to hide it anymore won't change the fact that you had a one-night stand with a stripper whose name you didn't even know. You're nine weeks, Kels. Too much longer, and they'll figure it out for themselves. I realize I don't know your mom as well as you do, but I'm willing to bet she'll be more hurt if she finds out any other way than from you."

"You waited until you were twelve weeks, so can you allow me that same time span?"

The light changed to green, and as I slowly crept forward, easing into an even acceleration behind other vehicles, I regarded her through the phone's camera, awaiting her response. Finally, she nodded and added, "Take as long as you want. I'm just being selfish, wanting the family to know there'll be *two* babies."

"I get it. And I want that, too. But honestly, if I say anything in the next couple of weeks, it'll look like I'm trying to rain on your parade. I'd rather let them smother you with excitement before adding more to their plates. Lord knows my family doesn't need overstimulation."

She laughed, which drew a smile to my own lips. "Okay, so get on with it. How'd you find the stripper?"

"I told you—I ran into him." Knowing her next question would be *where* I'd run into him, I decided to beat her to the punch. At least this way it kept me from having to make something up. "I was on my phone, and when I looked up, there he was. We've seen each other a lot over the last several weeks, and I slept with him again."

"You did *what*?"

Telling her I'd jumped into bed with the stripper who had fathered my child was my get-out-of-jail-free card. And I knew it, too. It was enough to keep her from questioning me about things I wasn't ready to answer, and at the same time, it kept me from having to lie.

"You hooked up with him again? Why? And why haven't you told him about the baby yet?"

"It's complicated. I honestly did try several times to tell him, but each time I opened my mouth to spit it out, I got interrupted by him or someone else. If it wasn't that, there was some reason that kept me from saying anything, until I finally gave up. After that, I felt like it'd be best to wait and see how things went. The last thing I want to do is scare him off with news like that, and I kinda wanna get to know him a little better. He's really not that bad of a guy. And he's not at all dumb like I thought."

"So then why tell him today?"

I took a second to formulate the perfect way to explain this. "We talked last night, and the topic of babies came up. He wasn't at all freaked out by the idea of having a kid with me. I think that was what I needed, maybe what I was waiting for all along. A sign to let me know it would be all right. That he wouldn't run off and ruin everything."

"Well, that's good. Although, I'm not sure how you got into that kind of conversation. Then again . . . this is *you* we're talking about. I don't understand half the things you do—such as sleeping with a stripper to begin with."

My office wasn't too far ahead, so I kept my eyes on the road, refraining from looking at Tatum as I responded. "It started by me expressing how upset I was over my mom's reaction to your news."

"Why were you upset? Is that why you left?"

Pulling into the parking lot, I sighed and took my time answering her. "It's stupid, Tatum. I realize these damn hormones make me crazy. But when I saw her get all excited, I thought to myself . . . she won't act that way for me when I tell her. I know she says she wouldn't care *how* I got pregnant, but I'm not stupid. She would, whether she wants to admit it or not. And then there's my dad. He looked all happy last night. When I tell them about me, I'll have to see the disappointment in his eyes—not the joy you saw. And let's not forget Marlena's comment about how I don't have to worry about giving Mom a baby because she can fuss over yours. As if kids are replaceable and hold no value."

"Wow, I didn't even hear her say that. I'm sorry, Kels. But honestly, I don't think you'll have anything to worry about. You don't have to tell them who the father is if you don't want to, or even how you got pregnant to begin with. No one needs to know it was a one-night stand. Hell, if you can keep them from finding out . . . you don't even need to tell them he's a stripper."

"Don't worry about that one, Tater. They will never find out that part."

"So you're telling him today? When?"

My chest tightened, and my ears began to ring. Clearly, I was nervous, no matter how many pep talks I'd had with myself since waking up this morning. I just had to bite the bullet and get it over with, knowing and trusting it would all work out in the end.

"After work. I shouldn't have too much to do today, so when I leave here, I'll go see him. I figured it'll probably be best if I give him some time to digest it before . . ." I cleared my throat, correcting myself before I gave too much away. "Before I see him tonight. *If* I see him tonight, that is."

"Oh, do you have plans with him later?"

I pulled my lips to one side and glanced out the window, wondering how I could word this for her without saying too much or being too vague. "We don't necessarily have *plans*, but in the event he comes over to watch a movie or something, I just want to be prepared. You know?"

"Yeah, that makes sense. Well, good luck! You'll have to let me know how it goes. I'll be anxiously awaiting a phone call this afternoon. And if you need a pep talk beforehand, you know how to find me."

"Thanks, Tater. You're the best."

A giant smile stretched across her face. "I do what I can."

I disconnected the call, took a moment to pull myself together, and then went to work.

Surprisingly, it ended up being a busier day than I'd expected. Normally, Tuesdays were planning days. We had the schedule of upcoming open houses, as well as a list of future projects that would require more time and effort. It was basically the day we went through the inventory catalog and paired furniture with certain projects so we knew exactly what we'd need and have it ready ahead of time. But today, on top of my typical agenda, I also had a crisis with a builder to diffuse. And by the time I finished rearranging my entire calendar, it was almost five.

There went my early day . . . up in flames.

One of the reasons I'd decided to talk to Aaron today about the baby was because I figured I'd be done with work around four, which would have left me with time to stop by his office on the way home. I didn't want to tell him about it at the apartment, where neither of us really had anywhere to go in the event it didn't pan out the way I hoped. This way, he'd have time to wrap his mind around being a father before leaving work, giving us a better chance at discussing everything without the initial shock I was sure he'd feel.

Luckily, as I passed his office, I noticed his truck in the parking lot. There was only one other car, so I assumed that meant either he was with his last patient or the only people left inside were him and his receptionist. I was willing to take my chances.

My heart thundered inside my chest as I parked my car.

While walking toward the building, my throat nearly closed up.

And when I opened the door, the world began to tilt.

I stood inside the vacant waiting room, the cold air blasting my face, and took a moment to get a grip. There was no way I'd be able to tell him anything if I were on the verge of passing out or throwing up. And after a solid minute of nothing but standing alone with my eyes closed, taking deep breaths, and giving myself a pep talk, I was ready.

Or at least I *thought* I was.

No one sat at the front desk, which meant there was a good chance he still had a patient in the back. After peeking down the hallway, I noticed his door cracked open and voices coming from inside—a man and a woman. So I calmly made my way toward his office, unable to hear much of what was said as I approached due to the blood rushing in my ears. But once I stood on the other side of the door, hand in the air to grab the knob, I froze.

"Shit, Noel . . . I don't know how much longer I'll last," filtered through the crack, the words wrapped in a deep, desperate voice. It was followed up by a woman moaning, "That's okay, baby." Panting filled the quiet spaces in between, as well as the distinct sound of one person frantically slamming into another. But what made me abandon my mission was when he said, "Fuck, I love you so much."

I couldn't take any more. It was too much to handle. So I ran.

I ran, and I didn't look back.

I couldn't do this again.

Never ever again.

Chapter 14

Aaron

When it rained . . . it poured.

All day, I'd looked forward to getting done with work so I could see Kelsey. Last night had been intense, and I worried how she'd react today. I hadn't stuck around last time to see how she was the next morning. There was no way to know if she had freaked out, if she'd thought about it, or if she had gone about her life as if nothing at all had happened the night before. So I had nothing to go on this time. The one thing I did know, though, was that I didn't want her thinking I'd been gone all day to avoid her.

Because that wasn't the case.

I'd been called to the hospital to evaluate a patient. It wasn't unusual to have a doctor ask me to come in and give my opinion; I just wished they had picked another time to ask me. Then again, I doubted the woman had planned to be involved in a car accident today, so there was that. It was just frustrating because the last thing I wanted this evening was to get home late.

It had been one thing after another—my truck wouldn't crank, so I'd had to take Noel's car to the hospital, leaving her to call her husband to pick her up. After the consultation, I'd dropped off my old battery, bought a new one, and then swapped Noel's car for my truck at the office. Now, it was almost eight, and I was finally climbing the steps to the apartment.

I found Kelsey on the couch, curled against the armrest with a blanket, the TV glowing in front of her. She barely made eye contact before returning her attention to the screen, not saying anything to me. That wasn't a good sign. So I decided to ease my way into this, feel her out, evaluate the entire situation before coming to any conclusions.

"Oh, I love this movie." I didn't. In fact, it had to have been the worst film ever created, but if I had to pretend it was amazing just to be in the same room as her, then I'd make this movie sound like it was worthy of an Oscar. "Let me get the ice cream."

"It's all gone."

I stilled behind the couch, where she couldn't see me—as if she would've seen me had I been in front of her, considering she refused to take her eyes off the TV for two seconds. "You ate it all?" I asked with a laugh, trying to act like nothing was *off* with us, even though it would have been obvious to a stranger that something wasn't right. "Want me to go to the gas station and see what they have? I can be back in, like, five minutes. Or I can run up to the store, but that might take me longer. You're about to get to the good part."

"I don't care, Aaron. Do what you want." There was something in her voice that I couldn't ignore. It called to me, drawing me closer until I was on the couch next to her, and once I was close enough, it was impossible to miss the glassy appearance of her eyes, even without her looking at me.

I pinched her chin between my fingers and eased her neck to the side, forcing her to face me. "What happened? Are you okay?"

My throat closed up at the possibility I had caused this. Whether it was what we'd done last night or my absence all day, I was to blame. But what worried me the most was how closed off she seemed. If I couldn't get her to open up to me, I wouldn't be able to make it right.

"Do you remember me telling you about my ex? The cop who was married?"

My face flamed with heat, anger burning within me at the mere thought of that douche. "Yeah. What about him? Did you run into him again today? What'd he do?"

She shook her head slowly and dropped her gaze to her lap. "Nothing. And no, I didn't see him."

"Then what's wrong?"

"So I told you that we were together for two years. That's two Christmases, two sets of birthdays—his and mine. Two Valentine's Days, two Thanksgivings, two of everything. There wasn't a holiday in those two years that I didn't see him. There were many nights he stayed with me. Weekends he didn't leave other than to go to work, but he'd come back to my place and fall asleep with me in his arms." She paused to take a deep breath, the raw emotions from dredging this up pooling in her eyes.

I grabbed her hand to offer her support or comfort . . . yet she yanked it away.

When she continued with her story, she made sure to meet my gaze, contempt shooting daggers at me while she spoke. "We had talked about marriage, about kids. We even discussed a destination wedding, possibly going to the Caribbean or Hawaii. He'd told me he wanted three kids, and I told him I only wanted one . . . even though I would've had as many as he wanted."

My heart ached with every word that fell from her lips, but I didn't do or say anything. I simply let her get it out, let her lay it all on the table so I could figure out what she needed from me. As of right now, she clearly wasn't interested in anything I could offer.

"So imagine my surprise when I learned that he was married—*had* been married the entire time we were together. I felt like an utter fool.

But the worst part was that I didn't leave him when I found out. I confronted him, we fought about it, and in the end, had he told me that he would leave her, I would've stayed." Kelsey wiped an errant tear from her cheek. "He made me weak. He made me stupid. And because of him, I swore I'd never allow myself to be that vulnerable with someone else ever again."

"That doesn't make you weak or stupid. People do all kinds of things for love—or should I say the *interpretation* of such, since it's nothing more than endorphins and emotions that create the concept of love. I'm sure most people would've been willing to stick around in that same situation, Kelsey."

She glared at me, making me retrace every word I'd spoken in case I had said something offensive without realizing it. "I was the other woman, and even if *she* had been the other woman, it wouldn't have changed anything. I was willing to stay with a cheater, someone who had no problem lying to my face. That's *weak*, Aaron."

I wasn't sure what to say to that, because it seemed she wasn't happy with anything I could come up with to justify her actions. So instead, I chose to sit there and listen until she was absolutely done talking.

"After I confronted him about it, he told me that he wasn't happy with her. That she never wanted kids and he did. I heard about what a bitch she was to him all the time, and how nothing he ever did was good enough. I felt bad for him. I *wanted* him to leave her—not necessarily for me, but because he was a good person who deserved better than that."

"I take it he didn't leave her?"

She shook her head yet chose to answer anyway. "He stayed because she had money. He was a cop, so it wasn't like he was bringing home the bacon. She came from old money, and I guess he wasn't willing to give up the bank account, no matter how miserable he was with her. It wasn't until later that I started finding out more of the truth than he'd let on. She wasn't a bitch. Oh, and they didn't have kids because he had gotten snipped before they got married. From what I've heard, she actually wanted a baby and had even contemplated adoption. *He's* the one who said no."

"So everything he told you was a lie?"

"Pretty much. He had two different Facebook accounts, both with super high privacy settings to keep either of us from finding out about the other. The one I knew of had tons of pictures of us together. And apparently, the one she knew of was filled with photos and posts of her. It was like he knew *exactly* what he was doing, playing us both, using his job as a way to keep us from finding out where he was sleeping at night. I wanted to tell her, and I almost did, but he reminded me of what that would look like to everyone. No one would believe for one second that I didn't know about her. I'd be dismissed as the woman he didn't choose, the one he didn't leave his wife for. And because of that, it'd look like the only reason I told her was to get back at him."

The more she explained about this asshole, the worse I hated him. And I hadn't thought I could hate him more after finding out he'd been married while seeing Kelsey. Apparently, I was wrong . . . because I'd found a new level of loathing.

"I'm not sure where this is all coming from, Kelsey."

She sighed and stood from the couch. "I just wanted to let you know that no matter what has happened between us, my mind hasn't changed. I still have no desire to get married. I don't wanna play house and raise babies with anyone."

"Is this about last night?" I stood and followed her, stopping a couple of feet behind her when she reached her bedroom door. "If it is, tell me so we can talk about it, please. Don't just make assumptions and verbally slam a door in my face without giving me a chance to discuss it first."

"Yes, it's about last night. And the very first night. But I don't want to talk about it, because we're pretending it never happened. Right? Isn't that what you said? Act as if we've never slept together? Well, that's what

I'm doing, Aaron. And I suggest you do the same." She didn't waste a second before closing herself off in her room, leaving me alone with more questions than answers.

Maybe it was good that I hadn't seen her the day after the bachelorette party.

"You're gonna have to start over, Aaron." Noel moved around the waiting room, cleaning up after a busy day, while I sat in a chair and listened. "Last I knew, you were desperately trying to find somewhere else to live so you didn't have to move in with the—and I quote—man-hater. Now you're asking for advice on wooing her? How do you go from wanting nothing to do with her to wanting to make her like you?"

"I never said *woo*. That word would never come out of my mouth."

She perched her fists on her hips and glared at me. "What word you used or didn't use is irrelevant, asshole." Thank God for the smile on her lips and slight lilt of humor in her tone. "How long have you lived with her?"

"Almost five weeks."

"And how many times have you slept with her?"

Nothing got past her. I felt bad for her husband. "Twice . . . including the first time, which shouldn't really count because I didn't know who she was at the time. The other one happened a little over a week ago, and let's just say that didn't turn out so well."

"I told you this would happen." She didn't have to look at me to make her point. Her eye roll was implied. "But you assured me it wouldn't. You said she hated men, and she was your best friend's little cousin. But I know you, Aaron." Her stare literally pinned me to my seat, making it impossible to move.

"Can we skip the *I told you so*s? It just kind of happened. She got upset last week at dinner when Tatum told everyone she's pregnant.

Her mom and sister made her feel like shit, and when we got home, she made a comment about how her mom would love Tatum's baby more than her own."

"More than Kelsey's?"

"Yeah."

"I didn't know Kelsey was pregnant."

"She's not."

Noel plopped into a chair in front of me with narrowed eyes and a cocked head. "Then why's she upset about a baby she's not even having? I'm highly confused here, Aaron."

"It was more hypothetical. Like *if* she were to ever have a baby, it would just be a baby to everyone. No one cares who the mother is or how they're related to it. I guess her mom has been making comments about her settling down and having a family, and now that Tatum's fulfilling that role, she doesn't care what Kelsey does. That's her interpretation of it, at least."

"So how did *that* lead to sex for the second time?"

This would've been much easier to explain to Jason, considering he knew about the role-playing concept from the first time. Now that I knew Kelsey was his cousin, there was *no* way I'd go to him about this. Which left me with either filling Noel in on the bachelorette party or keeping the entire thing vague. I doubted she'd be able to help me if she didn't have the details . . . so I decided to start from the beginning.

"And that's how we wound up in bed for the second time."

She stared at me with wide, blinking eyes, a combination of disgust and mortification on her face. "There's something severely wrong with you, Aaron. I'm concerned. The first, sure. I can kind of understand how that might've happened. But this time? Who in their right mind gets off on the thought of knocking someone up?"

I shrugged, having figured this would be her reaction. It was why I hadn't wanted to go into the whole story with her, but I doubted she'd be able to offer much advice without it. And now that she'd basically condemned me in my own office, I wished I'd never told her in the first place. No one would understand, because I doubted many people were in my shoes. She certainly wasn't. "You should ask your husband. I bet the idea of you carrying his baby turns him on."

She softened a little bit. But that didn't last long. "Okay, but we're married. And we're trying to get pregnant. Of course the idea of me having his child would excite him . . . but I doubt it would make him wanna have sex with me."

"You'd be surprised. You should text him and ask."

Even though she rolled her eyes and laughed at me, she pulled her phone out of her pocket and began to tap on the screen while carrying on with her conversation with me. "Regardless, you aren't married to her. You aren't in love with her. So your theory is flawed."

"Maybe. Maybe not."

After sending her text, she met my eyes again. This time, they were soft, full of sympathy—which I hated. "You're in love with the *idea* of being in love. That's dangerous, Aaron. It can't just be anybody, but it's like you're too impatient to let things naturally happen."

I pushed out of the chair and walked around her toward my office. "Forget it."

I'd learned this lesson before, but it seemed I needed a refresher course—never tell a woman to forget it. She wouldn't. *Never mind* should also never be uttered to a female. All it did was make them *more* interested in your business. And this time, it led Noel into my office with her arms crossed and face pinched with that "don't brush me off and then walk away" expression.

"What am I missing here, Aaron? You slept with the girl twice; both times were fulfilling some sort of fantasy, whether it was hers, yours, or somewhere in between. Either way, it wasn't real, yet you seem to have missed that part."

"I haven't missed any part, Noel. I know it wasn't real, okay? I'm not confused about anything—I'm not in love with her, and she's not

166

having my baby. I'm not delusional." That could be argued by some, but that was a moot point. "I just needed advice on how to get her to talk to me. Prior to last Monday night, we were good. We joked, spent time together, watched movies on the couch while eating ice cream from the carton. But now . . . she can't stand to be in the same room as me."

"So this has been going on for a week?"

"Yes. The only time she talks to me is when she finds new houses for me to look at. And the conversations aren't even pleasant. I feel like she's telling me I need to find something soon and get out of her apartment."

Noel's brows dipped. "She wasn't ever pushy before?"

"No," I said, shaking my head. "She'd let me know when she found something, but we'd always go together to look at them. Granted, there weren't many that I wanted to see, but at least she drove with me, and we'd walk through the houses together. She doesn't even do that anymore. Now, it's just, 'Here, let me know if you need the Realtor's info for any of these,' and then she's gone, locked in her room where she's spent the last week."

"And this all happened after the night you had sex?"

"Yes. I came home that next day from work—which was the day I had to go to the hospital and my truck broke down, and then I had to get a battery on my way home and swap your car for mine after getting mine to crank. It was, like, eight o'clock before I got home, so I don't know if she thinks I was avoiding her or what. I don't have a clue what to do or how to fix it. Which is why I came to you . . . not to get a lecture about how fucked up I am."

She lowered herself into the chair across from my desk and gestured for me to do the same. And once I sat next to her, she relaxed in her seat, her expression soft and comforting. "Start from the beginning, Aaron. Tell me everything."

"I'm not sure, could be wrong, but I believe the sauce is supposed to go in the pasta. Not on the floor." I glanced down at Noel, who was currently on her hands and knees in my kitchen, cleaning alfredo sauce off the tile while I worked at getting the splatter off my work pants.

After telling Noel everything yesterday, she'd offered to help me cook Kelsey dinner tonight. We'd rushed to leave the office, making sure we gave ourselves enough time to get everything done before Kelsey came home from work.

"Well, if you weren't rushing me, I wouldn't have dropped the spoon," she argued from the floor. "I never claimed to be a cook. You should've called your friend's wife. Isn't she good at this kind of crap?"

"Tatum? Yeah. She used to be a chef. Now she writes cookbooks. But I can't ask her, because she'd want to know why I'm doing this, and I can't tell her what I've done with Kelsey."

"You seriously think Kelsey hasn't already told her? Aren't *they* best friends, too?"

"Yes, but she's also married to Kelsey's cousin . . . so I can almost guarantee that she hasn't told her anything. If she has, I would've gotten a phone call from Jason by now. And he hasn't said anything to me about it."

Noel finished wiping off the tile, sat back on her haunches, and pointed to my pants. "You might want to take those off and throw them in the wash. You're only making it worse."

Glancing down, I took note of the wet spot near the zipper where I'd scrubbed the material with a damp paper towel. She was right; it looked bad. But before I could concede and change into something clean, the front door opened.

I whipped my head around to find Kelsey walking in, but Noel didn't move until the door closed. Noel popped up in my peripheral, but with my eyes on Kelsey, I didn't miss the transformation from surprised to pissed.

"You're home early." And I sounded guilty as fuck. Then again, I was—she'd specifically asked me not to bring anyone over, yet I had, even if my intentions were good. "We were, uh . . . just making dinner." Kelsey didn't say anything. She just stood near the door and nodded.

"Hi, I'm Noel. It's so nice to meet you." Noel tossed the sponge into the sink and then walked around the breakfast bar with her hand out to greet Kelsey.

"N-Noel?" Kelsey glanced from the woman in front of her to me, then back to Noel again.

"Yes, and you're Kelsey, right? Aaron's . . . *roommate?*"

She once again turned her eyes to me. "Yeah. Something like that. His parents finally kicked him out of their house, so he needed a place to stay for a couple of months. I have a tendency to take in strays. Although, I'm starting to feel like this one won't ever leave." She took Noel's hand and shook it hard. "And how do you know him?"

"Oh, I'm his receptionist." Noel giggled—a sign of her discomfort. "I'm basically his right-hand man at the office. He'd be lost without me."

"I bet he would. Maybe I should just start sending you the listings of houses I find for Aaron. Maybe you could get him to find a place relatively soon."

I prayed I wasn't about to get evicted . . . for a second time in less than two months.

Picking up on Kelsey's resentment, Noel glanced at me from over her shoulder. "I should probably get home. You've, um . . . you got it from here, right?"

"Yup. I sure do. Thanks for all your help, Noel." I walked out of the kitchen and met both women near the door, fully aware of the daggers Kelsey launched at me from her heated glare. "Let me walk you out."

"It was nice meeting you, Kelsey," Noel called out after Kelsey had walked away, heading toward her room to likely lock herself in there for the rest of the day. Once we got outside, Noel stopped me cold with wide eyes. "I think you drastically underestimated her anger, Aaron. I doubt dinner will be enough to warm her back up. She's like a block of ice in a freezer."

"Now do you see why I asked for help?"

She laughed and patted my arm. "Oh, honey . . . you need more than help."

"I don't know what else to do."

"Find a house and get out as fast as you can. Stop being picky about what you buy. Anything can be fixed up. And if it's in a bad neighborhood, just get a security alarm for the doors and bars for the windows. I'm sure that'll be safer than staying here."

"Thanks, you're a lot of help."

"Sorry, but you're on your own with this one. Without knowing what her deal is, I can't possibly begin to offer advice or suggestions on how to make it right. It seems she's pissed about something, and without knowing what it is, there's nothing you're gonna be able to do about it."

I nodded, not wanting to concede her point but knowing she was right. "Thanks anyway, Noel. I'll let you know on Monday what happens."

"If you don't show up, I'm calling the cops and sending them here." She stepped away and waved. As she headed down the hall, she called over her shoulder, "Good luck, my friend. Good luck."

I'd need more than that to get Kelsey to talk to me.

If this was how relationships were . . . I no longer wanted one.

It was far too much work, only to be left feeling like the ball in a world-championship game of Ping-Pong. I couldn't keep up. It was impossible to fix something or apologize for doing something wrong if I didn't know what the issue was.

It'd been twenty minutes since Kelsey had come home from work, and she'd spent the entire time in her room. Rather than knock or try to talk to her, I'd finished making dinner. But now that it was time to eat, I wasn't sure if I should bother her or just let her know her plate would be in the microwave when she was ready to come out.

In the end, I chose to call her out, refusing to let this go on any longer. "Kelsey," I said while rapping my knuckle against her closed door. "Dinner's ready. Come eat before it gets cold."

"I'm not hungry."

"Yeah . . . this from the girl who could eat a horse and then wash it down with a bucket of ice cream. I made you a plate; just come eat it, and then you can go back to locking me out as if I've done something wrong."

Apparently, that was all I had to say to get her to leave her room. She whipped the door open and stood before me in a long, oversize T-shirt and yoga pants that didn't reach her ankles. "*As if* you did something wrong? Are you kidding me right now, Aaron?"

I held up my hands in surrender, though I wasn't about to back down that easily. "No, I'm not. I get that you're pissed about Noel being here without your knowledge, and I'm sorry for that. I asked her for help because I wanted to make you something other than Hamburger Helper for dinner, and I don't know the first thing about cooking a real meal. I honestly didn't think about it, and for that, I'm truly sorry."

She crossed her arms over her chest and leaned into the doorframe. However, she didn't utter a word or even make a gesture that would offer any clue to what went through her mind. She gave me nothing to go on other than heated anger pouring off her rigid body and pain emanating from her sad, confused eyes.

"*But*"—I took a step forward—"this has been going on for over a week. Your resentment toward me didn't start today. It's not about me having someone at the apartment without your consent. And it'd be nice if you offered me *something* so that I knew what the hell I've done wrong."

"You're an idiot." She wasn't wrong, though I would need more specifics. Eventually, she caved and gave me what I sought—kind of. "You must think I'm stupid. That I don't know what I walked in on."

Yeah, that didn't help. Like . . . *at all*. "You walked in on us making *you* dinner. What am I missing here?"

She pointed to my pants, the same pair of khakis I'd worn earlier with the mess still decorating the crotch. "If you want your *right-hand man* to suck you off, fine. Go for it. You do you and all that. But don't you dare disrespect me by having her on her knees in my fucking kitchen."

"*Whoa.*" It took a few seconds for me to form coherent words after that accusation. "What? No. Baby, that's not what she was doing."

Kelsey balked, eyes wide and mouth dropped open. Every emotion that had coursed through her a minute ago amplified. The heated anger began to boil, and the pain intensified into a deep ache that would bring the strongest man to his knees. "Don't ever call me that again. I'm not your *baby*. I have a name, and if it's too hard to keep all your women straight, then mark me off that list. Get the hell out and don't ever talk to me again. That way, you won't have to remember what to call me."

I had no idea what I'd walked into, but now there was no way out. I had to see this through, no matter how confusing and muddled it had all become in a matter of seconds. "I'm sorry, Kelsey. I didn't mean . . ." I shook my head, realizing she didn't care about my excuses. "It won't happen again. I swear. But that's not what Noel was doing here. My God . . . she's *married*."

Her top lip curled, disgust radiating off her in waves. "That's even worse."

"No. That's what I'm trying to tell you. Nothing happened with her. *Ever*. She's like a little sister to me. She's worked for me for years. I was at her wedding. Her husband is a great guy. I would never . . ."

I eventually stopped talking when I realized she wasn't listening to a word I said.

"You could at least come up with better ways to lie. They're always *like a sister*, aren't they? Which, if you think about it, is really fucked up. I can't tell you how many times I've heard a guy refer to a woman as a sister yet sleep with her anyway."

"That's just it, Kelsey. I've never slept with her. I have *no* desire to. Where is this coming from?" I glanced down at my pants again, following her line of sight. Shit. Noel was right . . . this looked way worse than it was. "This is alfredo sauce."

"And she was on her knees . . . why?"

"She was cleaning up the mess—the *alfredo sauce*. The spoon fell and splattered all over me. She was wiping up the floor while I was trying to clean it off my pants. That's when you walked in. We weren't doing anything." I'd never thought I'd have to defend myself where Noel was concerned.

"Whether or not that's true, it doesn't mean you aren't sleeping with her. I caught you, Aaron. I went into your office last week to talk to you, and you were bending her over your desk."

That stunned me silent for far longer than an innocent man should be. Finally, I shook off the shock and attempted to make sense of this. "When? I've never had sex with her, let alone bent her over my desk for *any* reason."

"It doesn't matter when. The point is . . . you did. And then you brought her here, after I've asked that you don't have *anyone* over aside from Jason." She dropped her arms and closed her eyes for a moment. When she opened them again, a softer side shone through. "I just don't like to be disrespected, Aaron. That's all. And that's exactly how I feel right now."

"But I'm telling you . . . nothing happened."

"And my ex told me his wife was a horrible person." She shrugged, the will to fight no longer present in her posture. "I don't put much stock into what guys say anymore. You're all the same. You all must share tips on how to lie or what to say to pull on a woman's heartstrings. Unfortunately for you . . . it no longer works on me."

I didn't know what to say or do. It seemed nothing would make this right. I doubted even the truth from Noel would make Kelsey second-guess her assumptions. And that's exactly what they were—assumptions. The same thing I had to battle with every other female I'd ever encountered.

Silly me for thinking Kelsey was any different.

"I'll go through the listings you gave me this week. And if I don't find anything, then I'll figure something else out. You won't have to worry about me disrespecting you anymore." I grabbed her plate off the counter and took it two steps to the kitchen table. "I tried to make the asparagus the same way it was done at the wedding. I remember you saying you liked it." Then I took my plate, tossed it into the sink, and went to my room, disregarding the silence that came from Kelsey the entire time I was walking away from her.

I spent the rest of the evening and night looking at houses—some on her list and others I'd come across while searching online. One stood out above the rest, though. It had been at the bottom of Kelsey's email, a note attached to it pointing out how it was big enough for a family and how the front room could be a nursery or a home office.

After a few emails back and forth with the Realtor, I made an appointment to check it out the next day, as well as others he thought I might be interested in. But rather than the excitement I'd felt when walking through houses with Kelsey, I felt empty. And I couldn't begin to understand why. Maybe Noel had been right that I was in love with the idea of love.

Too bad that wouldn't keep me warm at night.

My mood had progressively deteriorated since Friday night, and come Monday morning, I walked into my office a zombie—or that character from Oz without a heart.

"I take it your weekend didn't get any better?" Noel asked from her desk. Based on the purse that still hung on her shoulder and the way she sat almost sideways in her chair, I assumed she had gotten there a minute or two before me.

Normally, I'd hang around the front for a few minutes, chatting with Noel. Especially on a Monday, when we had more to catch up on. But this time, I didn't care to hang out or fill her in on anything. Instead, I passed by her with a simple, "I bought a house."

"Wait up." She chased after me, her purse still on her shoulder. "You *bought* a house? Why aren't you excited? Why are you walking around like someone killed your cat?"

"Why do I have to be a cat person? Why can't I be a dog owner? Or maybe a beast like a lion or a tiger?"

"Oh my." Sarcasm didn't look good on her—it looked much better on Kelsey. "Let me rephrase. Why are you walking around like someone killed your abominable snowman?"

I glared at her, not in the mood for her mockery this morning. "I've had a really crappy weekend, Noel. No thanks to you. So if it's all right, I'd like a little time to get my day started so I don't scare off my patients."

She stood motionless, only blinking rapidly for a few moments before shaking it off, revealing her utter confusion. "No thanks to *me*? What's that supposed to mean?"

"For some reason, Kelsey is under the impression that you and I are sleeping together. She went off on me Friday night about how I disrespected her by bringing you to the apartment. Then she accused us of having sex, saying she caught me bending you over my desk. I don't even know what the hell she's talking about, but I'm fucking sick and tired of everyone making assumptions, acting like they know the first thing about me, and then holding it over my head as if I've done something wrong just because they *think* I did something that I didn't." I leaned back in my seat and took a deep breath, needing to calm down before I had a heart attack.

Noel was quiet for too long, only to come back with, "She said she caught us having sex in here?"

"Really? That's the only thing you have to say?"

"Did she, uh . . . did she happen to mention anything else about it? Like, perhaps, when?"

I was over the women in my life, ready to take a vow of celibacy and silence, surrounding myself with nature, as that seemed to be the only way to avoid this mess. "I didn't exactly question her, Noel. It never happened, so why would I press a nonexistent issue? She's clearly crazy."

"Well . . . what if she's not?"

"Not what? Not crazy?" I laughed, even though I found none of this funny. "Am I missing something here? Did I somehow fuck you and block it out? Do I need to perform a neuropsych eval on myself?"

She fell into a chair across from my desk, fear staring back at me. "So . . . do you remember that day last week when you asked to borrow my car and I had to have Pete pick me up from work?"

"Yeah." I already didn't like where this was going.

"Well, you see . . . the doctor said we shouldn't let sex become clinical."

"That makes no fucking sense at all."

She huffed and hung her head. "The doctor said there's nothing wrong with Pete or me and that we should just stop worrying about it, lose the stress of it all, and have fun with each other. Rather than pay attention to ovulations and periods and positions—"

"I don't need to hear any more. Really. I think I understand."

"No one was in the office that day, it was after hours, and I thought it wouldn't hurt if we tried to spice it up a little."

It took too much effort to get the words out, but eventually, I was able to say, "Are you saying you had sex with Pete in my office?"

"I could've sworn the front door was locked. I don't know how she could've *caught* me unless she was looking through the window, but honestly, you keep the blinds—"

"That's enough, Noel." I ran my hands through my hair and gripped the overgrown strands until my scalp ached. "It doesn't matter how she caught you or what she saw, because she thinks it was me. And that was the day after I'd spent the night with her. No wonder she thinks I disrespected her. What the hell were you thinking?"

"I was thinking I want a baby with my husband, and after over a year of trying with no luck, I guess I got desperate. I saw an opportunity and I took it, not thinking about how it could affect you. I'm sorry. If you're going to fire me, I understand. Just let me finish getting the files ready for the day, and then I'll be gone."

"Noel . . . wait." I caught her before she exited the room. "I'm not firing you. But that doesn't mean I'm okay with what you did. For your sake, I really hope it worked. I'd feel better if one good thing came out of it."

"It'll work out for you, too. I just know it."

I didn't believe it. My luck had always been shitty, and I didn't see it ever getting better.

"At least you have a house now."

"Yeah, there's that."

And in a month, I'd move into that house alone. Live there alone. And fill the room at the front with a desk and office supplies, knowing it'd never be the nursery Kelsey had suggested.

Chapter 15

Kelsey

For the first time in eight years, I played hooky.

Unfortunately, I couldn't blame it on alcohol, the pregnancy, a death in the family, or even an emergency such as a car accident on the way to work. The reason I chose to stay home today was purely selfish— I needed a little best friend time. So rather than drive to the office this morning, I headed straight to my cousin's house.

"You can't avoid this forever," Tatum said from the other side of the bed, passing me the bag of cheese puffs. "He has a right to know about his kid, no matter who or how many women he's sleeping with."

"I know, but I'm just not ready yet."

"Well, you're gonna end up running out of time before you're ready, Kels. I hate to break it to you, but you can't put this off forever. That little bean sprout will come in no time, and then you'll be stuck having to explain why you never told him."

I shoved a handful of artificially flavored crap into my mouth and spoke around the processed food. "I don't have to explain shit. He doesn't deserve it. He'll be lucky if I even put his name on the birth certificate. I'll give my baby the last name Pitt and tell everyone its dad is Brad. He's got a litter anyway; I doubt he'd notice one more."

"Really? Brad Pitt? I'd go with Tom Hardy."

I rolled my eyes as I handed her the bag—technically, she snatched it away from me—and grabbed the remote to find something else to watch. Commercials messed with my attention span. Honestly, if TV would cut out the ads, I bet shows would have more viewers.

"These cheese puffs aren't making me happy," I said around my orange-colored fingers between my lips. "What kind of pregnant woman doesn't have ice cream?"

"This pregnant woman. And stop changing the subject. Does this mean you don't plan to ever tell him? Or did you just put it on the wait list once again?"

"I don't know why the topic of my baby's father is so fascinating to you."

"Because you're so damn wishy-washy about it. It's like a soap opera. And now that I'm home way more than usual, I need something to entertain me. Your drama does that." She popped another orange puff into her mouth. "Plus, you're the one who came here crying about it. I'd be a shitty friend if I didn't keep us on topic."

"There's nothing more to discuss, Tatertwat."

She laughed so hard I worried she'd choke on the crap she'd shoved in her mouth. Luckily, she didn't. If she had, I wouldn't know how to explain it to Jason, since he was under the impression that Tatum had been on a rather healthy diet since she found out she was pregnant.

I stared at her with a straight face, waiting for her cackles to end so I could finish speaking and, hopefully, put an end to this conversation. "Seriously, though . . . I've fully caught you up on all the baby-daddy drama."

"Don't lie. There's still so much more to tell. Such as . . . you still haven't admitted that you have real feelings for the guy. And *that's* why you ran last week instead of telling him about the baby. It had nothing to do with catching him bending some chick over his desk, and *every-thing* to do with feeling rejected."

Rather than look at her—knowing she'd see the truth in my eyes—I kept my attention on the television that sat on her dresser and continued to flip through the channels. I thought if I acted calm, cool, and collected, she'd believe me when I said, "I feel nothing for the heartless, arrogant, lying sack of sperm."

"Wow, Kels . . . you almost had me. I was this close to taking you seriously." She held her fingers so close together I couldn't see through them.

I smiled and shook my head, wondering why I even bothered trying to keep anything from her. "What was it that gave me away?"

"'Sack of sperm.' If you truly hated him, you wouldn't have wasted your time with such colorful words." She raised one eyebrow, chin tilted to the side.

I must've zoned out while contemplating what she said, because I'd stopped flipping the channels without realizing it. It wasn't until she muttered something about a house that I snapped out of it. "What?"

"Aaron's new house," she said, as if I knew what the hell she was talking about. When she realized how confused I was, she pointed to the screen and continued to explain. "That house, it looks like the one Aaron just bought."

"Yeah . . . I got that part. I guess I was a bit lost at the news that Aaron bought something. Last time I checked, he was still looking." Then again, it wasn't like we'd spoken to each other since our big blow-out on Friday.

She regarded me with a furrowed brow. "I assumed you would've known. He told Jason it was one you had found for him. I think he said his offer was accepted this weekend. Do you not ever see him?"

I shook my head. Because that was about all I could do. I worried that I'd cry if I attempted to form words, and if I did that, there was no way I'd be able to keep this secret from her. As much as I wanted to unload and just tell her everything, spill every buried thought, I couldn't. No matter how I felt about Aaron, he still deserved to be the first one to know the truth.

That, and there was no way Tatum could keep it from Jason.

And Jason would *never* keep it from Aaron.

"It's been hit or miss with him lately." More miss than hit, though I hadn't complained until now. I was still angry with him. Well, *angry* wasn't the right word. Upset. Hurt. Those were much closer to how I felt about him, yet anger was the emotion I projected. "By any chance, do you happen to know which house it was that he bought? I've shown him a bunch."

She hummed while keeping her eyes glued to the TV. "It's on Relic Road. That's all I know."

My heart sank at the thought of Aaron buying my favorite house, the one I'd imagined us in together. And he'd done this *after* what had gone down in my kitchen Friday night. Part of me thought he'd done it on purpose, but the rest of me wasn't stupid—he wouldn't have purchased a home just to spite me.

He clearly didn't care enough about me to do that.

I stayed for almost another hour before heading home. I told her I didn't want to be there when Jason got off, but in truth, I needed a few moments to myself before Aaron walked through the front door. If I didn't organize my thoughts, this would all blow up in my face.

As luck would have it, I managed to word vomit in my journal before Aaron arrived. Doing so allowed me to zero in on what my real problem was so that I wouldn't accuse him of things he would never understand—such as purposely taking my favorite house to keep me from buying it. That wouldn't go over so well.

"Hey," I said, almost too quietly, when he walked in.

He stilled with his eyes locked on mine, wide with fear, as if I'd just caught him sneaking in after curfew. And when he said, "Hey," it was hesitant and forced, obvious that he didn't know how to respond.

"Do you have a few minutes to talk?"

Peace seemed to wash over him in that moment. It started with his eyes, softening them until I could recognize the man in front of me. The tension fell away from his shoulders, and the most relieved sigh filtered past his lips. He nodded and rasped, "Yeah."

We moved closer to one another—me from the doorway to my room and him from the foyer—and met at the back corner of the couch. His eyes implored me to start the conversation off, so I did. Just after I gulped down my own insecurities.

"I heard you bought a house. Why didn't you tell me?"

His gaze narrowed just slightly. "I haven't really seen you to tell you."

"Oh," I whispered. It wasn't a bad excuse, and one I probably could've come up with on my own. "Well, I heard it's the one off Relic? The one I starred on the paper with the office in the front?"

"Yeah, I remember. You noted it could be an office or a nursery."

I nearly choked when I swallowed, hearing him mention a nursery. "Yeah. That one. Why did you choose that house over any of the others?"

The easiness that he'd worn like a cape began to fall away. His spine stiffened as he stood rigid, his eyes hard and boring holes into my face. And when he spoke, his lips seemed tight, as if he had to hold himself back from saying something else. "You think I had some ulterior motive for it? Like I'd buy something that big for any other reason than I liked it and wanted it?"

I shrugged. Because apparently, I hadn't thought this through enough. "No. That's not what I was getting at." I blew out a huff and dropped my chin, hoping that when I opened my eyes, I could start over. "I just wanted to make sure you didn't jump the gun and make an offer simply to move out of here faster."

"I guess I took the whole thing more seriously after last week, but no. I didn't buy it just to get away from you. I've done that just fine without packing my bags."

That was a punch straight to the heart.

I nodded while searching for the other words I'd wanted to say. It seemed he'd knocked me off my axis and made me lose my balance. "Well, when's closing? How much longer are you stuck with me?"

"Four weeks from today—May twenty-eighth. And don't worry; I'll get out of your hair soon. You won't have to deal with me for that whole time. I just have to find somewhere to go in the meantime."

"Don't be ridiculous. I think we can deal with each other for another four weeks."

He opened his mouth but quickly closed it, obviously changing his mind on what he wanted to say. After pulling in a deep breath and briefly closing his eyes, he finally said, "Thanks, Kelsey. But really, you won't have to worry about it."

And with that, he turned and headed for the room he occupied.

I wanted to call out to him. Beg him to come back. Tell him everything I'd bottled up inside while screaming at him for breaking my heart. But I didn't do any of that. In fact, I didn't do *anything*, period. I stood there and watched him leave. Then I went to my room, where I cried into my pillow and unloaded my every emotion onto the pages of my leather-bound therapist.

Chapter 16

Aaron

If I hadn't already known I was a fool, this certainly proved it.

I stood on the dance floor while some hot chick rubbed her body all over me. My hands were on her hips, my eyes set on her lips—lips that promised to do bad, *bad* things to me. Things I wanted her to do, for no other reason than to get Kelsey out of my head. But my mind . . . well, that wasn't on her or the things she did. Or the things she *wanted* to do.

No. My mind was on a certain redhead.

More specifically, on the ache in my chest she'd caused.

"My place or yours?" the woman in front of me asked with her lips to my ear so I could hear her over the music.

I smiled as I grazed her cheek with the tip of my nose and then yanked her closer to my body, her earlobe between my teeth. But I loosened my hold, knowing she'd take off running when I answered her question. "Considering I don't have a place, I guess yours would be best."

She didn't run, but she *did* push against my chest to stare into my eyes, confusion tugging her thin brows closer together. "What do you mean, you don't have a place?"

My smile grew larger—proving my point that something was wrong with me. "My parents kicked me out of their house. Said I was too old to live with them anymore. Who does that? I mean, I'm only thirty-two. I'm a spring chicken!" This officially made me a masochist. "Although, I'm currently staying with a friend's younger cousin. We've slept together on occasion. I've told her I love her a couple of times. But she's mad at me right now because she *caught* me fucking my secretary. Receptionist. Whatever the hell she is. I don't even know. She's just Noel to me. Her husband's Pete. Really great guy. They're trying to have a baby, but it's not working, so she thought I could help her out."

Her eyes grew large, assumptions dancing in the light bouncing off them. And then she ran off, exactly what I'd known she'd do. Then again, I hadn't made it difficult. I'd almost purposely made my life sound like a fiery train wreck.

There would be others, though.

And as I sat at the bar, tipping my head back while gulping yet another beer, my next victim came to sit next to me. Where the last one was tall and leggy, this one was short and curvy. I was a lover of all types. Some guys were ass men; others cared more about the bra size. Me? I loved every part of the female body, no matter the size, shape, or color. The only part of a woman's body I didn't particularly care about was her feet. And this specific lady had heels that hid her toes—just the way I liked it.

"Wanna buy me a drink?" Damn, she was bold.

"Wish I could, sweetheart, but I'm broke. You see—"

And she was gone. Go figure.

"You're wasting your time, Aaron." Good ol' Cheryl, always coming at the right time to say the right thing when I needed it most. "I've seen you with four women now, and you've struck out with each of them. Not saying that's out of your skill set or anything, but it's clear you're doing this on purpose. Why?"

Setting my beer down, I shrugged. I knew the answer, though I chose to keep it to myself. "It seems I lost my game."

She leaned against the bar to bring her face closer to mine and laughed. "Aaron, I hate to break it to you, but you've never had game. I should know—you tried it on me."

"And it would've worked, too. You said so yourself."

One brow arched high, matching the one corner of her quirked top lip. There was something she wasn't telling me, and she had five seconds to spit it out before I'd have to drag it out of her. Finally, she shook her head and dropped her gaze to the counter. "It never would've worked. I thought you were a great guy—still do—but you were too nice. That's your problem. You know that, right?"

"Do I know what? I don't understand how being nice is a problem."

"No." She tucked her pink hair behind her ear and smiled sweetly at me. "Being nice is good. Being *too* nice is where you go from a contender to a cheerleader."

I still didn't understand.

Luckily, Cheryl knew me well, noticing the confusion in my eyes— or all over my face, though it was hard to tell without looking over her head into the giant mirror behind her. "You're a great friend. And—at least for me—it was hard to see you as anything else *because* you were too nice."

"You want an asshole?"

"No, but if you don't have at least *some* edge to you, then you kinda come off as weak. And no woman wants to sleep with someone they assume is weak. We want passion, to feel like a guy is crazy desperate for what we have. Nice guys don't give us that impression."

All I could do was shrug and tip my bottle back again. She didn't know how I was in bed because she'd never given me a shot. Much like the others. Assumptions made the world go round. And they made mine stop.

"So are you saying I need to be meaner?"

She laughed. Apparently, she'd mistaken my question for a joke. "I doubt you'll ever be able to pull that off, Aaron."

I tipped my chin, taking her words as a challenge. One I'd totally win. "Game on."

Five or six beers later, I was back at the bar. Though this time, a different girl was next to me. By now, I'd lost track of how many I'd spoken to since taking Cheryl up on her dare. I just knew I'd land one eventually.

She had her hand on my thigh, working her way closer to my crotch. Lust brightened her eyes, which appeared to be purple, but there was no way that could be. Unless she wore contacts. In that case, it was totally possible for her eyes to be purple. It also made me question if she had a little extra in her bra, or if the long blond hair that draped over her shoulders was real or attached by glue. Or thread. I still didn't know how that worked, but I'd seen my share of fake hair.

Either I'd had too much to drink, or I'd taken Cheryl's advice *too* literally, because when she smiled, I found myself saying, "Your teeth are big."

She pulled her head back and frowned. "Excuse me?"

"Every time you smile, it makes me wonder if you have any gum. Not chewing gum, but the kind that holds your teeth in your head. All I see are these big Chiclet-looking things. Nothing else. I bet you get that a lot, huh?"

"No. Actually, I don't."

A hum vibrated my lips as I nodded. "You probably hang out with people who are too nice to tell ya. I've heard the nice ones suck in bed. Weak or some shit like that. But the mean ones, the ones who'll tell you that you have horse teeth . . . they'll rock your world."

"I'm not sure that's right."

"Wanna test that theory out?" I wagged my brows, a wide smile burning my cheeks. "I deleted the Uber app from my phone, so it looks like you'll have to give me a ride . . ." I leaned closer to her ear and added, "Pun intended."

Her hand vanished from my thigh as she pulled away, repulsion dripping from every pore while she regarded me with pinched features. "I think I'll pass. But thanks for the, uh . . . the *offer*."

"Anytime, sweet cheeks." I nodded when she slipped off the stool to leave. "She'll be back," I said to Cheryl, who'd watched the entire thing from her station behind the bar. "I made sure to let her know just how good I was in bed."

"Yeah . . . you're a real rock star, Aaron."

I had an epiphany. "That's it. I could totally get laid if I said I was a rock star. Good thinking, Cheryl. Now . . . I just have to find someone willing to believe it."

"So you've resorted to lying?"

"You know . . ." I leaned forward as though I had a secret to share with her. "Tatum says if you don't make *all* of it up, it's called a half truth. Not a lie."

"She sounds like she's got it all figured out. Go for it, Aaron. Let's see how that works for ya." Cheryl didn't have much faith in me, but I'd show her. Right after I finished the beer she'd just placed in front of me with a telling smile lightening her eyes.

Before I knew it, I was in a room somewhere inside the club. At least, I assumed it was in the club, considering music thumped through the walls and the couch I was horizontal on smelled like stale cigarette smoke. I'd lost count of how much I'd had to drink, but at some point, I'd taken shots. Lots of shots. And just like they always said . . . beer before liquor, never been sicker.

It was embarrassing.

"How are you feeling?" Cheryl came into view when I peeked one eye open. Although, she was a little blurry. And there seemed to be two of her. "Do you think you're gonna throw up any more? Or are you done?"

"Done." That one word burned my throat, which had become raw with the bile that I'd started to believe would never end. "For now."

She giggled, and it made me wonder how she could stand being around drunk people all the time. I never enjoyed being the sober one in a group. I'd hate to have her job, though she seemed to like it.

"Things are a little fuzzy. I'm not sure what's real and what isn't. So tell me . . . did I get laid?"

Cheryl sat me up and handed me yet another bottle of cold water. "I was almost convinced you'd get 'er done with that last one. But unfortunately, it just wasn't in your cards tonight. Maybe next time. You really mastered the art of asshole, though."

I smiled, proud of myself for overcoming the stigma of the nice guy. "So you think I would've gotten with that last chick if I hadn't thrown up?"

Her brows dipped, gaze narrowed. "Uh . . . the vomiting didn't start until after she left. Luckily, no one but me saw that."

"Then why'd she leave?"

"Gee, Aaron . . . it might've had something to do with you calling her Kelsey and telling her that you wanted her to have your babies."

"But I was mean about it, right?"

"You sure were. When she corrected you—for the sixth or seventh time—that her name is Emily, not Kelsey, you told her you'd call her what you wanted, and if she didn't like it, she could . . ." She covered her lips and ducked her head, stifling her laughter long enough to finish speaking. "She could sprout wings and fly like a bird . . . 'faw, faw, faw away from here.'"

I stared at her, blinking, unsure why she couldn't stop laughing. "I don't get it."

"Yeah, she didn't, either. I'm pretty sure she's too young, because she didn't understand why you kept saying, 'Life is like a box of condoms.' I thought it was clever. I laughed. She didn't." Clearly, considering she was *still* laughing.

I leaned forward, pressing my elbows into my thighs while I cradled my head in my hands. "I need to get out of here."

"Don't worry . . . I called someone to come pick you up."

Dropping my hands, I stared at her—more like *tried* to stare at her, since my vision was still off, but stared all the same. "Who'd you call? Uber?"

"I would've, but you deleted the app, and I couldn't get it reinstalled without your password. So I went through your contacts and found someone willing to get out of bed at one in the morning to come get your ass and take you home."

"Who?" *Please say Jason.*

"Kelsey." Wrong answer. "She's on her way."

"Kill me now. Why the hell would you call *her*? Of all people, why her? I have, like . . . a lot of people in my phone. You had . . . a lot of options to choose from. Are you *trying* to make my life worse? I thought we were friends."

She took my hands in hers and drew herself closer. Compassion curled her lips and dimmed her eyes. "It's obvious you came here tonight to drink away whatever issues you have with her. And it's not working. I don't have a clue what is going on or what's happened between the two of you, but I know it's big enough that it drove you here. The only way you'll be able to deal with it is if you talk to her. So yes, I called her because you live with her, and she's the best person to get you home safely—but also because there's clearly something you need to get off your chest, and she's the only one you should talk to about it. Not strangers at a bar. Not an empty beer bottle or shot glass. Her."

Just then, someone cleared their throat and caught our attention, drawing my focus from Cheryl's fuzzy face to the redhead near the office door. Double vision still troubled me, though I could see enough to notice the confusion on her taut brow. As I lowered my gaze, I became aware of the flowing tank draping over her perky breasts, the yoga pants accentuating her legs, and her flip-flops, which showed off the dark polish on her toenails. I'd rubbed those feet countless times, always contemplating if she wore black or some really dark shade on the perfectly manicured nails.

"What color is that?" I pointed to her toes without a care in the world that I likely made no sense to anyone. The question was out of the blue, but then again, I was drunk off my ass, so I didn't give a shit. "Is it black?"

Kelsey's toes wiggled, and I could picture her staring down at her feet, though I never glanced up to verify if she was or not. Instead, I kept my attention on the polish and awaited her response. A second later, I heard, "Yeah, it's black."

I sucked in a lungful of air and pushed to my feet, meeting her eyes for the first time since realizing she was here. "Good choice. Matches your heart." Passing her, I added, "Let's go."

Murmurs cascaded behind me, though I refused to turn around to see Cheryl and Kelsey talking, and I certainly didn't bother waiting around to find out what they had to say. I'd gone from hopeless to hopeful to drunk to sick and now to angry . . . all within a few hours. I was beyond ready for this night to be over.

"You could show a little more gratitude, you know. I didn't have to drag myself out of bed to come pick you up, so it'd be nice if you didn't act like me driving you home is a prison sentence," Kelsey called out as she followed me into the parking lot.

I had no idea where I was going, considering I didn't have a clue where she'd parked. I could've scoured the lot for her car, but that would've required focus and single vision. Currently, I was too busy fuming over Kelsey being here to pay any attention to anything around me. Oh, and my eyesight rivaled that of an elderly man with cataracts and glaucoma.

I turned around to face her, telling by the sounds of her steps that she wasn't far behind. I only meant to pivot on my foot, yet I likely resembled a ballerina with the way I spun, nearly losing my balance. "Maybe I don't want you to drive me home."

"Too late. I'm already here."

By now, we were face to face—couldn't have been more than a foot separating us. Anger fueled our fight, though betrayal burned in my veins, igniting more than an argument. Resentment kindled within me until my breaths were labored and ragged.

"Why are you so mad?" She held up a hand and shook her head, keeping me from responding. "You know what? I don't care. Be pissed. Throw a temper tantrum until you're blue in the face. I don't have the time or patience to deal with it. For a thirty-two-year-old, you certainly don't act like a man. You're acting far more like a little boy who didn't get his way. Find your own ride home, and don't wake me up when you get there."

I wouldn't let her get away with this that easily, so when she turned to walk off, I followed. Every step she took, I matched with my own until I was a breath away, suffocating in the scent wafting off her clean hair.

"For your information"—no, I wasn't aware at the time how my choice of words proved her right about the way I was acting—"I came here to forget about you. So excuse me if I'm pissed that the *one* person I wanted to block out of my mind is here to drive me home."

She stopped suddenly, nearly causing me to run into her back. Shifting on her heel, her body only slightly angled toward me, she peered at me, as though studying my expression or attempting to read my mind. "Why were you trying to forget about me? What'd I do to you other than prevent you from doing to me what my ex did?"

It seemed I'd never be able to escape the assumptions, the preconceived notions that took on a life of their own. No matter who it was, what it was about . . . they'd always be there. They were my skeletons in the closet. Inescapable. Always there, hiding in the dark corners, waiting to take me down every time I thought I was about to move forward.

"I'm so hung up on you, and you can't even see it because *you're* too hung up on what someone else did to you. You say you want a good guy." I held my arms out and leaned my chest forward. "But you wouldn't recognize one if they stood right in front of you with a sign around their neck. If you'd stop looking behind you, stop focusing on what *he* did, and turn to look at what's ahead, you'd see it. I'm right here. I'm constantly turned down for being the *nice guy*, yet you, someone who might actually want that in a person, dismisses me because you can't accept the fact that there just might be a guy out there who doesn't wanna fuck you over."

Without a word, she dropped her gaze, shuffled her feet, and continued to make her way toward her car. Or at least, I assumed that was where she was headed. I didn't really know, though I doubted she'd wander through a parking lot at night for any other reason. In her pajamas, no less.

Taillights flashed ahead of us after Kelsey pressed a button on her key fob. She went to the left, making a beeline to the driver's side, while I made my way to the passenger seat. And as soon as we were both in, doors closed, all outside noise blocked out, she muttered, "I know what I saw, Aaron. I know what I heard." She cranked the engine and turned toward me while pulling the seat belt across her chest. "It doesn't matter what you say—you won't convince me that I'm wrong about you."

"I wasn't even there." The truth burned the back of my throat so badly I wasn't able to keep it in any longer. Defending myself had never been something I'd bothered with—it was pointless to prove someone wrong when they never gave me the benefit of the doubt to begin with. "I was at the hospital, evaluating a patient in the ER. I'm sure there are lots of people who can confirm that if you don't believe me."

She drove in silence, keeping her thoughts and arguments to herself, likely waiting until I finished speaking so she could metaphorically hang me with what she presumed to be a lie. Little did she know, the noose actually hung around her neck—not mine.

"You know what? I don't give a shit if you believe me or not. You're the same as everyone else. You see something, hear something, and without taking a second to question it, you make assumptions. No one ever assumes I've got a big dick or that I can make a woman come like no other. They don't assume I'm capable of loving someone with my entire heart, giving my all to one person. No . . . they hear my name and conjure up an image of me performing brain surgery, only to think less of me when they discover the truth. They hear me admit that I lived with my parents and then run before they can learn why. You hear someone having sex in my office, and you automatically slam the gavel without once recognizing that not everything is as it seems."

Her hands grew tighter around the steering wheel. It was obvious she had a lot to say, but she wouldn't get a chance until I was done.

"I told you Noel was married. But since one guy fucked you over, lied to you about who he was—cheated on his wife with you—the only conclusion your brain could come up with was that she had to be cheating on her husband with me." I quit speaking, hoping she'd take the stage and fight back.

I needed a fight. I needed her rampage. The amount of resentment that burned within me would be catastrophic if I didn't find an outlet for it. As much as I hated to admit it, I needed her to make this pain go away.

Kelsey cleared her throat, though she never turned my way. Instead, she kept her attention on the road ahead while lacerating me with her sharp words. "The only reason I stopped on my way home was because your truck was in the parking lot. Two people were having sex in *your* office. If it quacks like a duck . . ."

"Have you ever heard a duck call?"

She stilled for a moment but then said, "A what?"

"It's a whistle that hunters use to lure game birds. When they hear it, they come closer, not realizing they're about to be shot and killed, likely someone's next meal. It quacks like a duck . . . but it's not a duck."

I turned my head toward her, making sure she didn't miss the meaning of my next words. "Assumptions can be dangerous."

Thank God for TV. Anyone who said reality shows were ruining our culture was wrong.

"Then why was your truck there?" she asked, her words thick in her throat.

"I couldn't get it to start, so I took Noel's car to the hospital. She had her husband pick her up from work. This all happened the day after Jason's dinner announcement, right? The day after we slept together?"

Still, without taking her eyes off the road, she nodded.

"Do you by chance remember that I came home late? Around eight o'clock, I think. Do you recall that I walked in with my sleeves rolled up, my hands greasy? Probably not. You were too busy stewing on the couch. Anyway, that's because I stopped to change the battery after leaving the hospital. I returned Noel's car and drove my truck back to the apartment. I wasn't there."

Nothing more was said for the next three minutes. But when she pulled into the parking lot, she remained behind the steering wheel, the engine still running. It seemed she had something to say, maybe had to work her way up to speaking the words aloud. Yet I didn't wait around for it. She was a week too late.

Instead, I climbed out of the car, closed the door, and left her behind.

I might not have successfully pushed her from my mind, but with time, I would.

Chapter 17

Kelsey

When I was in fourth grade, my teacher had shown us all a picture. She'd kept it on the screen for sixty seconds, not telling us what it was or why it was up there. After taking it down, she'd gone back to her desk, ignoring the class for two full minutes. She didn't tell anyone to stop talking or even give directions about what we needed to do. After those two minutes were up—twice as long as the picture had been on the screen—she moved to the front of the class and asked us all to get out a piece of paper. On that paper, we had to describe what we'd seen, using adjectives to draw the image she'd shown us a couple of minutes before.

I'd felt confident I was right. *Beyond* right. And as my classmates had read their assignments out loud, I had become more and more impatient for my turn, knowing how pleased my teacher would be at the details I'd remembered. The parts of the image no one else had mentioned—or that they'd gotten wrong. The woman had worn a green dress with feathers along the bottom and black shoes with silver buckles, her purse clutched in one hand while she held on to a child with the other. The little boy, a towhead, squatted at the woman's feet, petting the belly of a beige-colored dog.

No one had mentioned these things. And I couldn't wait to be praised for my memory, my perception, my incredible attention to detail. I'd never forget it, the way all the other kids had stared at me as I read my assignment aloud. When I finished, several of them had called out rebuttals, arguing with me about how I had gotten things wrong. But I knew I hadn't. I knew that out of the entire class, I had been the only one who'd gotten it all right.

Until our teacher filled the screen with the image again.

Her dress hadn't been green but blue. And there were no feathers at the bottom of the long skirt—it was snow piled around her feet. The silver buckles on her black shoes had turned out to be light reflecting off pieces of ice that sat upon two small rocks. She held on to a purse, yes, but the little boy turned out to be a little girl, a bonnet on her head. The dog wasn't a dog at all; in fact, it wasn't even an animal. Just more snow.

I'd been so sure of myself. Only to have it all come crashing down with one more glance at the same picture.

Last night had been a reenactment of that day in fourth grade. And as I lay in bed, exhausted from a long night, I couldn't help but compare the two different yet similar situations, once again baffled at how I had been so wrong when I'd felt so sure.

Yes, his truck had been in the parking lot. And yes, there were two people having sex in his office. However, I hadn't *seen* him, only assumed it was him based on what I knew—and heard. But when I stopped and thought about it, thought about what had been said, the voices, the words, the *tone* . . . it became rather obvious that it hadn't been Aaron in that room.

I'd always thought Aaron had a rather normal voice for a guy— deep and manly without the burly gruffness that came with super deep baritones. The man in his office had grit, like his words had been dragged along a gravel road as he spoke. Even though I'd only had sex with Aaron twice, I couldn't ever forget the way he sounded in the heat of the moment, during both rough and sensual times. His voice became hoarser the closer he got to his orgasm, and when I came, he growled. The sounds—what I'd heard in his office that day and what I knew of Aaron during sex—weren't even close to the same.

Also, Aaron had told me he loved me. He'd said those exact words to me a few times. Granted, he'd been pretending I was someone else, but that didn't mean I was deaf to what that sentiment sounded like falling from his lips while in the throes of passion. And as I thought back to how the man in his office had sounded as he told Noel he loved her, I realized it was a far cry from the strong, powerful way Aaron had spoken those words to me.

I dragged myself out of bed, knowing there was a lot I had to make up for and with no idea where to begin. Glancing at the clock on my nightstand, I noticed it was just after eight. With how intoxicated Aaron had been last night, I figured he'd still be in bed. So I took a quick shower, threw on the first outfit I pulled from my closet, and went to him.

Only to be gutted at the sight of his empty room.

I was too late.

I'd woken that morning with a sliver of hope on the horizon, and I rested my head on my pillow that night in total darkness. No sliver of anything, just an invisible weight that wouldn't relent. And the later it got, the heavier the weight became until it was crushing.

I'd stayed up all day and all night waiting for Aaron to come home.

In the end, the sun rose, yet he never came.

My phone buzzed from the coffee table, but I was too scared to look at it. Aaron had pretty much been gone for the last five days, so I'd sent him a text a few minutes ago, asking if he'd be at the apartment tonight. This was probably his response, but I was no longer sure I wanted to see it.

If he said yes, that meant I'd have to come clean, tell him the truth about the baby. I'd gone to my twelve-week appointment today, and in a few days, I'd officially be in the second trimester. I couldn't keep this from my family—or Aaron—any longer.

However, if he said no, my world just might crumble at my feet.

He'd barely been home since I'd been dragged out of bed at one in the morning to pick him up from Boots. He'd left the next morning before I got up and hadn't come back for more than a change of clothes since.

I'd stupidly thought he'd come back tonight, at the very least to take a shower like he had the last two nights before leaving and sleeping somewhere else. Yet it was almost nine, and he hadn't come home. I didn't want to think about where he'd been staying. I already knew it hadn't been at Tatum and Jason's place, and the only other *friend* of his I knew of was some chick who worked at the bar. I didn't have a clue how to get ahold of her, considering she'd called me last week from Aaron's phone.

Giving in, I grabbed my phone to read his text.

Aaron: No

My heart sank. It wasn't until that exact moment that I realized how badly I'd screwed this up. I didn't want to tell anyone else until Aaron knew, but he wasn't making it easy on me. My plan was to announce my pregnancy on Sunday at my parents' house, which meant I had about two days to let Aaron know, and I refused to give him that news in a text.

Me: We really need to talk. When will you be home?

Aaron: Not sure

His response had been almost immediate, which made me wonder if he had his phone in his hand, possibly waiting for me to reply. That also made me wonder where he'd be or who he'd be with that he would rather stare at his phone than entertain someone else.

Logic told me he wasn't alone.

Experience told me he was with a woman.

Me: Where are you?

Again, his response was instant.

Aaron: Doesn't matter

Me: Can you come over tomorrow please?

Aaron: I don't get the keys to my place for another nineteen days

As irrational as it was, reading those words hurt. My apartment had always been *mine*—except when Tatum was here—and his stay had always been temporary. I'd never referred to it as his home, nor had he ever called it *his* place. It'd always been mine. So it shouldn't have bothered me that he refused to acknowledge this as his home . . . yet it did.

I took a deep breath and moved on. It was the only option I had left.

I couldn't dwell. I *refused* to dwell.

Me: Are you alone?

Aaron: no

Me: We need to talk.

Aaron: Ok? So talk

I should've known he wouldn't make this easy on me. Then again, I didn't blame him. Things had been good with us. We'd found a comfort level between us, and as soon as we'd gotten to a place where we might've actually stood a chance to move forward, I'd fucked it up.

Needless to say, I didn't text him back. And he never pushed.

By eleven, I'd given up on sleeping. Tossing and turning didn't equate to slumber, so I got out of bed and did yoga. And by *did yoga*, I mean I paced. While eating ice cream—straight from the carton with the scoop. The only reason I stopped and put it away was because it had started to melt and drip down my arm.

And as I stood in front of the sink, rinsing off the rocky road that made my fingers stick together, I realized something. Something that shouldn't have taken me this long to figure out. Apparently, while I could learn a lesson, it didn't stick with me for long.

"I think I'm going to throw up," I said after Tatum answered the phone. I had her on Bluetooth as I drove over the bridge to Aaron's office.

"You woke me up to tell me that? Unless you *are* throwing up, it's not considered an emergency." She no longer sounded sleepy. "And even then . . . it's only a cause for concern if it's bloody or something. Or black. I don't think black vomit is healthy."

And that was why I'd called her, even knowing I'd wake her up. In a crisis, Tatum could always make me laugh. And even though I only had a slight curve to my lips now, that was all I needed to keep me sane.

"I'm on my way to tell him about the baby."

She was silent, not even her breathing audible through the line. Then there was a bit of rustling, a door closing, and her echoing voice as she asked, "What? Like right now?" It was clear she was in the bathroom—as if that wouldn't raise suspicion if Jason woke up.

"Yes. Right now."

"Why? Did something happen at your appointment today? Is the baby all right?"

I moved one hand from the steering wheel and held it against my softening belly. I still wasn't showing, which was a good thing, but my body had definitely changed. I wouldn't be able to go much longer before people would just know.

"The baby is fine. I've decided to tell my parents on Sunday before everyone gets there, and if I'm going to do that, then it's only fair he knows first. I tried to get him to come over earlier, but he was being an ass, so I'm going to him."

"It's almost midnight. On a Thursday. Don't most people have jobs they have to go to in the morning? Won't he be asleep?" She sighed, keeping me from answering. "Never mind. I forgot he's a stripper."

I chose to ignore that. "Anyhooter, I'm freaking out."

"Don't. It'll be fine. Just spit it out and get it over with. If you think about it, it worked out for the best that he didn't go to your place. I mean, imagine having to kick him out after telling him. At least this way, you can leave as soon as those words are out of your mouth."

Her optimism made me feel better.

"So you're going to tell everyone on Sunday?"

"No. Just my parents. *Before* everyone gets there."

"Which means Jason still won't know." Defeat rolled through her voice like thunder through the clouds. "Can you just tell me when everyone will find out? I don't want to say something thinking that the cat's out of the bag, just to find out it's only out of the bag to, like, one person."

She was tired of keeping this from Jason; I didn't have to read her mind to know that. And I understood the predicament she was in. "Soon. Once this guy knows and I can talk to my parents in private, then you can say anything you want. Deal?"

A soft squeal leaked through the line. "So . . . Sunday?"

"Yes. Sunday." My laugh was genuine, and the smile on my lips burned my cheeks. "But I'm about five minutes away from him, and I think I need to get my head in the game. Shit . . . I still don't even know what to say."

Let the freak-out commence.

"It's easy. All you have to do is say *I'm having your baby* and leave."

"Good thinking." I shook my head, amusement still dancing on my lips. "Where would I be without you, Tater?"

"Lost." Her soft giggle flooded my ear just before we said our goodbyes.

And then it was just me. And the road. On the way to Aaron's office, where I found his truck in the parking lot. The otherwise *empty* parking lot. And through the slats on the closed blinds, I could see slivers of light from inside. Why it had taken me almost a week to realize where he'd been sleeping was beyond me.

My heart hammered with each step I took, my throat constricting further the closer I got to the door. And as I raised my hand to knock, my head grew so light I worried it'd float away like a balloon. Somehow, between the car and the front door, I'd developed vertigo, and I was on the verge of falling over when movement from the window next to the door caught my attention. I must've knocked, though I didn't recall doing so. Either way, someone had separated the blinds to peek out.

And after several—*long*—seconds, the door opened.

Aaron stood in front of me in gym shorts, nothing covering his intoxicating chest. He'd always worn shirts around the apartment; the only times he hadn't were when he was in my bed. It was a glorious sight . . . until I made my way to his face and noticed the scowl.

"What are you doing here, Kelsey?" His voice was hard and sharp, capable of holding me down and cutting into me like a scalpel.

"I told you . . . we need to talk."

"How'd you know where to find me?"

I stepped closer to him and placed my hand on his chest. His heart raced beneath my palm. His body heat seeped through my pores until flames licked just beneath my skin. But what got to me more than anything else was the combination of pain and hope in his tired eyes.

"Well, the obvious guess would be that you've been staying with a girl—or more than one. And once I stopped looking at the obvious, I wasn't left with many options." Using his shock to my advantage, I leaned even farther forward until I could fit through the door and into the office. But I wasn't prepared for what I'd find. "What the . . . ?"

"Can we not do this right now?"

I stared at the blow-up mattress in the middle of the waiting room, chairs pushed aside to make room for his mock bedroom. "Why are you sleeping on the floor of your office?" I asked, peering at him from over my shoulder. At the very least, I'd expected him to have a couch or something more than this.

He slowly closed the door and turned to face me, chin tucked and gaze downcast. But with a sharp breath, he returned to his normal height, with his shoulders back and eyes boring holes into mine. "Where else was I supposed to go? You made it clear you didn't want me at your place."

"I specifically told you to stay until you closed on the house. Why would you say I didn't want you to if I'd *told* you to?"

He shook his head and laughed, though not with humor. "Telling someone to stay out of pity is *not* the same as *wanting* them there. I'm not going to be where I'm not wanted, Kelsey."

"Fine. I get it, but I asked you to come home tonight. Doesn't that mean I *want* you there?"

"To talk. And to be honest with you, I'm not entirely sure I want to hear what you have to say. I heard enough last week. I don't know how much more I can take coming from you."

It took me a minute to speak, his words bombarding me on repeat in my mind. And when I finally found my voice, the softness surprised us both. "What do you mean . . . coming from me?"

"It doesn't matter."

I grabbed his wrist to keep him from moving away. "No, it *does* matter, Aaron. What did you mean? Don't hold back now."

"You were different. At least . . . I thought you were. I had fun with you, and I didn't feel like I had to be someone else. Whether we were sharing ice cream or just hanging out watching TV, your feet in my lap, it felt natural. Easy. Maybe it was *too* easy. Maybe that's what was wrong, and it's my fault because I didn't see it from the beginning. I thought we were getting somewhere, and then you did exactly what everyone else does. You assumed the worst without once giving me the benefit of the doubt."

I heard every word, but there were certain parts that stuck out more than others, and until those were addressed, I wouldn't be able to move forward. "You thought we were getting somewhere . . . where did you think we were going?"

"I don't know, Kelsey. I honestly don't. It could've been a really strong friendship. Closer than a friend but not as close as a lover. Or maybe more. I couldn't tell you because you shut me out too soon. All I know is something seemed to change that night—after we got home from dinner with your family. But before I had a chance to dig deeper into my feelings toward you, you accused me of . . . hell, I don't even know what you accused me of. Cheating? Lying? What was it exactly?"

I slid my hands along his warm skin—up his arms, over his shoulders, linking my fingers behind his neck—and held him still until he saw the truth in my eyes. "I felt the same way, Aaron. That's why I came here that day. To talk to you about . . . *us* and what was ahead. What I heard in your office killed me. No, I never should've assumed. I saw your truck, I heard what was going on in there, and I didn't bother to discuss it with you. I'm sorry. I allowed my emotions to get the best of me, and I hate how that affected you."

"Is that what you wanted to talk about?"

I swallowed, suddenly feeling nervous and incapable of speaking. I'd come here to tell him about the baby . . . but that was before I saw the sleeping quarters he'd set up in his waiting room. I'd thought he had been staying here, but apparently, thinking it and seeing it were two very different things. Because now that it was more than an idea in my mind—and now that I'd witnessed the warring emotions in his eyes—everything changed.

I cupped his cheeks and brought his lips closer to mine, thankful he didn't object. "I wanted to tell you that I'm sorry. I didn't mean to let you down or hurt you. I shouldn't have let my own feelings dictate how you were treated."

"That's just it, Kelsey . . . had you come to me then, I could've explained." He grabbed my hips and pulled me closer. "Had you called me, you would've known I wasn't at the office. I could've put those hurt feelings to rest right then and there, long before now."

"Is it too late?"

He took so long to answer that I worried I'd pass out from holding my breath. But he breathed life back into me when he said, "No. It's not too late."

My lips met his. Urgency and need spilled between us like molten lava, burning their way through my veins. I couldn't keep my hands off him, couldn't dig my nails into his shoulders any harder, and no matter what I did, I couldn't slow my racing heart, my labored breathing, or the desire that pulsed between my legs.

I needed him.

And based on the pressure against my lower stomach . . . he needed me, too.

But just as I thought we'd explode with untamed desire, he pulled away, breaking the kiss. He didn't let go of my hips or put distance between our bodies. Instead, he dropped his forehead to mine and said, "I want to be with you tonight, Kelsey."

"Then be with me."

"No." Not only did he drop one hand from my side, but he pulled his face away. Granted, he then used his free hand to cradle my cheek, which was enough to calm my nerves. "I mean . . . no pretending. No make-believe. *I* want to be with *you* tonight. Without the act. Without the fantasies. Can you do that? Can you just be with me as we are?"

God, I thought I was about to climb this man like a ladder.

Standing on my tiptoes, I tightened my arms around the back of his neck and pressed my chest to him, our mouths so close his breath kept me alive like an oxygen mask. "I don't want anything else. Only you. And me."

That was all he allowed me to say before grabbing the backs of my thighs and lifting me off the floor. In one dizzying sweep, I was on the air mattress, and Aaron was above me. A flash of worry crossed my mind, hoping we hadn't popped the bed. But when nothing happened—other than his lips claiming mine—I promptly forgot about anything other than Aaron's hands, his mouth, his tongue.

The only thing that existed was *him*.

And then he loved my body in a way no other man had before. He didn't take charge like he had the first time, though he maintained control over every move—his *and* mine. Nor did he make love to me like he had a few weeks ago. Yet that didn't mean he didn't *make* me feel loved. Cherished. Taken care of, like I was the only thing in his world that mattered.

He told me everything I needed to know with his mouth . . . just not with words. And he used his hands to show me everything I *wanted* to know. There wasn't a single part of me—inside or out—that he didn't reach.

And when he dragged me off the cliff, I could see my whole future. I saw him. I saw our baby. Our whole life stretched out in front of me, waiting for me to take hold of it and secure it close to my chest.

The one thing he didn't give me, something he'd offered both times before, was his profession of love as he followed me over the ledge. Though I didn't doubt for a second that it was there . . . he just didn't utter the words.

Then, afterward, he wrapped me in his arms and held on to me while I fell into the most peaceful sleep I'd had in a long time.

Chapter 18

Aaron

"Why is your alarm going off so early?" There was nothing sexier than Kelsey's voice first thing in the morning. She rolled off my chest and groaned. "The sun's not even up yet, Aaron."

It might have been early, but that didn't stop me from laughing while silencing the alarm on my phone. "I need time to deflate my bed, get it stored in my truck, and put everything in here back where it was. And that has to be done before I go to the gym so I can take a shower and get ready for work. That way, by the time I get back to the office, Noel won't have a clue that I've been sleeping here."

Kelsey curled along my side, her palm pressed against the center of my chest. "Come home today. Please. You still have about two more weeks before you close on your house. You shouldn't be sleeping here."

Running my fingers through her hair, I stared at the dark ceiling and contemplated my response. "If I do . . . where would I sleep?"

Airy confusion filled her voice when she asked, "What do you mean?"

"Well, I've now spent two nights sleeping next to you. And after last night, I don't think I'd make it a whole night in a separate bed, let alone a separate room."

She tilted her head back and lifted her hand to cup my cheek, gently directing me until I turned my face toward hers. "Are you saying you'd want to stay in my room with me?"

"I wish there was more light in this room right about now."

"Why?"

"So I can see your eyes. If I only go by your voice, you sound freaked out. And I don't want to freak you out. I want you to be sure of whatever decision we make. After last night, I guess I assumed this was something you were ready for—wanted, at least."

Letting go of my cheek, Kelsey wrapped her fingers around my wrist and brought my palm to her face. After a moment of molding my touch to her features, she released a breath and said, "Do you really want to sleep in my bed? With me? Every night until you get the keys to your own place?"

Fuck it.

I pushed up on my elbow and dropped my forehead to hers, our lips a breath apart. My fingers spread across her cheek as if to keep her face close to mine. "If I had my way, you'd come with me in two weeks. But I understand if this is too soon or too fast for you. I'll go as slow as you want, Kelsey. You tell me what you're comfortable with, and I'll follow. I don't want to scare you off."

She didn't respond. Instead, she covered my mouth with hers and pulled my body between her parted legs. I really didn't have time to slide into her, but I couldn't find the strength to deny her.

In the end, we both got what we wanted. Unfortunately, I had to all but kick her out of the office so I could get everything picked up and put back and then leave before Noel showed up. The only thing that made it better was knowing I'd see her after work.

But then I moved the blankets out of the way to deflate the mattress.

Kelsey had left her phone. I quickly checked the parking lot in case she hadn't left yet, but her car was no longer there. My thumb must've accidentally hit one of the buttons on her cell and turned the screen on. Normally, I wouldn't have even looked, but the excessive texts from Tatum caught my attention. If she'd tried to get ahold of Kelsey that many times, I worried something was wrong, and with her being pregnant, I became even more worried—especially when I happened to see the word *baby* on the screen.

It wasn't about Tatum's baby.

Although something was definitely wrong.

Tater Salad: I haven't been able to go back to sleep thanks to you. Are you still with him?

Tater Salad: Seriously Kels . . . it's been almost an hour. How long does it take to say "I'm having your baby"???

Tater Salad: Fine . . . I'm going back to sleep. Text me in the morning.

As I held the phone in my hand, it began to vibrate with more texts.

Tater Salad: I'm getting concerned. If you're missing, the only thing I know about him is he's a stripper. That won't give the cops much to go by. Text me back.

Tater Salad: Or CALL me!! That's even better.

The room spun and tilted around me. My knees grew weak. The temperature in the room rose about ten degrees until beads of sweat ran down the back of my neck. My stomach twisted into knots, bile rising in my throat.

If this was true—if Kelsey was pregnant with *my* baby—this was not the way I would've wanted to find out. And the more I thought about that, the more I worried that I'd gotten it all wrong, that she wasn't pregnant with my baby. In which case, the thought of her having another man's baby made me sick. I wanted to assume it was mine— if she truly was pregnant—but I knew exactly what happened when assumptions were made with only pieces of information. And as much as I wanted to be happy about the prospect of this being real, I really didn't care for the destruction of my hopes if it wasn't.

There were too many questions floating around in my head and no one here to answer them. Not to mention, I had no way of getting ahold of Kelsey to even ask. The only thing I could do was go about my day and wait for her to show up looking for her phone.

By some small miracle, I managed to get the waiting room put back to normal, stuff the blow-up mattress and bedding into my truck, and make it to the gym before Noel pulled into the parking lot. But through it all, I couldn't get my thoughts to switch to anything else. I was in a perpetual tunnel that did nothing but echo Tatum's texts all around me. I felt like I was drowning, the world closing in on me.

There was only one thing I could do.

Twenty minutes later, I pulled into the parking lot of Kelsey's apartment and noticed her getting into her car. She didn't see me, so I parked my truck behind her, blocking her in. I needed to keep her from leaving before she told me everything.

As soon as she saw me with her phone in my hand, her shoulders dropped, relief flooding her posture. "I was just about to head over to your office to see if I left it there. I didn't even remember taking it inside with me, so that was the last place I thought to check. Thank you so much for bringing it over, but you didn't have to. I could've come to get it."

Without a word, I handed her the device and then carefully watched her expression as the next few moments played out.

Rather than look at the screen, she moved closer and tilted her head back, silently requesting my lips. But I wouldn't give them to her until I had answers. Until I could breathe again, and the only way that would happen was if I heard her tell me the news and then explain everything to me. Most importantly, I wanted to make sure that her visit last night had been sincere. If she'd only come to tell me about the baby, I needed to understand why she had changed her mind and slept with me instead.

I cradled her cheek in my palm, running my thumb in soothing strokes along her porcelain skin. "Tatum texted you several times. I think she's worried about you. You should probably let her know that you're okay—that the stripper who knocked you up didn't kill you after you told him the news."

Her hazel eyes widened, darkened, matching the shock and fear that was written all over her face. Panic filled the gasp that escaped her quivering lips. Anxiety brightened her cheeks until they were a cherry red, just a hint at the fire flooding her system while she stood there, staring at me like I were a ghost.

She took a step backward and dropped her attention to the device in her hand. Her body shivered as she attempted to unlock the cell to read the messages. And the entire time she did that, I just stood there and watched, reading her expressions and body language.

"Aaron . . ." she whispered, lifting her glassy eyes to mine after pulling up Tatum's messages. "I don't know what to say."

"The truth is a pretty good place to start."

She nodded and then stared at the ground for a moment, pulling herself together. When her eyes met mine again, fear danced in the dark outer edges of the irises while hope blossomed in the golden striations.

"Are you pregnant?" I hoped I could move this conversation along.

"Yes," she answered with a slow, almost uncomfortable nod.

"Am . . . am I the father?"

"Yes, but just hear me out."

Warmth spread through my body, starting in my chest and ending in my fingertips and toes. My face flushed, and I wasn't sure I'd be able to get through the rest of this without sweeping her off her feet and carrying her inside to kiss away her nerves and assure her that everything would be okay.

But somehow, I managed to steel myself long enough to gently catch her chin between my thumb and forefinger. "I'm here to listen to you, Kelsey. I didn't come to confront you. I'm just really confused why you didn't tell me last night."

"I wanted to. That's what I had planned to talk to you about, but once we finally got in the same room, and we weren't yelling at one another . . . I just wanted to be with you, Aaron. I didn't want you to think it was only because of the baby. So I figured we could have our night together, and then I could tell you when you got home today."

"Who all knows?"

"Just Tatum. I plan to tell my parents this weekend, but I wanted to tell you first."

I lowered my hand from her chin to her neck, tracing the dip in her clavicle with my thumb. Her gravitational pull was too much to resist, and honestly, I didn't want to. I sucked in a deep breath and pressed my lips to hers. Soft at first. Then harder, claiming her. Reminding her of how good we were together. And once I felt satisfied that she'd gotten the hint, I broke the kiss, resting my forehead on hers.

"I appreciate that you wanted me to know before your family. And I understand why you didn't tell me last night . . . I just wish I hadn't found out from anyone but you. I would've rather it'd been *you* who told me, but I know it's not your fault."

Her breath rushed out at the same time she tucked her face into the crook of my neck and gripped the sides of my shirt. "I'm so sorry, Aaron. I really wanted to be the one to tell you. It's just been so hard with you moving in and everything being up in the air—then the whole

Noel thing and you leaving. I just kept waiting for the right time, and the longer it went on, the harder it became to tell you."

The whole world stopped spinning, and I froze. Not a single muscle in my body working properly. My arms dangled by my sides, and my hands balled into fists, all while Kelsey curled into me, expecting support. Comfort. Acceptance. Hell, I had no idea what she sought from me, because I couldn't think past the words she'd just uttered to even consider what she needed.

"How long have you known?" My mind whirled. It didn't make any sense. "We had sex a little less than a month ago, so my moving in shouldn't have had anything to do with it." More questions hit me, almost knocking me off my feet. "And how could you have possibly known the next day when you came to my office? When you found Noel and her husband having sex?"

She cleared her throat and pulled away, just enough to peer up at me without taking a step back. "I found out right before the wedding."

The bachelorette party.

Our first night together.

"So you've been pregnant for . . . over two months?" Heat flamed my face, and no matter how hard I tried, I couldn't keep the anger from reaching my voice. "And you never told me? You've known this whole time, and you never said anything to me? We've spent almost every evening together for weeks. *Weeks*, Kelsey."

"I didn't know it was you at the time, Aaron. All I knew was that I'd slept with a stripper, woke up the next morning with a condom wrapper stuck to my face and bits and pieces of our night together floating around in my head. And when I called the entertainment company I'd used to hire the stripper, they told me that he never showed up. At that time, I didn't have a clue who I had slept with. I didn't have a clue who the father of my child was."

"Okay, fine. I get why you didn't say anything when you first found out. But you knew it was me the night of the rehearsal. You've had *plenty* of time and opportunities to come clean. Why haven't you?"

She shrugged. She fucking shrugged as if this weren't a big deal. As if keeping me in the dark for nearly two months about being a father was no different than forgetting to mention that a telemarketer had called looking for me.

I retreated one step, then two, shaking my head. Full of pain and anger and disappointment. Heavy with betrayal and resentment. Looking at her now, I almost didn't recognize her. This wasn't the same person I'd spent those last seven weeks with. The one I'd shared evenings on the couch with. This wasn't the girl I'd dreamed about being with.

"I tried. Several times."

"Oh yeah? When, Kelsey? When did you *try* to tell me? And what stopped you?"

Tears welled in her eyes, and as soon as she spoke, the pain ran free—flowing in rivers down her cheeks and flooding her voice with unfeigned agony. "The night of the wedding, when you came to the lobby and we sat on the bench to talk. I tried to say it then, but you kept cutting me off. And again later that night when you came to my room. You told me to just forget it had happened."

"And you couldn't have found any other opportunity to mention the fact that I'm going to be a dad? That you and I were having a baby together?" I froze, a lump in my throat threatening to silence me forever. "Were you . . . did you . . ."

"Did I what?"

I cleared my throat and fisted my hands. "Were you planning on getting rid of it?"

"No, Aaron. That never crossed my mind."

"Then I just don't understand why you've kept it a secret. It's not like we haven't gotten along or spent any time together. I could see you not wanting to tell me if I was an asshole to you. But I wasn't. What more did you want from me?" Betrayal ate away at me from the inside out, like a parasite that wouldn't relent until every ounce of me had rotted away.

"I was worried about how you'd react. And since we were living together, I figured it'd be best if I waited until after you moved out. That way, if you didn't take the news well, I wouldn't have to see you every day. Then we slept together again, and I thought . . . maybe this could work. Maybe we could be something. You acted like you wanted that—but then the next day happened. I thought I had heard you tell Noel that you loved her. How was I supposed to say something then? I felt like a fool."

My heart wanted to relate to her, wanted to understand how hard it must've been for her to hold on to this for so long. But I couldn't. While my heart wanted to accept her reasons, it was far too broken to win the war against my mind—the part of me that wanted to turn away from her, from the betrayal she'd delivered.

So that's what I did. In the end, my mind won, and I left. I didn't bother to look in my rearview mirror, to see her standing exactly where I'd left her. And as the day went on, I didn't care to reach out to her, didn't care to see how she was or try to talk about anything.

Noel asked me several times if I was all right, and each time, I dismissed her concern. It was unlike me, and she knew it. I'd always been a happy, fun-loving guy, even when things were tough or I had something on my mind. So the fact that I didn't care to share anything with her was a big red flag, one she clearly noticed.

"Listen, if you don't wanna talk about it, I won't make you. It's obvious that whatever has you down is a big deal. I just want you to know that I'm here if you need advice or just a listening ear." Noel had always been like a kid sister to me, except I could share private, personal things with her without the disgust of *actually* being siblings. Leaning on her for advice—especially advice on women—had become a regular occurrence.

I doubted I'd be able to talk to her about this just yet. I still hadn't processed it, and until I did that, there wasn't anything she could advise me on. "I appreciate that, Noel. I honestly do, but right now, I just need to absorb it all. I'm sure you'll get an earful on Monday."

Her gentle smile did enough to warm my heart and give me hope.

If only I could make it through the weekend in one piece—which would've been a hell of a lot easier had my parents not called me on Saturday.

"Mom, move the phone down a little." Staring at the screen, I could see only my mother's eyes and forehead. Even though she had no clue how to use FaceTime on the phone, she insisted on video calling me to see my face.

"There . . . is that better?" It was not—unless looking at her chin was better than her forehead.

"You should be able to see yourself in the small square in the corner of the phone." As soon as those words came out of my mouth, she pulled the camera closer to her face, likely to see this square I spoke of. "Yeah, Mom. It's better."

"Can you see me now?"

I couldn't, but there was no point in wasting my time with her on her videography skills. "Yes, and you look beautiful. As always."

"Are you getting excited about the house? It's only two more weeks, right?"

A long, harsh sigh blew past my lips. And somehow, *that* managed to get her attention enough to pull the phone away until I could see her whole face in the picture. Go figure.

"Oh no. What happened with the house?" The concern in her voice nearly gutted me.

"Nothing, Mom. It's not the house."

"Then what is it?"

Here went nothing . . .

Before, every time I'd been to the Petersons' house for Sunday lunch, I'd come with Kelsey. This was the first time I'd gone alone, driven myself, shown up before Jason and Tatum.

I'd avoided Jason all weekend, telling him I was busy getting things set up for the closing. It wasn't all a lie—I did have things I needed to do, just not *this* weekend. The truth was, I couldn't face him. Not yet. There was a chance he'd be pissed and want to take his anger out on me. And he had every right to, yet that didn't mean I deserved it. I guess I needed to truly face everything before defending myself to him.

And the first thing I needed to face was Kelsey telling her parents.

Like hell I'd let her do that alone—for several reasons. I was just as much a part of this as she was, and no matter how I felt about her right then, I refused to let all the burden fall on her shoulders. I had to take responsibility for my part as well. The other reasons were more selfish; I didn't want to offer Kelsey the opportunity to lay blame at my feet or allow anyone to think less of me if I wasn't there to correct any misinformation.

The truth was . . . she'd been pregnant this entire time and never told me.

Rather than just walk in like I had every other Sunday I'd been here, I knocked and waited for someone to let me in. My stomach had lodged itself in my throat, threatening to spew what little contents it had at the thought of Kelsey having already told them. I had no idea what I would face when someone came to the door—or *who* would be the one to open it.

Luckily, it was Diane, Kelsey's mother. And she had the brightest smile on her lips. I assumed that meant Kelsey hadn't told them anything. "Oh, come in, Aaron. I didn't think we'd get to see you this weekend."

"I guess I'm a sucker for your pasta salad." I leaned over to return her hug and then followed her down the hall to the living room, where I noticed Kelsey sitting in an armchair, her back to me.

Diane led me into the room without so much as a hint of hesitation, pretty much confirming that nothing had been said yet, but by the way Fred, Kelsey's father, sat on the edge of the couch across from her, I could tell she'd already prepared them to hear something. "Look who decided to come after all," Diane announced once we made it past the kitchen.

Fred glanced up while Kelsey turned in her seat, her shocked eyes meeting mine.

"Good morning, everyone. I hope I'm not too late." I made sure to direct that last part at Kelsey, ensuring she'd picked up on the meaning. "Sorry for intruding, but I really wanted to be here for this."

Kelsey stood and placed both hands against my chest, pushing me away slightly while whispering, "Why are you here?"

With a downy touch along her lower back, I dropped my lips to her ear, not once caring if the signals I was giving her were mixed. "If you think I'm going to let you make me the bad guy with your family, you might want to think again."

Her breath hitched in her throat as she pulled away, turning to face her parents.

Diane clapped, eyes wide and bright as if expecting good news. "Oh, are you two dating? Is that what you wanted to tell us? This is just . . . ah, so amazing."

"No, Mom. That's not it. In fact, Aaron has decided to stay somewhere else until he closes on his house in two weeks."

Oh, hell no. I wasn't about to let her throw me under the bus like that, knowing the next thing she would tell them was that she was having my baby. That'd make me look like a piece of shit, and I wasn't about to let that happen. "It wasn't by choice, and you know it. So please, don't make it sound like I ran out on you. I'm here, am I not?"

While I spoke low so that my words were aimed at Kelsey, I didn't bother to keep her parents from overhearing. It was important to me that they understand more about the situation than I knew she'd let on. Because the last thing I wanted to do was defend myself after the fact; that would only make me look like more of a piece of shit by pointing a finger at their daughter right after they learned that I had knocked up their little girl. Yeah . . . not happening.

Kelsey cleared her throat and resumed her seat in the chair, leaving me to stand next to her. I didn't bother to move or step away, only rested my hand against the back of the seat and waited for her to share the news.

"I'm sure this will come as a shock to you, but I can assure you that it was just as much—if not more—of a shock to me." Her voice quivered, and I had to fight against my desire to touch her, comfort her, let her know she wasn't alone. "And I wanted to come here early so that you two were the first to know."

It was in that moment that I realized my reason for being here for this wasn't at all to defend myself. It had nothing to do with ensuring she didn't bury the blame at my feet. No. My need to be here, to listen to her tell her parents, went beyond that. I had to hear her say it, because I hadn't heard those words come from her mouth. Even when I'd confronted Kelsey, she hadn't come out and actually said that she was pregnant. With my baby. I'd asked her, and she'd told me yes; however, she'd still never uttered the one phrase I deserved to hear fall from her lips.

"I'm pregnant." She gulped, her throat dipping deep with the harsh swallow. And without glancing at me, she added, "Aaron and I are having a baby."

Before I could absorb her words or figure out how I genuinely felt about them, I was caught off guard by Diane's reaction. Her trembling fingers covered her parted lips, the same thing Kelsey did when she wanted to conceal a gasp or hide her overwhelming emotions. An exploding star had nothing on the blinding elation in her eyes, and even though a tear slipped free, slithering over her cheekbone, it shone with the happiness it'd been born in.

This was a far cry from the reaction I had expected, as well as the one she'd had on hearing Jason and Tatum's news. Rather than boisterous excitement, she appeared to be filled with unmistakable pride, overflowing joy, and the purest love rooted in her marrow. Not one ounce of rejection or hesitation registered on her face.

Fred, on the other hand, had a slightly different reaction. There was no denying the happiness in his eyes, but I had to look past the shock, confusion, and disappointment to see it. Then again, he was her father. I'd almost anticipated that to be his response. If my child was a girl, I'd probably react the same way.

I had to stop myself for a moment, recognizing how that had been the first time I'd thought those words. *My child.* It brought up a swelling sensation in my chest and left my body scalding just below my skin.

No matter how badly I fought it, I couldn't stop myself from reaching down and placing my hand on Kelsey's shoulder. Although, I did have enough strength to keep myself from looking into her eyes—but maybe that had more to do with fear than strength.

Chapter 19

Kelsey

"Are you guys going to say anything?" Worry strangled me as I sat there and watched my parents stare at me in shock. If my heart sped up any faster, I'd be in cardiac arrest at any moment. I wasn't sure how much more of this I could take. And if Aaron thought his touch was calming, he couldn't have been more wrong.

While Mom sat there and stared at me with wide, glossy eyes, my dad sat forward, his elbows dug into the tops of his thighs. He glanced between Aaron and me, but I couldn't quite read his expression. His brows were drawn closer together, yet the lines in his forehead were mere hollows, not yet the valleys they became when he was mad. However, his lips were pressed into a flat line, which generally indicated his unrest.

"You said he moved out?" Dad's question might have been directed at me, and his attention might have pinned me to my seat, yet there was no doubt in my mind that this was meant more for Aaron.

"I did, sir," Aaron answered from over my shoulder, his strong, unwavering tone nearly begging me to look at him. "I'm not sure how much you both know, but I have recently bought a house."

"And do you plan to move Kelsey and the baby in with you?" Dad wouldn't let up, but at least he had his sights on Aaron this time instead of speaking to him through me. "Or are you going to make her raise this child on her own?"

At this point, I had to take a stand—literally. I was on my feet in less than a second, positioning myself between Aaron and my dad, though I had no idea why, other than to protect him any way I could. "That's enough, Dad. This is between Aaron and me, and we haven't gotten that far yet. Okay? Let us work that part out, and we'll keep you guys in the loop."

Everything fell apart after that.

The front door opened, and Aunt Lori came in. She was always the first one here, which meant it was only a matter of time before Jason and Tatum would show up. If I had to guess, we had less than ten minutes—five if Marlena and her brood were on their way.

Mom wrapped me in her arms, hugging me so tightly I wasn't sure I'd ever be able to catch my breath again. And while my mom squeezed me, Dad took Aaron to the side, as if this had all been planned to keep me from defending him to my parents. And then there was Aunt Lori, setting her stuff in the kitchen without a clue what was happening.

"Oh, congratulations, Kelsey!" Okay, so maybe she did have a clue.

I planned to kill Tatum and her big fat mouth.

Mom released me and turned to her sister—their resemblance was uncanny sometimes. Generally speaking, someone might guess they were related, though not sisters. But then there were moments like these when they'd look at each other with complete opposite expressions on their faces, yet they could've been twins.

That was it—Mom's shock was identical to my aunt's excitement. Which didn't say much about either one of them. If anything, it made me want to take a look in the mirror to make sure I didn't get that gene.

"You knew?" Mom gaped at Aunt Lori, then swung her betrayed eyes to me. "How did she know before we did?"

I was just about to open my mouth and explain to her how best friends work—how Tatum and I typically tell each other everything before anyone else—when my aunt cut me off. She flicked her wrist and fluttered her lashes, a rapid eye roll that she reserved for moments of dismissal. "Oh, Diane . . . I didn't know. But I do now."

"So you just guessed she was pregnant and went with it, hoping you were right?" Mom propped her fist on her hip, no longer paying any attention to anyone else in the room. If anything, she appeared to be in awe of her sister.

Then it dawned on me.

Aunt Lori was sneaky. Her sweet and innocent persona was just that—a facade.

With a hand on my mom's shoulder, I carefully turned her just enough to face me. "She didn't, Mom. All she said was congrats. That could mean so many things. You're the one who just told her what it was."

I wish I could've seen the look my mother gave her sister as she peered to the side, but I couldn't, because right then, my attention was pulled to my dad and Aaron. Technically, it was pulled to Dad's growly voice, but once I noticed how Aaron had dropped his head forward, almost in shame, I couldn't look away.

And again, before I could address that situation, more people came down the hall into the kitchen. Connor, my nephew, ran into the room and latched on to my dad's leg. "Paw Paw! I got a new truck, Paw Paw! Wanna play it wif me?" And just like that, my dad's entire demeanor changed.

He picked up Connor and swooped him into the kitchen, leaving Aaron behind with his chin tucked to his chest. I desperately wanted to go to him, make this right, but I wasn't sure if he even wanted me to. It wasn't a secret that he was angry with me, but that didn't mean I felt the same. Truthfully, I felt the complete opposite. I hated how I'd hurt him, and anytime he set his betrayed eyes on me, it only made the knot in my stomach tighten. The ache in my chest deepen.

I wanted to go to him, but I couldn't, because Marlena chose that instant to shout, "Oh my God, you're pregnant? How far along are you?"

"Two months," Aaron answered for me, suddenly finding his voice.

"Are you kidding me? Two months? Why would you keep that from me?" My sister could be perceptive when she wanted to be. "Wait. This is the first time you've told anyone?"

Aaron stepped up, and the thought of what he'd say terrified me. "Technically Friday was the first time she told anyone, and that was me."

"What about Tatum?" I had no idea who'd asked that, but whoever it was had impeccable timing, because just then, my best friend appeared in the kitchen and froze in shock at the sound of her name.

Her eyes shifted between everyone in the room while she stood frozen, like a deer caught in headlights. "What about me?"

"Did you know she's two months pregnant?" Marlena turned to my best friend. "Oh, why am I wasting my breath? Of course you did. I bet you knew from the beginning, didn't you?"

Tatum said, "I'm not sure if I should answer that," at the same time Jason turned his bugged eyes to me and asked, "You're pregnant?"

This couldn't have been better scripted for a comedy show.

"Well, I guess the cat's out of the bag." Tatum clapped her hands and moved farther into the kitchen, feigned confidence straightening her posture. "And I gotta say . . . it's about time."

"So you've known all along?" Jason pinned her with a stare.

"Well, yes, but only because she needed someone to read the stick for her. I've been trying to get her to announce it, but she didn't want to do that until she told the father, and for some reason, that's taken forever and a day."

And when Tatum was nervous, she didn't stop talking.

"Then again, I don't really blame her. She developed feelings for him, but then he kinda smashed those dreams when she caught him—"

"Tatum, that's enough." I needed her to shut up. *Now.*

"I'm sorry. I don't want to make him out to be a bad person or anything; I haven't even met him. So he could be a really great guy for all I know. I guess only time will tell."

"Wait." My mom finally spoke up, moving toward the center of the circle created by the members of my obnoxious family, arms out at her sides like she was warding off a brawl. "I thought you said you and *Aaron* were having a baby. Is he not the father?"

"*What?*" Tatum shrieked—I'm pretty sure Marlena harmonized with her, too. "Aaron Baucus? *That* Aaron? The one standing right there?"

"Yes. Aaron's the father. *This* Aaron."

Before anyone could say or do anything else, Jason turned cold eyes on his best friend, who refused to look at him. "*You* knocked up my baby cousin? The one thing I told you before I even asked if you could stay at her place was that you didn't touch her."

Silence fell over the entire room. Seconds later, my dad carried Connor to the back patio while my mom followed with my niece in her arms. Aunt Lori wasn't far behind, leaving the four of us—plus my sister—in the room alone. Marlena stuck out like a sore thumb, yet there was no way she would've missed this opportunity. She wasn't one who enjoyed drama in her life, but she sure as hell ate up everyone else's anytime she could.

"It's not what you think." Aaron finally spoke, his hands up as if surrendering. "She was already pregnant when I moved in."

That was all it took to drag Jason around the breakfast bar into the living room, closer to where we stood. "And you didn't bother to mention that when I suggested you stay with her for a few months?"

"I didn't know, man. I swear. She just told me two days ago. Trust me . . . this is as much of a shock to me as it is to you."

"If she was already pregnant by the time you moved in, and you two hadn't met until the night before the wedding . . . how could you be the father?"

With this, Marlena sat on a barstool to witness it all, no doubt planning to use this to fill Mom in on what she'd missed. My life was seriously becoming the next episode of *Jerry Springer*.

Aaron turned his attention to me, silently asking me to step in and explain the parts he couldn't—considering this likely wasn't the most comfortable thing to discuss with my cousin, best friend of his or not.

"We met at Boots the night of Tatum's bachelorette party." I took a deep breath and lifted my gaze to the ceiling, unable to look at anyone as I gave as much information as I could without dirtying my image. "I didn't know who he was, and he had no idea I was your cousin. So while we technically met a few weeks before your wedding, we didn't realize who the other was until the night of the rehearsal. When we ran into each other at the elevators."

"Back up a second . . . I think I'm missing something." Marlena couldn't just sit there and listen. No. She *had* to get all the details, even when it had nothing to do with her. "How did you two *not* know who the other was? I guess you both have rather common names, but come on. It was a bachelorette party—one I now wish I'd gone to. Did you not once stop and think of the coincidences? You know . . . like how you had a friend who was about to get married, whose cousin's name is Kelsey, who also happens to be the bride's best friend? None of that came to mind?"

Again, Aaron refused to answer, only regarded me with pleading eyes, begging me to save him. I couldn't deny him that, especially after all I'd already put him through, so I huffed, shoulders dropped in resignation, and filled in the missing pieces as best as I could. "It's not like we stopped to think about much, Mar. We were both in somewhat of a shitty place that night and found a way to get each other through it."

"Oh my *God.*" Jason cringed, disgust dripping from every pore on his face. "The necktie?"

I whipped my head to the side to regard Aaron. "You told him about that?"

"Don't pretend like you didn't give details to Tatum."

"Hey, don't bring me into this," Tatum called from the other side of the breakfast bar, too worried to come much closer, likely out of fear of getting burned. "I'm an innocent bystander here. I had no idea you were the stripper."

"Stripper?" Dammit, Marlena.

"He only pretended to be one that night. It's a long story. No point in rehashing it now." I just wanted this to be over already. "Can we maybe finish this conversation another time? It seems we're all caught up on the important stuff—I'm pregnant; Aaron's the father; I kept it a secret from everyone for two months. Oh, and apparently, I'm a slut."

I turned to make my way back to the chair I'd been in before all this had fallen apart, needing a moment to myself, even though I'd still technically be around everyone—I just wouldn't have to see the judgment in their eyes. But I never made it to the recliner. Aaron caught me before I could take two steps, his large hand wrapped around my upper arm.

"Don't ever say that again." His hushed voice flooded my ear with heat, fueled by what I could only describe as aggression. The rawness of his words was enough to make me pause and look at him, but his eyes were what made me listen. "Regardless of the situation or how we got to this place, none of that makes you a slut, and hearing you say that about yourself pisses me off. You're not even close to one. I never want to hear you degrade yourself like that again."

My thighs clenched together as his demand filled my body with intense arousal. And once again, I hated the fact that he was angry with me, because I wanted nothing more than to haul him into one of the back rooms and let him have his way with me.

Oddly enough, all I could say was, "I'm sorry."

He released his hold on me and took a step back, though he kept his voice just as low as when his lips had been against my ear. "Don't apologize to me. I wasn't the one talking shit about you just now . . . that was *you*." And then he walked away.

I was in too much of a mental fog to grasp everything as it happened, but he apparently left. Jason followed him out to the driveway while Tatum made her way to me. Marlena voiced a few questions, none of which I responded to, yet Tatum answered what she could—which wasn't much, considering I'd left her out of the loop as much as everyone else.

And before I knew it, my parents and aunt were back inside, the kids running around as if nothing had happened. Jason headed down to the dock to help my dad with the grill, Marlena took Connor and Lizzie to the patio with Mom, and Aunt Diane helped Tatum in the kitchen. All in all, this was a normal Sunday.

Except for the whole having-Aaron's-baby thing.

Oh, and Mom fawning all over me—though it seemed my having a baby only made her play matchmaker even harder than before.

I didn't even bother to get off the couch when Tatum opened the front door. She'd always just walked in before, so there was no reason to change things now. Not to mention, I was elbow deep in mint chocolate chip, and at this juncture, nothing was worth putting the ice cream scoop down.

"Really?" She waved her hand around the room, closing the door behind her. It wasn't often my apartment was a mess, but when it was, Tatum was the *last* person I wanted to see it this way. She was probably calling me a hypocrite to herself. "This is how you solve your problems? Feet on the coffee table, reality TV on the screen, and a tub of ice cream in your lap?"

"Is there a better way?"

"Yeah . . . it's called *get off your ass and do something about it.*"

"What am I supposed to do about it, Tater?" I sat up, though I didn't put the giant spoon down. That would not leave my hand anytime soon. "Please, tell me, because it's pretty apparent that I can't make decisions for myself these days. I swear, this baby is making me irrational and stupid."

She slowly lowered herself onto the cushion next to me. "Kels . . . put down the spoon and move away from the carton. Everything will be all right. I promise. But nothing will get solved with ice cream and a stained . . . is that a Justin Bieber T-shirt?"

I swung a small couch pillow at her and laughed. Damn, it did feel good to feel the rumbles reverberate through my chest and the heat of the smile strain my cheeks. After today, after the ups and downs at my parents' house, I hadn't been sure when I'd experience that again.

"I messed up, okay?" Just because I'd decided to talk did *not* mean I'd give up my mint chocolate chip. "There's nothing I can do to fix any of this. If there was, I would've done it already. This isn't how I imagined any of this would go. I don't know what to do."

"Well, considering you've left me out of most of this loop, why don't you start from the beginning?"

I gave her a side-eye while scooping another spoonful into my mouth. "The only part of the loop I didn't fill in for you is that Aaron's the father. Other than that *one* piece of information, you know everything."

"Why didn't you tell me about Aaron?"

"At the time, I had no idea."

"You're seriously gonna have to start from the beginning. So you brought the stripper home the night of my bachelorette party. That's when you got pregnant . . . right?" Tatum waited for my nod before continuing. "That phone call in the hotel, right before we headed downstairs for the rehearsal . . . was that real? Or did you already know at that point?"

"The phone call was real. I didn't know who he was until a few minutes later when I got to the elevators—when you were doing what you were doing in Jason's room. In fact . . . I didn't know that was Aaron until you showed up and mentioned it. I just thought I'd randomly run into the stripper that I was looking for, not at all realizing who he really was."

"And how did he end up the stripper at my party?"

I shrugged and fought hard to keep the smile off my face. It wasn't funny. Shouldn't have been funny. Yet the irony got to me every time. "Our guy never showed up . . . as you know. So I guess someone who works at Boots, one of Aaron's friends, called him to fill in—except he didn't know what he was filling in for. I'd asked for a doctor, and apparently, since Aaron's a doctor, she thought he would be a good stand-in. It didn't hurt that he has a hard time getting women, and we were a group of drunk women . . . stone, meet two birds."

Out of *everything* I'd just said, the one thing she picked up on was Aaron's inability to get a date. "What do you mean, he has a hard time getting women? That man is with someone new every time I turn around. It's why we never meet them, because they—" Her mouth fell open, eyes wide with realization. "That little sneak."

"Let me guess . . . he makes it seem like he's a ladies' man?"

"Oh yeah. Big-time. I never would've guessed. Although . . . Jay has always made a joke of it. I don't think he's ever believed Aaron when he talks about his conquests. I'm pretty sure he just plays along."

Yup. This bloodsucking fetus inside me had officially made me lose my mind, because the thought of Aaron lying to his friends about being a player when the truth was far from it made me fall for him even harder. It made me think of a little boy, alone on the playground, watching everyone around him have fun. And that only fueled the hurt

I already felt for him, for all I'd done to him, kept from him, accused him of.

"But still . . ." It seemed Tatum had spent too long with my sister, because she'd adopted Marlena's way of beating the same thing to death. "Why didn't you tell me after you found out? You continued to let me think you were having a stripper's baby."

With my eyes closed, I rested my head on the back of the cushion and blew out a long sigh. "Because I knew there would be no way you'd keep that from Jason. And if Jason knew, he'd tell Aaron. I wasn't ready for that to happen yet. Granted, I guess that backfired, huh?"

She placed her hand on my knee and waited until I opened my eyes and met her stare before saying anything. "I'm sure he'll come around. He just needs to sort through it. The only thing you can do is prove to him that your heart was in the right place. Be honest with him, Kels."

"I don't know how to do that." The best way to keep people from knowing that you're crying is to shove more ice cream into your mouth. You can always say that the tears in your eyes are from the brain freeze. Foolproof excuse.

"Go to him. Tell him how you feel."

"Been there. Done that."

"Did he not listen?"

I needed to put the carton away before it leaked through the cardboard and drenched my perfectly good shirt in melted ice cream. But I didn't want to be too far away from it in case I needed more, so I chose to put it on the coffee table instead. That was about as far as I could go.

"I fucked up. Okay? The night of your dinner, we slept together. I told you about it, just didn't tell you who it was. Anyway, the next day, I went to tell him about the baby."

"Yes, I recall. This was the first time, right? When you caught him having sex with someone else?" At least she retained the things I told her. That was a plus. Kept me from having to repeat myself.

"Correct. Except he *wasn't* sleeping with anyone else. In fact . . . he wasn't even there. Long story short, his assistant, Noel, is a freak—and I mean that in the really good way. She and her husband were getting it on in his office while he was at the hospital for some consulting thing. I'm not entirely sure what he was doing, since his job still doesn't make a lot of sense to me. But that's not the point."

"Then get to the point, Kels. I'm growing grey hairs over here."

Arching just one brow, I glared at her, then gave up when she laughed. At me . . . not with me, because I wasn't laughing. "The *point*, which you're so eager to hear, is that when he came home that night— completely unaware of what had taken place at his office earlier that day—I shut him out and basically accused him of being no different than my ex."

"The prick? Ew. That's gotta be the dirtiest insult ever."

"Yes. And he didn't even fully understand it at the time." My chest tightened as I recounted all the ways I'd hurt that poor boy on the play- ground. "He tried for, like, a week and a half to break down my walls, but I refused to let him. In the end, I was wrong. Clearly. And when I went Thursday night to tell him everything, we got caught up in our feelings for each other, so I never got the words out."

"What do you mean . . . your *feelings*?"

I shrugged and stared at my fingers twisted together in my lap, sticky from ice cream. "I think I'm in love with him."

Silence.

When Tatum was nervous, you couldn't shut her up with a mute button. But when she was stunned, it was like someone had stolen all the words from her pretty little head. Too bad there wasn't a balance in between.

"Say something, Tater," I pleaded, finally giving in and looking into her eyes so she could see the desperation in mine. "I've needed my best friend for weeks, but I haven't been able to go to her because of the hole I dug myself. It just kept getting deeper and deeper, and now I'm suffocating in it."

She finally snapped out of it and wrapped her arms around me, pulling me to her. "One of these days, we'll learn to stop keeping things from the other person. Trust me . . . I know all too well how lonely it is to live with a secret you can't share with your bestie."

I sniffled and wiped my cheeks with the back of my hand. "I fucked up, didn't I?"

"You never know." She took a deep breath and leaned away a little bit, which meant she didn't believe her own words. "Aaron's a really great guy. I never would've asked you to let him move in if I thought differently."

Laughter curled my lips. "You just got done telling me how you thought he was a player."

"That doesn't mean he can't be a good person." She waved me off and rolled her eyes. It was like old times all over again. "And if I'm being honest, I thought the whole womanizer thing would prevent you from sleeping with him. I know how you feel about players."

"Yeah, well . . . that might've worked *before* I slept with him."

"You mean before you got pregnant."

"Same thing." Not really. Aaron had to be the most skilled lover I'd ever been with. Pregnant or not, there was a good chance I would've found myself tangled up in his sheets again—even if he *were* an avid collector of bedpost notches. "But you're right. He is a good person. Unfortunately, it took me too long to be as open and honest with him as he's been with me, and now he's gone."

"He's not gone, Kels."

"Yeah, he is. He's not even staying here. He's sleeping on an air mattress on the floor of his office. He'd rather take showers at the gym every morning than stay here. I've lost him."

The only sound in the room was Tatum's deep inhalation, which she held for longer than usual. "He's seriously living in his office?"

"Waiting room floor, but same thing."

"Does anyone else know?" Concern stuck to her voice like cement, weighing it down.

I shook my head, yet I decided to give her more than that. "I don't think so. He gets up early so he can be out and have the chairs all moved back before Noel shows up in the mornings. I couldn't begin to guess if he's told anyone else."

"Why didn't he ask any of his friends to stay with them? We have a spare room he could've stayed in until the sale of his house goes through."

I glared at her. "Really, Tatum? If he had gone to Jason, he'd have to explain why he's not staying here anymore. Even before he found out about the baby, what was he supposed to tell him? That we slept together and then I turned on him? Um, no."

"Hmm . . ." She quirked her mouth to the side in thought. "You're right. Jay probably would've killed him."

"That's a little hypocritical, don't ya think, Tater? Jason, my cousin, worried about his best friend sleeping with me? When . . . oh, that's right, Jason, my cousin, had no problem at all sleeping with you . . . *my* best friend."

"It's not the same."

"Oh, it's *exactly* the same."

"Fine. It's literally identical. Except for the part about you getting pregnant after a one-night stand with *his* best friend, prior to you knowing he was your cousin's best friend. And then him moving in with you, where you continued to have sex with him while keeping it from him that you were carrying his baby. That's nothing like what happened with Jay and me."

I blinked a few times, wondering how she'd managed to get one up on me. That never happened. It was a sure sign of the apocalypse. Too bad I'd never taken those prepper shows seriously. I could've used a buried school bus and a massive stash of astronaut food right about now. "Let's go back to my cousin, the hypocrite, shall we?"

"No . . . we shall go back to you fixing things with Aaron."

All humor died on my lips. "I don't know how, Tatum."

"I have an idea. But it won't happen overnight. Are you willing to put in the time?"

"Of course. We're going to be tied together for at least the next eighteen years. All I have is time at this point." I realized at that moment how badly I didn't want to *only* be tied to him due to having a child together. I wanted more. With him.

"All right. This is what you need to do . . ."

Chapter 20

Aaron

I flung the office door open, expecting to find Kelsey, but I found Jason instead.

As if seeing him and his entire family earlier today wasn't enough.

"What is with everyone coming to my office at almost midnight and waking me up? Don't you know there are plenty of daylight hours you could use to talk to me? Oh, and a phone? You should try that next time."

"I did, asshole." He pushed past me and invited himself in—just like Kelsey had. If he thought we'd cuddle on my mattress, too, then he needed to think again. "You didn't answer, which left me no choice but to come here."

"If I didn't answer, there's probably a good reason for that. Like, maybe I was . . . *sleeping*?"

Thank God he chose to take a seat in one of the chairs instead of on my mattress. Things had already gotten weird between us earlier today at the Petersons' house. I wasn't sure how much worse they could get, and I wasn't in the mood to find out.

I stood in front of him with my arms crossed over my chest—at least I'd had the forethought before lying down to put a shirt on. Didn't need him gawking at my body the way Kelsey had. And it would be lovely if I stopped comparing Jason to Kelsey. Or better yet . . . just stopped thinking of Kelsey.

Yeah . . . I doubted that would happen anytime soon.

Or ever.

"What do you want, Jason? Didn't you say enough this morning in your aunt's driveway?" I couldn't take another verbal beating from him. The things that guy could come up with at the drop of a dime would likely make a hitman shit himself. Okay . . . maybe not that bad, but hearing my best friend call me a *fucking piece of shit* wasn't the highlight of my day. Or week.

Jason leaned forward and covered his face with his hands, a long, dramatic exhale rushing out. "Listen, man . . . I'm sorry about that. Okay?" He met my stare, and I couldn't miss the honesty that reflected back at me. "It's one thing to find out you've been sleeping with my cousin after you adamantly swore you wouldn't, but it's another to find out you got her pregnant."

"I don't mean to poke the bear, but do you really have room to point fingers at me?"

He shook his head, and I breathed a sigh of relief that I hadn't pissed him off. Nevertheless, that didn't stop him from glaring at me while conceding. "No, not really. Which is another reason I shouldn't have come at you earlier. It caught me by surprise, and to make it all worse, I had the unfortunate knowledge of hearing the things you've said about her, not knowing it was *her*. So forgive me if I lost my shit for a second. I'm sorry."

Well, I couldn't really ask for much more than that. "You're forgiven. But is that really the reason you came here? At"—I checked my watch and groaned—"eleven thirty at night. My God. Do you people not care that I have to work in the morning? And that I have to get up even earlier to make this place look like I haven't used it as my bedroom for the last week and a half?"

Jason stood and took two steps, stopping when he was a couple of feet away, his hands deep in his front pockets. "Come stay at my place. There's no reason you should be sleeping on the floor."

"It's not on the *floor*, in case you can't tell. I have a mattress."

"Yeah, filled with air."

"What's wrong with that? Remember when waterbeds were the big thing? Well, watch out, bro, because air will be the next craze. And you'll be jealous of what I have."

He couldn't fight back his grin, and I'd never been happier to see another man smile in my life. Guys were easy—if they were pissed, they'd tell you; you'd hash it out, and then it was water under the bridge, never to be spoken of or remembered again. However, the exception to that was when you did something to someone they cared about. Fuck with a family member they actually liked—or creep up on his woman—and your ass was grass. Luckily, Jason knew me well enough to understand the complex situation we'd found ourselves in. He'd had his moment and flipped the fuck out, and we'd moved on. I only hoped this meant it'd never be brought up again. Or remembered.

"Get your shit, asshole, and let's go. Tatum has the spare room made up for you."

"How'd you even know I was here?"

He shrugged and cocked his head. "Kelsey."

"Is it too early to say anything about her big mouth?" I pretended the punch to my shoulder didn't hurt, when really, I'd be surprised if I could move it tomorrow. "Got it. Good to know. I'll keep those thoughts to myself until the time's right."

"Dude . . . the time will *never* be right." His words were harsh, his voice low with impending rage, yet the slight uptick in the corners of his mouth proved that, beneath it all, we'd be all right.

"Does this kinda make us related?"

"Not at all."

"I think it does. Our kids are going to be cousins."

"Third cousins or something ridiculous like that."

"So does that make us cousins-in-law thrice removed? Got a catchy ring to it."

He laughed. Actually laughed. Which made my chest rumble and shoulders jump as I joined in the amusement. Moving into the weekend, I'd had so much against me—my issues with Kelsey on top of finding out I was going to be a father—that adding one more thing to the pile had nearly knocked me down. What had made it worse was that the one more thing happened to have been my best friend cornering me outside to tell me how disgusting he thought I was. How I was scum and didn't deserve Kelsey. That whatever had happened between us was my fault, and she was better off without me.

I'd never seen him so angry, and there'd been many things in high school that should've made him rage, yet it'd never happened. So to see him so pissed and have that fury directed at me had sent me running.

Granted, I hadn't engaged, which had probably only irritated him more. Had I defended myself, then maybe we could've hashed it out and been done with it before I left the driveway this morning, but I hadn't seen a point in it. As mad as he'd been at me, I'd been just as angry with myself.

"Come on and get your shit together. I don't have all night. I have to work in the morning," he said with a slap on my back and a smile across his face.

"You're such a dick." I laughed and stepped away. "I'll stay at your place, but *only* because my back has been killing me. However, I'll head that way tomorrow. I'm dead on my feet, man. I don't have the energy or care to pack all this up and drive to your house before getting back to sleep."

"Not a problem. I get it." And with a solid nod, he left.

The (Secret) Baby

As much as I wanted to fall back asleep, it wasn't that easy. I tossed and turned, unable to get Kelsey off my mind. The final straw, though, was when my phone buzzed next to me, and her name flashed across the screen. That was enough to get me up . . . and keep me up.

Kelsey: Thank you for being there today. I wasn't expecting you to come, but I'm glad you did. Sorry if my dad and Jason made things worse on you.

It took a few minutes, but I eventually found the words I wanted to say.

Me: You didn't have to do that alone. And it's all right. I kind of expected it. From your dad, I mean. Not so much from Jason

Me: BTW thanks for telling him where I'm staying

Kelsey: I thought you'd be sleeping.

Kelsey: And I didn't tell him. I told Tatum. Blame her for blabbing.

Me: If you thought I would be asleep, why did you text me?

Kelsey: Did you not read the first message?? To say thanks. Also . . . I figured you'd see it in the morning, which would save me the awkwardness of an uncomfortable conversation. But here we are . . .

My smile only grew bigger.

Kelsey: I didn't wake you up, did I?

Me: No. Jason did. When he stopped by. I came here so I wouldn't be bothered, but I think I've had more visitors in the last five days than I had the entire time I lived with my parents

Kelsey: Speaking of your parents . . . have you told them yet?

Falling back into easy banter with Kelsey wasn't hard to do. But the reminder of our situation put an end to that. I wasn't sure how we would move forward or what our relationship would look like for the next eighteen years, but for now, I needed a breather. And I couldn't do that while talking to her.

Me: Yeah. I talked to them yesterday

While they were happy to have a grandchild, they weren't thrilled about *how* it'd happened. Then again, these were two people who'd probably thought I was still a virgin, considering I wasn't married. They had their opinions, and they'd advised me on what to do and how to handle the situation. But I wasn't about to tell her any of that. She didn't need to know how everyone—even my family—seemed to be on her side. Granted, they claimed they weren't on a "side," yet I wasn't sure what else it would be called when they told me to give her a chance.

Me: Listen, I have to go. Sleep beckons

A response never came, so I put the phone down and rolled over, praying slumber would come. And just before I dozed off, my cell buzzed once. I didn't need to look at it to know it was Kelsey, and I knew if I read her message, it'd be that much longer before sleep would come again. So I left it for the morning.

It was a sock emoji.

"Are you ever gonna tell me what's going on with you?" Noel invited herself into my office after the last patient left. "Something happened on Friday; it's now Tuesday. You said you'd probably talk to me after the weekend. Well, the weekend's over. Talk to me. You're starting to worry me."

"I'm having a baby."

I expected shock to color her face, yet that's not what happened at all. A smile stretched across her lips, her gaze softened, and her arms—crossed over her chest—relaxed. "That's amazing news, Aaron. How far along are you? You look great, by the way. Would've never guessed you were with child."

My shoulders shook with the humor that filled me, and had I not been in the middle of typing up notes, I probably would've laughed out loud. Instead, I picked up a pencil out of the pen holder and threw it at her. "You're a dick."

"See . . . that's what I *thought* you had, but it seems I was wrong. Granted, I've never checked, but I'd like to believe that if you didn't have one, I would've figured it out by now. I guess it does make perfect sense, though—you don't date much, can't get laid too often. I always chalked those up to you living with your parents, but now it's all so clear."

"What the hell are you going on about?" I stopped what I was doing and turned to give her my full attention. "And don't say you're still hung up on the bullshit that I'm the one who's having the baby, because we both know that's not the case."

She shrugged and then took a seat across from me, leaning into the desk with her elbows. "I figured this way you could tell me without making me pry it out of you. I don't want to be nosy and ask, so I thought this would be a better way."

"When have you *ever* been worried about butting into my personal life? You've done it for the last four years. Just ask, Noel."

"I don't butt into anything. You've always offered it up, and I'm clearly not going to stop you and tell you that I don't wanna hear the comedy show that is your dating life. So I listen. And laugh—behind your back, of course. Never to your face." Her gaze narrowed when I glared at her. "Okay, fine. I've laughed *at* you a few times. But in my defense . . . well, I don't really have a defense. Carry on."

I covered my face with my palms, hoping she couldn't see just how big my grin was. This was ridiculous. I'd had a shitty few days, more stress than I ever cared to have again, and this woman had me laughing like a teenager, like I had no reason to be so high strung.

After recovering, I shook it off and sat forward, matching her posture with my elbows on my side of the desk. "Kelsey's pregnant." I ignored her gasp and continued. "Apparently, it happened that very first night—when we met at Boots and then went back to her place. She's known since before Jason's wedding, before I moved in with her. And she's kept it from me this whole time."

It wasn't until I saw the sorrow in her eyes that I remembered her struggle with getting pregnant. I felt like an asshole, like I was complaining about my situation when I knew damn well she would've given her left arm to be in my shoes.

"I'm so sorry, Noel. I didn't mean—"

"Don't apologize. It's not like you could control any of this—well, I guess technically you could've controlled getting Kelsey pregnant by wearing a condom. But I think it's a little too late to revisit that lesson from health class."

"I did wear one. I've never *not* worn one."

"And you're sure it's your baby?"

I took a moment to contemplate that theory. "I'm about as sure as I can be without a DNA test. I don't see why she'd lie about it, especially to her family. Jason wasn't happy when he found out, and I'm just waiting for her dad to show up with a shotgun and either shoot me or demand I marry her. So really, nothing good could've possibly come from her lying about me being the father."

"And you're *sure* you wore one?"

I shifted on my chair and pulled my wallet from my back pocket. Right behind the credit card slots was a small pocket, where I'd always kept a few condoms just in case. You could never be too prepared. I pulled one out and tossed it on the desk. "I've *always* worn one."

Noel picked it up, examining the wrapper in the light at all angles, and then threw it at me with a large, ridiculous smile on her face, eyes bright and filled with amusement. "I don't understand how you can be such a brilliant professional, yet so damn stupid in the real world. Seriously, Aaron, what the hell happened to you in grad school?"

"What do you mean?" I examined the foil packet she'd tossed at me, but I didn't see anything wrong with it. I even tilted it in the light, but I didn't find any holes or puncture marks, so I didn't have the slightest clue what she'd seen when she looked at it.

"You do know they put expiration dates on those for a reason, right?" She grabbed the condom from my hand, slapped it onto the desk between us, and pointed to the numbers along the ridges at the top.

"That's fucking stupid. Why in the world would they put that there? And why is it stamped instead of printed? You think I could see that?" I picked it up for a closer look. "Eh, it's not *that* out of date."

Noel giggled, leaning back in her chair with her arms stretched over her head. "It's about as out of date as curdled milk."

I rolled my eyes and tossed the packet into the trash beneath my desk, then thought better of it and put it back in my wallet to toss it somewhere else. The last thing I needed was to have someone see it in my office and question why I'd have it there.

"What I don't understand is how you could possibly keep those things for that long." She didn't have to come out and say it, as her question insinuated it enough—it definitely made me look like I *never* got laid.

"I found them when I was packing up my room. They were always my favorite kind, so I put a few in my wallet just in case. It's not like they've been in there since I bought them."

"Let's hope not." She smirked and pulled herself to her feet. "Anyway, if you need to talk to anyone, I'm here. I'm sure you have other people to go to, but figured I'd offer in case you wanted a different view on it."

"Wait," I called out, stopping her before she left the room. "What do you mean, a different view on it?"

"Well, I'm sure your guy friends have their opinions, and I'd be willing to bet your parents have their own—I just might be able to provide a female's perspective on it. You know, say, let you get a glimpse into what it might be like in her shoes."

She made a good point, though I wasn't ready to hear it yet. "I think I'll take you up on your offer, but not now. I'm not there—mentally. As much as I want to have an idea of her motivations, I need a bit to wrap my mind around everything."

"No worries. You know where to find me when you're ready." And with that, she was gone, leaving me with my thoughts and her words.

While I was grateful that Jason had given me a place to stay for the last two weeks—one with a real bed—that didn't mean I spent much time at his house. Things were still a little . . . *off* around him, and for the first time ever, I actually felt uncomfortable around Tatum. She hadn't done anything to make me feel that way, other than being Kelsey's best friend. I had no idea what those two talked about, but I definitely didn't care to be the topic of any conversation.

As I stepped out of the bathroom, hair still wet from my shower, I was surprised to see Tatum standing in the hall, a cold beer in her hand. I pointed at it and asked, "Should you be drinking that? I may not be a *real* doctor, but I'm fairly certain you should avoid alcohol while pregnant."

With an easy laugh, she extended her arm and held the beer out for me to take. "I grabbed it for you."

"And then waited for me to get out of the shower? You don't find that the slightest bit weird? What if I don't want it?"

"Too bad. It's already opened, so it looks like you'll have to drink it. And while you do that, maybe we should sit down and have a chat?"

I dropped my head forward and groaned. "Will this *chat* be over when the beer is gone?"

"Yup."

With that, I took the cold bottle from her hand and followed her to the couch. If all I had to do was finish this one drink before I could leave the room, then she was about to have the world's quickest conversation.

"Why have you avoided Kelsey since she told you about the baby?" At least she didn't waste any time getting straight to the hard questions.

"I haven't avoided her." That wasn't completely true. Over the last two weeks, anytime she'd texted me about the pregnancy or the baby, I'd responded. And recently, she'd resorted to sending emojis. But every time I saw that pair of blue socks pop up in a text, I broke a little more. Became weaker. Thoughts muddled and off track. I couldn't handle that, and the only thing I could do to safeguard myself was not respond. At all.

"Really? Then what would you call it?"

"What am I supposed to say to her, Tatum?" I glanced around the quiet room in search of some sort of backup. "And where's Jason? Shouldn't he be out here for this? You're in your pajamas, for Christ's sake . . . and I just got out of the shower. This seems rather inappropriate."

She laughed and glanced down at her outfit. "I'm in a T-shirt and yoga pants. And we're not even sitting next to each other." She had a point there—while I'd taken the recliner, she sat on the sofa with *plenty* of space between us. "Not to mention, we're talking about Kelsey. Nothing inappropriate here, so stop deflecting and start talking."

I dropped my head against the back of the recliner in a desperate attempt to melt into the cushion and disappear. "It's not that I'm ignoring her. I just don't have anything to say. It's not like she was overly chatty for the weeks on end that she knew she was pregnant with my child and never told me. So why am I the bad guy for not reaching out to her about it?"

"That's not what I mean, Aaron." Her eyes softened as she relaxed into her seat, likely assured I wasn't going to jump up and leave. "But this was the reason she was so scared to tell you about it in the first place, and in a way, you're proving her right. All you're doing is justifying her fears."

"Except it wouldn't be like this had she been honest with me from the start."

"Is that all you're pissy about? That she didn't tell you when she found out?"

I picked at the label on the bottle, trying to sort through the last couple of weeks. "This is my first child, Tatum. She stole moments and memories from me that I'll never get back. I feel robbed of the excitement of finding out I'm going to be a dad for the first time. That first doctor's appointment. Hearing the heartbeat. And honestly, I wouldn't be surprised if she would've found out the sex before telling me. So no, this is more than being pissy that she waited so long. She took things I'll never be able to get back."

She was quiet for a moment, but when her eyes met mine, I could see the sympathy that flowed through her veins. "Do you think you'll ever be able to get over that? Or will you hold this against her forever?"

"No, not forever. Honestly, the only reason it's gone on for this long is because I've been swamped with the house stuff—the appraisal, inspection, on top of furnishing the entire place. I haven't had a lot of time to process it all." There was also this issue of not being ready to delve into those feelings, but that was irrelevant.

"Why haven't you just told her these things? You found out that she'd kept it from you, and you left. Don't you think she deserves a conversation—or, at the very least, to hear why you're so angry? As it stands right now, she has no idea what your reasons are for ignoring her."

I nodded, though it was more to myself as I absorbed her opinion on the matter. "You're right . . . she does. But I guess I haven't been ready to discuss it with her yet. It's not like I'm trying to punish her or anything. Honestly, Tatum, I've been busy. I've had a lot on my plate, and I don't think it's fair or right to go to her about what I'm feeling until I've fully dissected *how* I feel."

"Agreed. But you're closing on your house tomorrow, and I think I overheard you tell Jay that the furniture company is delivering everything by four. So about how much longer do you think it'll be before you'll be in a place to explain it all to her?"

I rubbed my eyes, already tired of the pressure. "I don't know. I guess that all depends on how long it takes me to get settled in and back to a somewhat regular routine where I'll have a few moments to analyze the entire situation. I don't want to have to keep going back and forth with it. I would like to sit down, explain it all, and then move the fuck on."

"Is there anything she could do or say that would make this better for you?"

I shrugged. "I doubt it. It's not like she can give me these things, allow me the chance to experience it all with her. I think it more or less comes down to me taking the time to move through the emotions and put it behind me so I can move on."

Her smile was sad, though her eyes held understanding. "I get it. I just hate seeing my best friend so broken, you know? I don't condone her actions—I tried to get her to tell you before I even knew you were the stripper—but that doesn't mean I think she deserves to be isolated during this time. She's having a baby. *Your* baby. And above all else, that kid should come first. Not your resentment; not her fears."

Well, wasn't that a punch in the gut.

"I agree, and I promise, I'm doing what I can to move past this with her. But the last thing I want to do is open a discussion about it before I've sorted through it all. She's had her time to process it. Now it's my turn. It's not my fault she didn't allow us to do it simultaneously."

"All right. I'll leave you to it, then. But if this goes on for more than another week, expect me to beat down your door and force you to face it. Got it?"

"Yes, ma'am."

"Good. Now you may finish your beer in peace." And with that, she got up and walked out of the room, leaving me with a full drink, uncomfortable silence, and thoughts of Kelsey.

Chapter 21

Aaron

A week after I'd closed on the house, Kelsey had sent me a message about a last-minute doctor's appointment, asking if I'd be able to make it. It had concerned me, considering she'd told me that her regular checkup wasn't until Thursday, so I was confused why she'd need to go a few days earlier—and at the last minute.

Regardless, I'd told her I'd be there, and I was.

The problem was . . . she'd left me sitting in a small, cozy room all by myself while she was somewhere else getting the scan. And during all this, no one bothered to tell me what was going on. It wasn't until the lights dimmed and the giant TV screen came on that I realized she'd had something up her sleeve, and this wasn't a typical appointment.

Soft music played in the background as black-and-white pictures scrolled across the screen. At first, I thought they were generic, more of an advertisement for the office, but when Kelsey's voice came on, I realized they were sonograms of our child.

My baby.

"Tuesday, March twelfth," she said through the speakers. "I found out today that I'm pregnant, and I'm not sure how I feel about it. So I figured I'd write it all down to sort through the mess I've gotten myself into."

I swallowed, realizing she'd chronicled her pregnancy thus far—at least the beginning of it—and this was her way of including me in the steps I'd felt cheated out of. Had I known this was her plan, I doubted I would've shown up, but since I was here, and this gave me a chance to hear her out without having to face her, I decided it was worth sticking around for.

"A few weeks ago, I had a one-night stand. A really hot, incredible night with a stranger I never planned to see again. It was supposed to be that one time and that one time only. But now, I'm pregnant with his baby, and I don't even know who he is. I don't know how to find him, what name to list on the birth certificate, or if he'd even want to know. And while I realize I don't need to have all these answers right now, that I have time to figure it all out, I'm choking on all the what-ifs that continue to swarm me as each second passes me by."

My stomach twisted into knots at the sound of her confession. Somehow, through all this, I'd never taken the time to think about what it had been like for her. How scary it must've been. How alone she must've felt. And now, hearing her admit it all—even without looking me in the eye while speaking her truth—gutted me.

"Sunday, March seventeenth." A picture of her flat stomach came up on the screen. "Well, little one . . . I know who your daddy is. It was quite a surprise, but at least he's not a *dancer* like I originally thought. So that's good."

The slight giggle in her tone put a smile on my face.

"But the bad news is . . . he's going to be living with us for a few months. And as much as I wanted to tell him about you, I think it was divine intervention that it didn't happen. I have no idea how he'll take the news, and the last thing I want right now is someone or something making me doubt this. I won't be able to handle any negativity surrounding you."

And just like that, the smile vanished while a noose circled my neck.

"Sunday, March thirty-first. Your daddy came to lunch today at your grandparents' house—you'll understand what these are in time—and I think I learned more about him today than in the last two weeks of knowing him combined."

I thought back to that day. We were together until she went to bed. She must have written this entry then.

"He's not just a pretty face attached to a fantastic body . . . he's actually incredibly smart. I hope you get his intelligence. And eyes. And skin. If you're a boy, I hope you look just like him. But only if you get my feet—his aren't anything to look at."

I laughed, more curious now than ever before about what all she'd written that she'd never admitted aloud.

"He's making it harder and harder to keep you a secret from him. I only need to make it a couple of months until he buys a house and moves out, but if he keeps acting this way, I may not make it that long. And as much as I want him to know about you, I don't want . . . whatever this is between him and me to end. That's my worry. That he'll freak out and run, maybe accuse me of trying to trap him now that I know he's a doctor. And I'm just not ready to lose his company quite yet . . . especially after we finally had a real conversation today. Oh, and your grandma thinks I should marry him. I can only imagine what she'll say once she finds out about you. Lord, that will be entertaining, to say the least."

Hearing that made me recall the Sunday I'd gone to the Petersons' house to be with Kelsey as she told her parents. I couldn't get her mother's reaction out of my head—or her dad's, for that matter. It'd been weeks, and he apparently wasn't still angry with me, but that didn't mean I was ready to go fishing with the guy. He'd likely toss me overboard and take off.

"Tuesday, April ninth." She took a deep breath and then released it in a quick huff, making me worried about what had happened on this day. "I tried to feel him out tonight . . . to see where his head's at with having a baby or family. And I realize he doesn't know about you, but all he kept talking about was some woman he works with—about how she's struggled to have a baby of her own only for others who never wanted kids to get knocked up during a one-night stand. I couldn't handle it anymore and walked away. I don't think I can do this. I just wish I had a sign one way or the other so I can stop guessing how he'll take the news."

I'd forgotten all about that conversation, and now, hearing about it from her perspective, I wanted nothing more than to go back in time and change it all. I'd never meant to make her feel that way. No wonder she hadn't told me sooner. This entire time, I'd blamed her for keeping this from me, yet she'd tried several times . . . only for me to block her at every attempt. And not just block her but make her feel like shit as well.

"Thursday, April eleventh. I heard your heartbeat for the first time today." Just then, a rhythmic whooshing sound filled the room before fading out, just in time for Kelsey's voice to return. "It was the most beautiful sound I'd ever heard in my life. But it'd be a lie if I said I wasn't filled with sadness at the same time."

Her voice danced with a quiver, and I closed my eyes, imagining the tears that had lined her lower lids. Had she been in front of me right now, reading her innermost thoughts, I'd have pulled her into my arms and eased the ache that had spread from her lips to my heart.

"I was alone when the audible sound of your life inside me filled me with so much love. And as much as I wish your grandma or even Tatum had been with me, the one person I truly wanted there is your father. But he couldn't be . . . because I still haven't told him about you. I hate that he doesn't know. I hate even more that he's missing all of this. But I'm a coward. And I'm selfish. I don't want to lose him. I love you, my baby . . . I just hope he does, too."

I dropped my head into my hands and ran my fingers through my hair, whispering, "I do. I do love you." And as those words came out of my mouth, I had no idea which one they were meant for. Perhaps both—my child *and* Kelsey.

Her voice had cleared in time for the next entry to sound through the speakers, and more pictures of ultrasounds and her stomach, as well as ones of me, her, and her family, filled the screen. "Tuesday, April sixteenth."

I cringed at the date, knowing exactly what had happened that day.

"I'm going to tell him today, little one. I can't go into specifics with you, because it's certainly not age appropriate, but your father and I had a really good . . . *talk* last night. I think he'll be okay with the news. Maybe even more than okay—perhaps happy? I can only hope so. Regardless, I plan to talk to him after work and tell him all about you. I just pray he doesn't get mad that I've kept it from him for this long. If he does . . . I guess I deserve it. Right?"

My heart sped up, slamming into my sternum.

I didn't want to hear what came next.

Sorrow clenched her voice as she said, "I didn't tell him. Without going into the details . . . I don't think he's ready to hear that he's going to be a father. In fact, I'm not sure he even *wants* to be a dad. At least, not right now. Or . . . maybe just not with me. Unfortunately, he doesn't have much of a choice in that matter. But for now, I can't tell him. I can't even be around him right now. The thought of it makes my heart break."

I wasn't one to cry, but damn . . . that almost got me, hearing in her own words what she'd felt that day. All this time, I'd been angry that she'd made assumptions about what she'd walked in on, not once taking into account the pain she'd experienced. And now . . . it was almost too much to bear.

Then she cleared her throat. "Saturday, May fourth."

I stilled, held my breath, and waited to hear her version of that day.

"At this point, I'm not even sure if I'll ever let you read this journal. Not even when you're grown and married and having a baby of your own. I'm sure there are things in here you should never know about, and this will be another one." She paused to take a deep breath, her inhale shaking like a Jell-O mold during an earthquake.

I glanced up at the screen, as if I'd be able to see her face. I knew it wouldn't be there, but the sound of her pain called to me anyway. Instead of her face, though, I saw pictures of me as a kid—which she had clearly gotten from her sister or Jason, as they were mostly my teenage years—mixed in with some of her around the same ages. It was impossible to see those and not try to imagine what our child would look like. Who it would resemble.

"I screwed up. Badly. Not only did I hurt Aaron, but I think I might've ruined things for us—permanently. He's gone, and I doubt he'll ever come back. Even after he finds out about you, I don't think we'll ever be the same. And it kills me. It hurts so much, this pressure in my chest. It's like I can't breathe. And I don't know what to do other than tell him the truth. Which I will do . . . once I find the courage to face him again."

I closed my eyes and fought back my emotions.

"Friday, May tenth." Just hearing the date was a stab wound to my chest, straight through my heart. "He knows. I can't tell for sure how he feels about it . . . but he knows. And he wants nothing to do with me. If I screwed things up for you to have a relationship with your father, I'm so sorry." Emotion tightened her voice and filled it with sheer heartache. "That was the very last thing I ever wanted to do."

The background music broke away, and when I glanced up at the screen, I found Kelsey's face, tears glistening in her eyes. I stood, unable to remain in my seat on the couch, and moved closer to the video of her.

"Don't freak out, but Tatum told me what you said to her about feeling cheated out of everything up until now. Please, don't be mad at her. She's only trying to help, and without her sharing that piece of information with me, I never would've been able to find a way to at least *try* to make it right for you. The passages you just heard me read were from my journal. The morning after the bachelorette party, I found a notebook in my old bedroom at my parents' house, so I took it home with me. I didn't realize at the time that it would come in handy for this. But from the first day I found out that I was pregnant, I logged almost all my thoughts and feelings regarding the baby."

It wasn't until I gasped for air that I realized I'd held my breath as she spoke, as if inhaling would keep me from hearing what she had to say.

"I must've written in it almost every day, but I only pulled the most important ones for you. If you would like to read every passage, I'm more than happy to give you the journal to read. I would've given it to you now, but since I'm still pregnant, I thought it might be best if I continue to use it—at least until the baby's here."

I glanced around the room, as though I'd find her standing behind me. But still, the room remained empty. Just me and the prerecorded video of the mother of my child. If that wasn't depressing, I wasn't sure what was.

"You're probably wondering what you're doing here."

"You can say that again," I mumbled to the screen, not caring that no one could hear me.

"Well, since I kept you from all the early milestones, I thought I'd let you have one of the biggest . . . if you want it, of course. If not, you're free to go. Leave this room, and the woman at the front desk will give you a disk of all the 3D ultrasound images that were taken today. But if you want to know what we're having—if it's a boy or a girl—stick around. I don't know the results. Only you will get them, and if you choose to share it with me, that's your choice. Or you could keep it to yourself like I did with the first twelve weeks of the pregnancy. Either way, the receptionist will have the images on a disk for you."

I stood, stunned, motionless. Unable to speak or even blink. Shocked at the gesture she'd offered willingly. In all honesty, I hadn't yet decided if I wanted to learn the gender or not by the time I saw the results on the screen—I'd stayed so long that I'd lost my chance to leave. And after that, I couldn't contain the emotion that thrived in me.

I'm going to be a father . . .

It became real in that moment.

As if the last four weeks had never happened.

Chapter 22

Kelsey

"Any word from Aaron?" Tatum asked as we walked out of the grocery store, two carts full of food for her baby shower that would also double as their gender-reveal party.

"A letter came to the apartment yesterday, addressed to him. I called him about it, and he asked me if I could bring it to him. But other than that, no." It'd been five days since the doctor's appointment. I didn't want to bring it up to him, but I didn't know how much longer I could last before losing my cool and demanding he speak to me.

Shock raised her dark brows. "Nothing about the ultrasound? The journal entries? The gender?"

"Nope. Nothing." He'd gone with me to my regular checkup on Thursday, and even then, he'd never brought it up. I wouldn't lie . . . that hurt. "I told him that he didn't have to tell me if he didn't want to. I guess he's still punishing me."

We reached her SUV and parked the carts behind it while she lifted the back gate. She continued to talk while we moved the bags into the trunk. "Maybe he didn't stick around to find out."

"He did." My chest constricted, and tiny pins pricked the backs of my eyes. "Marlena saw him at the store and asked him about it, and he told her that he knew what we were having. But he wouldn't tell her, and I guess he didn't stick around long enough to let her pull it from him."

"Well, maybe he'll say something when you get to his house."

I rolled my eyes and laughed. "Doubtful. I'm the one who told him that he had a letter, and it took him almost an entire day to get back to me about it."

Even though I tried to play it off like a joking matter, that didn't mean I wasn't ripped apart anytime I thought about his absence and avoidance. Foolishly, I'd believed things would change once he got his house. I thought he'd come around and find the time to talk to me after he got all moved in and unpacked. But he'd been there for a week and a half, and from what I'd heard—based on the things he'd told Jason—he'd been settled in since the end of the first week. So I'd given up hope that we'd ever move past my mistakes.

I hadn't just made my bed to lie in it.

I'd set the house on fire . . . and now I had to sit in the soot and smoke.

Tatum put the last bag in the trunk and then stepped away to close the hatch. "How long are you gonna let it go on before you say something?"

"What can I say? I don't have any right to bring it up, so I can't."

She huffed before setting her sad eyes on me. "Want me to say—"

"Don't you dare say a word, Tater. I appreciate all you've done to help me and be there for me through all this, but really . . . I think this would be better left alone." I meant it—there was no way I would've made it through the last month without her.

"Well, let me know if there's anything I can do." She pushed the shopping cart to the front of her SUV and unlocked the door with the key fob. "You're still coming over before the party next weekend to help me set all this up, right?"

"I wasn't planning on it." I winked when she rolled her eyes. "Of course I'll be there."

I moved around her vehicle to mine and settled in behind the steering wheel. As long as I was around Tatum, my nerves were fine. But now, when I was alone and knew I would see Aaron in about ten minutes, they were fried. I was so anxious that the drive to his new house went by in the blink of an eye.

And before I knew it, I stood on his front porch, my heart hammering in my chest.

I rang the doorbell, and a second later, my phone vibrated with an incoming text. One look at the screen, and my stomach flipped. It was from Aaron, telling me to come in. I had to read it about eighty-four times to make sure I hadn't misunderstood *I'm in the back . . . just walk in.* Because, you know, those words could mean so many different things. And eventually, I grabbed the cold doorknob and turned, carefully pushing it open as if sneaking in.

But the second I made it inside, my heart stopped.

Air left my lungs.

Oxygen couldn't reach my brain.

There was a good chance I'd died on the way here, and this was my heaven.

Aaron stood about ten feet in front of me, hands deep in his pockets, eyes hesitantly meeting mine. If nerves had a voice, they'd sound like his when he said, "Hey." If they could smile, it'd look like his when I moved two steps closer—short and lopsided, cautious. And if nerves had eyes, they'd be the deepest green, imploring me to go to them like an outstretched, offered hand.

My stomach twisted into knots, and then *those* knots twisted into more with each step I took from the front door to the man in front of me. This had to be a dream . . . or a trap. I'd barely spoken to Aaron in *weeks*, and now, he waited for me in the middle of a room, gaze glued to me like he wanted to pour every thought, every emotion, every want and desire, into that one stare in the hopes I'd read and understand them.

However, as soon as I came to a stop less than three feet away, my fear overrode all other emotion and flipped me on my head. I held out the envelope that had come to the apartment addressed to him. My tongue wouldn't form words. My chest wouldn't expand to pull more air into my lungs. And my knees were on the verge of giving up, threatening to make me fall to the floor at his feet. But luckily, none of that happened before he could say, "Open the letter, Kelsey."

"It's your mail, though."

"Open it," he repeated, more sternly this time.

I hesitated, hoping my thoughts would settle on something coherent to say. In the end, I went with, "If you wanted me to read your mail, why make me come all the way here? You could've just asked me to do that the other day when I told you about it in the first place."

Rather than issue more demands or argue back, he lunged toward me, held my cheeks in his hands, and without pause covered my mouth with his lips. It was intense yet short lived. Although, even when he pulled his face from mine, he never dropped his hands or shifted his attention away from my eyes. "Kelsey, please open the letter."

As if I couldn't think on my own, I did as he said, not bothering to look at what I was doing as I slid my finger beneath the flap and tore through the envelope. It wasn't until he took a step backward, giving me space to focus on the letter in my hand, that I dropped my chin and unfolded the piece of paper that had been neatly tucked inside.

If you want to know what gender our baby is, open the double doors.

I flipped the paper over, looking for more instructions, as if the one sentence printed on the front wasn't enough. But as soon as I stopped questioning it and met his stare once more, peace washed over me. It stirred through my body, coursed through my veins, and took control of my every movement, starting with my feet. It was like I wasn't in control of my actions and had no defense against each step I took toward the room behind the French doors just off the entryway. When I'd pointed out this house to Aaron, this room had been a selling point—the perfect space for a home office. I'd also mentioned its use as a baby's room in the event I ever found the courage to let him know about ours.

Standing in front of the double doors, I closed my eyes and took a long, deep breath. I wasn't sure if I should turn the handle and find out the sex of my baby, or back away and leave. Most of that confusion came from the uncertainty of his reasons. He'd had *days* to tell me what we were having, yet he never had. He could've called, come over, sent a text. But still, he hadn't done any of those things. Instead, he'd waited for me to come to him, as if this were no big deal.

Just as I fisted my hands at my sides, the sound of crinkling paper caught my attention. It yanked me out of the twisted, insecure thoughts enough to remind me why I was here in the first place. Why I stood in front of these doors. It brought to mind his kiss, the lingering tingle on my lips left behind from his.

He hadn't waited for me to come to him.

He'd orchestrated the whole thing.

And once I realized that, I no longer cared that I hadn't received a phone call or text, or that he hadn't reached out to tell me what we were having. If this was the way he wanted to tell me—to *show* me—then I had to be the luckiest girl in the world.

Heat covered my back like a warm blanket on a cold night. And when I glanced over my shoulder, I found him behind me, practically molding his body to mine. "Do you want to know?" he asked in my ear, and the second I nodded, he opened the door.

I gasped and covered my lips at the sight of the pastel walls. Instantly, the room blurred beyond my tears, so I turned to face him, meeting his eyes, holding his stare. Needing to see his face, his reaction, his *emotion*.

"I didn't get any furniture," he started, as if that had even been a thought in my head. "I was hoping we could go together to pick it out. But only under one condition."

I nodded . . . then shook my head. Then I nodded again. "What condition?" I managed to get out past the knot in my throat.

"That we only buy one crib. One dresser. One set of clothes." He took my hands in his and lowered his head to bring his eyes closer to mine. "I don't want two houses—this one and your apartment. Only one. And preferably this one since I just bought it. I don't want shared custody or rotating weekends."

I stood motionless while his every word hit my ears, breathed life into my heart, and etched itself into my soul, where no one and nothing could ever take them from me.

"I want you . . . here. With me. *For* me." He lowered his lips to mine, but he kept the tiniest space between them as he continued to whisper the most beautiful promises I'd ever heard. "I fucked up, Kelsey. I blamed you for not giving me a chance, yet I did the same to you. Do you think we can start over?"

I nodded and closed my eyes, my breath passing through my lips only to heat my face as it blossomed between us.

He captured my cheeks in his hands and tilted my head back, forcing me to look at him again. With a smile that shone through his entire expression, he said, "We're having a baby girl."

I didn't waste a single second molding myself to him. And he didn't try to stop me. In fact, his hands and mouth were as frantic as mine as we tore at each other's clothes, needing to be closer. Needing to put the final pieces of ourselves back together . . . as one.

This time, when he kissed my bare stomach, whispering secret devotions to our daughter, I didn't have to pretend it was real. When he looked me in the eyes and told me he loved me, I didn't have to try to convince myself that he saw me—I knew without a doubt that he didn't see anyone else. And after it was all over, I had my ear pressed to his chest, listening to the beating heart of the man I loved.

"You really want me to move in with you?" I whispered as he held me against him.

"For now."

I pushed up on my elbow and stared down at him, waiting for him to explain more. When he didn't, I asked, "What's that supposed to mean? Like, you only want to live with me for a little while?"

"I never said that."

"You said *for now*."

"Yeah, because at some point, I'll want more." Sensing my shock, he fingered my hair out of my face and tucked the strands behind my ear. "I'll want you to take my last name. After that, I may want you to give me a son. Or another daughter. Or both. And then, when you think I couldn't possibly want more . . . I'll want to grow old with you."

My eyes burned from the tears that begged to be released.

He swiped one finger beneath my lashes, catching the lone drop of emotion that I hadn't been able to fight off, and said, "But I know that will take time. I'm well aware that you're only here because of some malfunction with the condom. You weren't given the choice. I just hope that, in time, you won't feel like you want a choice anymore, and the only thing you'll desire is to be my wife. My partner. Till death do us part."

I leaned over him and grazed his lips with mine. "I've always heard about people being blinded by love. But really, I think most of us are blinded by the pain of something we perceived as love, when it was never really love at all. And that keeps us from seeing what we need, *who* we need. That's when the choice is taken from us and decided by something greater—something that knows what we need more than we do."

"That sounds about right."

"I've always wanted a family, but after having my heart shattered and my dreams destroyed, I stopped believing in the picture. Everything felt like a lie. The idea of marriage and kids no longer seemed like a happy one, but instead one full of pain and uncertainty. It wasn't until you came along that I realized just how wrong that theory was. You make me happy, Aaron. I think I would've fallen for you even if you hadn't knocked me up while pretending I was someone else."

"Kelsey . . . I've *never* pretended you were anyone else."

My brow tightened as I regarded him with unspoken curiosity.

"I may not have known your name at the time, or known who you were—hell, I didn't know a single thing about you. But that didn't mean I wished you were someone else. The only thing I pretended that night was that you saw me for me, and that we loved each other."

"Then I guess you got your wish, huh?"

"I'm not sure. Did I?"

"Well, yeah . . . I see you for you."

"And?" No matter how hard he fought against it, his lips twitched with a hidden smile.

"And you love me." Laughter tore through my chest as he flipped me over, landing on top of me while holding himself up with one hand and tickling my side with the other. Barely able to breathe through the bursts of happiness that invaded my soul, I added, "And I love you, too."

His fingers immediately left my side, just as his mouth closed over mine in the most possessive kiss I'd ever experienced. And in the blink of an eye, the dominant side of him returned, warmed by the protective side and softened by his inner teddy bear.

He situated himself between my thighs, lifted my arms over my head, and pinned my wrists to the carpet beneath us. The entire time, he kept his eyes on mine. And as he moved into me, owning me, claiming me, there wasn't a single ounce of my being that questioned his love for me. I only prayed he could feel the same thing from me.

My orgasm climbed higher and higher, and as he tumbled off the cliff with me, he tattooed the words *I love you* against my shoulder with his teeth. And once I had calmed down enough to speak, I whispered, "Yes."

"Yes, what?" Confusion deepened his green eyes.

"Yes, I'll move in. Under one condition, though."

A coy grin tipped one side of his mouth. "What condition might that be?"

"You don't wait for *someday* to ask me to marry you."

"Are you saying you want me to ask you now?"

"I'm saying I'm ready when you are."

"I would just like to point out that I think it's utter crap that you trusted Rebecca with the sex of your baby and not me. She used to date your ex-fiancé . . . *I'm* your best friend." I lifted my middle finger in Tatum's face.

"Which is why Jason wouldn't let you be the secret keeper. He knew you'd give it away somehow." She made a good point—as did Jason. "Plus, we needed someone who could bake. I love you, Kels, but that's not you. Look at the bright side, though . . . we get to find out at the same time."

"Yeah . . . as does literally everyone else in the room. Way to make me feel special, Tater."

"Be happy you get to find out at all." That was a cheap shot, referring to the fact that Aaron and I had agreed to keep our own secrets for a while. After keeping things from each other so long, we'd decided to have a few secrets that no one else knew about—such as our baby being a girl.

I rolled my eyes and stuck the spoons into the various dips on the snack table. "I still think you should've gone with one of my ideas. Cutting into a cake is so anticlimactic."

"Every suggestion you came up with involved a mess."

"I don't know why you're complaining about that . . . you're a walking, talking mess just waiting to happen." I'd suggested the guests shoot them with paintballs colored either blue or pink, but then she'd pointed out that might hurt, so I'd compromised with Silly String. To which she'd given me an adamant no. After that, I'd gone with a few tamer ideas, like glitter bombs, fairy-dust explosions, confetti showers. Yet she'd turned them all down, using the ridiculous excuse that they'd make too much of a mess, and in the end, she'd gone with some stupid cake idea.

So lame.

"When you decide to reveal what you're having, you can do it any which way you want. Unfortunately for you, this is my party, and I want a damn cake."

"Here . . . let me cut you a piece." I almost had the knife to the frosting before she yanked my arm away, realizing what I was about to do. "What was that for? You said you wanted cake!"

"Aaron!" she yelled over her shoulder. "Come get your baby mama."

A few seconds later, the sexiest pair of arms came up from behind me, wrapping themselves around my growing waist. A strong chest pressed against my back at the same time his heated breath hit my ear, filling it with the deep rumbles of his intoxicating voice. "I can't wait for the day that I get to hear her call you my wife."

I turned in his arms and locked mine around his neck, lifting myself onto my tiptoes to whisper, "I guess you'll just have to settle for hearing me call myself your wife for now. I'm not ready to let anyone in our bubble just yet."

"You do realize they'll all be pissed at us when they find out that we went off and got married yesterday behind everyone's backs, don't you? Are you prepared for that?"

I pulled away just enough to stare at him with wide eyes. "Are you trying to say you want to tell them?"

"Nope. Just making sure you won't regret it."

"I ordered a stripper to help me feel better after seeing my ex and then took him home and let him have his way with me. Then I moved the stripper, who turned out not to be a stripper, into my place and—once again—let him have his way with me. All of which has led us here . . . married, pregnant, and happy. Aaron, there's not a single bit of any of that worth regretting. And the one thing I do regret more than anything else is already water under the bridge. So stop worrying about me."

"Get a room, you two," Jason said as he came up behind Aaron, slapping him on the shoulder. "Just not one of mine."

Aaron pulled away with laughter curling his lips and brightening his eyes. Happiness was a good look on him. And I'd do anything to keep it written all over his face.

Tatum sidled up next to me once the guys walked out back. Now, it was only the two of us in front of the kitchen table, surrounded by snacks and a cake that held the day's biggest surprise. She looked at me, and I looked at her, and without a single word spoken between us, we both knew what the other was thinking.

"I'm pretty sure if you stick a toothpick into the bottom, no one will ever know."

"That only works if the cake isn't done. Thank God I didn't leave the baking up to you."

I elbowed her and frowned. "Then how are we supposed to see what color the inside is?"

"I guess we wait until it's time to cut into it."

"Or . . ." I grabbed a plastic fork from the tray and stuck the very bottom of the cake in the back. "Oops. I accidentally fell into it with this here fork, and oh . . . look, it's—" I peeked at the small crumbs of cake that stuck to the frosting. "Oh my God, Tatum. You're having a boy!"

"Really?" Her dark eyes grew wide, glistening with excitement and surprise. "A boy?"

"How exciting is this? Too bad our kids will be somewhat related; otherwise, they could've gotten married." I was so happy for my best friend that I didn't once think about the words that came out of my mouth.

She froze midclap and dropped her mouth open. "Wait. You're having a girl?"

"It's crazy, right?"

"How could you keep that from me?"

As soon as I saw her eyes water, mine followed suit. "Trust me, it wasn't nearly as hard as keeping the wedding a secret."

"You're getting married?"

I shook my head, relieved that I finally got to tell Tatum the most exciting news of my life. "No. We already did. We went to the courthouse yesterday."

She jumped and wrapped her arms around me, both of us caught up in the extreme levels of happiness that poured from our eyes. Even when Jason and Aaron returned from the backyard, we still didn't separate.

"What's going on in here?" Jason asked, speaking over Aaron's concerned question of, "Is everything okay?"

Tatum sniffled and pulled away only enough to turn her head so that we were both looking at the guys. And like them, we spoke at the same time. While she said, "They got married at the courthouse yesterday and didn't tell anyone," I announced, "You're having a boy."

When the guys started to speak over each other again, my mother showed up out of nowhere and moved between the four of us, becoming the center of our circle. "One at a time. I can't possibly keep up when you're all talking over each other."

Apparently, Jason got to speak first. "They cut into the cake and found out what we're having before the reveal."

"I didn't do anything." Tatum held up her hands in defense. "That was all Kelsey."

Ignoring my mom's glare, I shrugged and said, "I tripped, and the fork I had in my hand accidentally nicked the bottom of it. There was no cutting. You all should be happy that I didn't fall over and hurt the defenseless unborn child in my belly."

"Wait one minute here." Mom glanced between all of us before bringing her attention back to me. "Is it a boy or a girl?"

"Girl," I answered, once again not contemplating the words that came out of my mouth.

Baby brain was a real thing.

And it made me stupid.

But I was with child . . . so it was excused.

Mom clapped and turned to Tatum. "You're having a girl?"

"No." Tatum pointed to me. "She is."

My mother's tears nearly gutted me, but the smile on her face brought me back to life. "I'm going to have a granddaughter?"

"You do remember Lizzie, don't you? Marlena's child? Your *granddaughter?*"

She waved me off just before wrapping me in her arms. "This is excellent news." Without releasing her hold on me, she craned her neck to see Tatum over her shoulder. "So you're having a boy, then? A baby boy and a baby girl. I feel so blessed."

"I guess there's no point in having the party now since everyone already knows what we're having," Jason muttered with an exasperated shake of his head.

"Sure there is." Tatum was amazing at getting out of trouble. I loved her for it. "We can use it to celebrate Aaron and Kelsey's wedding that no one was invited to."

Tatum had a big mouth. I couldn't think of anything other than shoving a sock into it.

"Your *what?*" Mom's tears returned, though this time, they weren't filled with happiness. "You got married and didn't tell anyone?"

"For the love of—"

"All the things," everyone around me called out, finishing my sentence.

"Yes. As a matter of fact . . . for the love of *all the things*." I quirked one side of my upper lip, which was the universal facial expression equivalent to the middle finger. "This isn't about me. It's about Tatum and her impatience to dig into the cake before everyone got here."

I had to be delusional if I thought I'd get out of that one.

"Your father is going to be heartbroken, Kelsey." Mom's dramatic, tear-filled remark would've worked better had she not waited until my dad had approached. "You stole his chance to walk his daughter down the aisle."

"Seriously, Mom . . . do you not remember Marlena? Your *other* daughter? Dad walked her down the aisle, so I didn't steal anything from him."

Dad cocked his head to the side and held me in his stare. "Why can't I walk you, too?"

"She ran off with this handsome doctor and got married without any of us there."

A beaming smile stretched across Dad's lips as he turned to face Aaron. "That's excellent news. Congratulations, son! Welcome to the family."

I couldn't do anything except roll my eyes and groan as they shook hands.

And when Aaron turned his attention to me, likely analyzing how I was holding up now that everyone knew the secrets we'd agreed to keep to ourselves—or questioning how I'd been able to keep the baby a secret for so long, yet had spilled the beans on the first chance I got—I just shrugged. "Too late now, Aaron. You're stuck with this. Forever."

Rather than answer, he winked and returned his infectious smile to my dad. "I couldn't be happier."

Me either.

Epilogue

Aaron

"It's too early. She's not ready," Kelsey cried as she cradled her round stomach in her arms, sobbing in the passenger seat.

"No it's not, and she's okay." Her due date wasn't for another two weeks, though at the last checkup, we'd been told it could be any day. Apparently, *any day* in pregnancy terms meant two days. "Just keep up with the breathing; you're doing great. We'll be at the hospital in no time."

I grabbed my phone from the center console and tried Jason again. I'd called Kelsey's parents several times, but no one had answered, and I didn't have Marlena's number in my phone. It wouldn't have been a big deal had we not accidentally left Kelsey's cell at the house, but I wasn't about to turn around for that. Someone had to answer a call at some point, and once that happened, I trusted the news would spread like wildfire.

But again, Jason's voice mail came on, and I hung up. I didn't want to drop Kelsey off at the hospital doors without anyone with her; I didn't want to make her walk up from the parking lot, either.

Luckily, I spotted an empty parking spot in the first row as soon as I pulled in. It was the best compromise I could've come across. Although, with as close as her contractions were, I doubted she'd make it to the front doors without having to stop and curse me out.

She'd gotten really good at that over the last hour.

By some small miracle, we made it inside and up to the second floor, where the labor-and-delivery unit was located, without much incident. But just as we came to the front desk, all hell broke loose. Ironically, it had nothing to do with the baby that fought to break free from Kelsey's womb.

No. The commotion was caused by none other than the Peterson clan. Her mom sidled up beside us, flanked by her dad and Marlena. A quick glance over my shoulder proved that the others—Jason's mom, Nick, and Marlena's kids—were all in the waiting room.

"It's about time you got here," Kelsey's mom said with concern lining her brow.

"Uh . . . we came as fast as we could."

"She's been in labor for hours!"

I glanced at Kelsey, who currently had my hand in a viselike grip while she spoke to the nurse behind the counter, and then back to her mother. "It's only been bad for the last hour or so. I wouldn't say it's been *that* long. And you're not supposed to get here until contractions are closer together anyway. Once that happened, we headed straight here."

"Oh . . ." Her eyes lost the bewilderment and opened wide. "You've been in touch with Jason?"

I shook my head and winced at the finger that my wife had likely just snapped in two. "No. I haven't been able to get ahold of him. I've tried to call him ever since we left the house."

"Then how would you know how close her contractions are?"

Again, I turned to assess Kelsey at my side, then swung my attention back to her mother. "Because I've been timing them?" It came out as more of a question than an answer, simply because I had no idea what this woman was getting at, and if she didn't hurry it up, I'd have to learn how to change a diaper with one hand.

"Why in the world would you be timing Tatum's contractions?"

Confusion stunned me silent, but as soon as Kelsey released her hold on me, it tore me from the news of Tatum's labor and brought me back to why we were here in the first place. I glanced to the side to see what was going on, and I noticed the nurse had come around the counter and had one hand on my wife's lower back. I wasn't sure what they were about to do, but either way, it required my attention and focus. But before I could ask what was going on, Kelsey peered over her shoulder, glared at her mom, and said, "*My* contractions, Mom."

And then I followed the nurse and Kelsey down the hall, leaving the frantic crowd behind.

A little over two hours later, I sat on the side of Kelsey's hospital bed, completely lost in the sight of my daughter in her arms. I'd never known a love like this, nor had I ever imagined it possible. But here I sat, happily drowning in the emotion.

"Did you know that all the nurses are convinced that we did this on purpose?" Tatum asked as Jason wheeled her and their new baby into our room. "I laughed and told them that if they thought I'd hold this giant of a baby in for an extra week just to deliver on the same day as you, then they were insane."

Kelsey laughed softly, as if she worried she'd wake the baby if she were any louder. "If I remember correctly, when you found out I was pregnant, you were most excited about having someone to share the experience with. You can't share it more than we just did."

"It would've been better to have had you at my side, and then to be at your side a couple of weeks later. But I guess you're right . . . best to have just gotten it over with so we can start sharing the experiences of motherhood together."

Jason helped Tatum onto the other side of the bed so that both women could sit side by side, each holding a baby in her arms. Once we had them situated, Jason looked at me and nudged his head to the side, motioning me to follow him to the other side of the room.

"They'll be here in about sixty seconds," he muttered beneath his breath with an eye on his wife, likely to make sure she didn't overhear him. "It's best to stay back and blend in with the room. They go after the women and children first."

I tried to keep my composure, but I lost the battle. Humor rattled my shoulders and burned my cheeks. And before it waned, the door opened, and in came a flock of Petersons, all cooing and smiling, oblivious to the two of us against the wall.

"Who do we have here?" Jason's mom asked as she approached the bed, as if she had no clue who those babies were.

I joked, but in all honesty, I was one lucky son of a bitch to be included in this group of people. My parents had planned to be here next weekend, not expecting Kelsey to go into labor two weeks early. And rather than change flights and Mom's doctor's appointments that had been scheduled for before their trip, they decided it would be best to come after we'd gotten back home and the local excitement had settled some.

Tatum shifted the little blue bundle in her arms and said, "Meet William James Watson."

And when Kelsey's mom slid around to stand next to her daughter, Kelsey glanced down at the pink swaddle in her arms and said, "Mom, meet Kimberly Diane Baucus." Even though we'd agreed on names long ago, my heart still grew larger at the sound of my mother's name. "But we're going to call her Kimmy."

"Why would you do that? Diane is such a lovely name."

"I'm not calling her Diane, Mom. You're lucky I even used your name in any part of it."

With a smile, her mom stepped back and held up her phone, causing the whole room to groan. "Just a few snapshots . . . please?"

"You've had a few. Now put the camera away."

Diane waved her daughter off and went back to fussing over the babies. "When might you give me a grandson?"

Kelsey pointed to the little boy at the foot of the bed standing next to his mother and sister. "Really, Mom? Connor's right there. Would you like me to introduce you to your grandson, since you seem to have forgotten him?"

"Don't be silly." My mother-in-law shook her head. "Of course I haven't forgotten him."

Jason leaned against my shoulder and lowered his voice so no one would overhear. "You've been around long enough to have an opinion on this . . . does it seem to you that Kelsey's the favorite and Marlena's the forgotten child?"

I bit my lip to keep from drawing attention our way. "Yeah, but for some reason, Kelsey believes her sister's the golden baby and she's the redheaded stepchild."

He slapped my shoulder with a smile stretched across his face. "Good luck with her, bro."

I didn't need luck.

I had all I'd ever wanted right here.

ABOUT THE AUTHOR

Leddy Harper had to use her imagination often as a child: she grew up the only girl in a family full of boys. At fourteen, she decided to use that imagination to write her first book, and she never stopped. She often calls writing her therapy, using it to deal with issues through the eyes of her characters.

Harper is now a mother of three girls, making her husband the only man in a house full of females. She published her first book to encourage her children to go after whatever they want, to inspire them to love what they do and do it well, and to teach them what it means to overcome their fears. You can learn more about Harper at www.leddyharper. com or find her on Facebook at www.facebook.com/LeddyHarper.